PRAISE FOR THE DCI RYAN MYSTERIES

What newspapers say

"She keeps company with the best mystery writers" – *The Times*

"LJ Ross is the queen of Kindle" – *Sunday Telegraph*

"Holy Island is a blockbuster" – *Daily Express*

"A literary phenomenon" – *Evening Chronicle*

"A pacey, enthralling read" – *Independent*

What readers say

"I couldn't put it down. I think the full series will cause a divorce, but it will be worth it."

"I gave this book 5 stars because there's no option for 100."

"Thank you, LJ Ross, for the best two hours of my life."

"This book has more twists than a demented corkscrew."

"Another masterpiece in the series. The DCI Ryan mysteries are superb, with very realistic characters and wonderful plots. They are a joy to read!"

OTHER BOOKS BY LJ ROSS

THE DCI RYAN MYSTERIES IN ORDER:

THE ALEXANDER GREGORY THRILLERS IN ORDER:

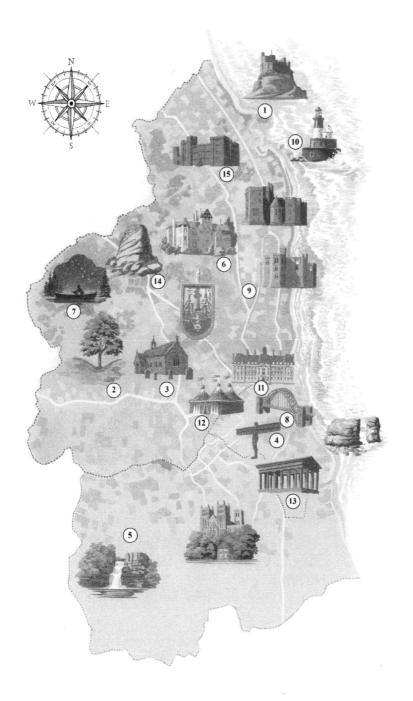

THE INFIRMARY

A DCI RYAN MYSTERY

—PREQUEL—

THE INFIRMARY

A DCI RYAN MYSTERY

—PREQUEL—

LJ ROSS

ISBN: 978-1-912310-11-1

First published in 2018 by LJ Ross

This edition published in October 2020 by Dark Skies Publishing

Author photo by Gareth Iwan Jones

Cover layout by Stuart Bache

Cover artwork and map by Andrew Davidson

Typeset by Riverside Publishing Solutions Limited

Printed and bound by CPI Goup (UK) Limited

"First, do no harm."

—Hippocrates

CHAPTER 1

Sunday 6th July 2014

The Sunday Market on Newcastle's Quayside was bustling. Traders touted everything from chocolates to knitted tea caddies, and the air was heavy with the scent of fudge and fried onions as John Dobbs fought his way through the crowd.

He walked with his head bent, avoiding the faces of those who jostled him along with impatient nudges and irritable sighs.

"'scuse me, mate."

A meaty hand thrust him aside and Dobbs stumbled backwards into the path of an oncoming buggy laden with children.

"Mind out o' the way, man!"

A rake-thin woman raced towards him, shoving the buggy out in front of her like a battering ram.

"Sorry," he muttered, ducking between the stalls.

Dobbs risked a glance between the flaps of colourful tarpaulin and waited. He searched the passing faces of the crowd and began to think he had imagined the creeping, paranoid feeling of being followed.

Then he spotted them.

A man and woman weaved purposefully through the stream of people and came to a standstill, craning their necks as they searched the faces with hard, focused eyes that set them apart from the common herd. It was the same pair he'd seen yesterday, and the day before that.

It could mean only one thing.

Police.

He felt his stomach jitter, one slow flip that brought bile to his throat. They had come for him.

"Oh, God," he whispered, and shuffled backwards, trying to make himself invisible. His chest shuddered in and out as he battled to remain calm, sucking in deep breaths of sickly-sweet summer air.

The policeman must have sensed him, because he turned suddenly and their eyes locked. Time slowed, the crowd became a blur and, in the second that PC Steve Jessop hesitated, Dobbs took his chance.

He spun around and burst through the brightly coloured canopies that billowed on the air, running along the quayside without any idea of where to go, driven only by the need to get away, to find somewhere safe.

"Hitchins! He's leggin' it!"

Dobbs heard the man shouting to his partner and knew they wouldn't be far behind. His feet slapped against the pavement and he'd barely gone a hundred yards before he began to tire, muscles screaming as he urged his useless body to go faster.

"We're in pursuit of subject heading west along the Quayside! Surveillance is blown. Request further instructions. I repeat, request immediate instructions!"

Dobbs cast a glance over his shoulder and saw the pair of them shouting into their radios as they gave chase. When he turned back, he lost his footing and careened into a group of teenagers, falling awkwardly to the sound of jeers.

He didn't stop to listen but scrambled up again, the pads of his fingers tearing at the rough paving stones as he fought to stay ahead. There was a buzzing in his ears as he leaped into the road.

Horns blared, brakes screeched as he ran beneath the enormous bridge connecting Newcastle and Gateshead. It towered high above his head in a graceful arch of painted green steel, its underbelly spattered with the faeces of a thousand birds who nested in its nooks and crannies. Their noise was deafening, a cacophony of squawks and cries as he searched for a way to escape, a quiet hollow where he could breathe and think clearly. He pressed his hands to his ears.

"Please, God," he muttered. "Make them stop."

Beneath the wide arches was a granite tower supporting the north side of the bridge. Usually, its doors were kept firmly locked to the public, but vandals seeking a new dumping ground had tampered with the chain and it lay in a heap of rusted metal on the floor, leaving the door tantalisingly ajar. Dobbs squeezed behind the barrier railing, yanked the door open with a creak of hinges, and hurried inside.

He blinked as his eyes adjusted to sudden darkness, retching at the overpowering smell of birds and mildew. Ahead of him, a staircase beckoned, and he followed it up to an enormous tower room. Its steel framework was still visible from the days when it had been used as a warehouse in the 1920s and, as the sun broke through the dusty window panes, he looked up to its high rafters in a kind of wonder. Tiny pigeon feathers and a haze of dust motes floated on the air and, to his fevered mind, it was a kind of cathedral, a place of sanctuary.

But not for long.

The sound of running footsteps followed him upstairs, and Dobbs flew up another staircase leading to the upper level. In the distance, he heard the long wail of police sirens outside and knew they were for him.

Sweat coursed down his face and into his eyes as he hurried upward. His legs burned, and his gasping breaths echoed around the high walls as he clambered higher.

"*Up there!*"

He heard them in the tower below, then the crackle of a police radio.

"Subject is inside north tower of the bridge and heading for the roadway exit on the top level. Requesting immediate support!"

"Where the hell is Cooper?"

Dobbs didn't stop to wonder who Cooper was. His lungs laboured, dragging stale air into his exhausted body. Clammy hands pushed against the crumbling wall as he struggled to reach the top of the stairs and whatever fate awaited him there.

"John!"

He heard the woman calling out to him, warning him to stop, to stay calm. All the things he couldn't do even if he wanted to.

He emerged from the stairwell onto a precarious gangway wrapping around the topmost level of steel frame and the height was enough to make him dizzy. His legs were shaking with fatigue and black dots swam in front of his eyes as he clung to the wall. He heard the rattle of metal as they climbed the stairs below and he searched desperately for a way out.

Dobbs spotted a door halfway along the gangway and began to edge forward, sweating as his feet slid against bird excrement and the gangway creaked beneath his weight. The birds were all around now, cooing and crying like the pealing of bells.

"John! Stay where you are!"

He clasped a hand around the heavy door handle that would lead him out onto the top of the bridge. On the other side, he could hear the thrum of traffic and he tugged harder, desperate to get out.

The door was locked.

A sob escaped him, echoing around the cavernous tower.

Frantic now, he put his weight behind it and kicked out at the old chain lock, but it wouldn't budge. He was almost beaten when he spotted a small hook to the side of the door with a set of old keys, coated in cobwebs and grime. His hands shook as he tried each of them in the lock until, miraculously, the chain fell away.

The police were only metres away by the time he prised the door open. When he burst onto the bridge, a gust of strong wind hit him like a fist to the face so that he almost fell backwards again. Cold air rolled in from the North Sea and whipped through the high arches, the metal screeching and moaning like a woman in torment. He shook his head to clear the sound, pressing the heels of his hands to the sides of his head to relieve the pressure.

"John?"

He backed away from the door as the two police officers joined him, red-faced and out of breath.

"John," the woman repeated, palms outstretched. "I'm Detective Constable Hitchins and this is Police Constable Jessop. All we want to do"—she paused to catch her breath—"all we want to do is talk to you."

But he heard fear and mistrust buried beneath the empty platitude.

"I don't believe you," he whispered and began to cry.

Jessop and Hitchins glanced at each other, neither sure how to handle a situation that was escalating rapidly out of their control.

Where was Cooper?

Vehicles and pedestrians moving in both directions across the bridge had come to a standstill and the road was blocked by the shrieking arrival of several squad cars. In his peripheral vision, Dobbs watched as more police officers swarmed out of their cars and began to set up makeshift barriers to protect the public from the madman on the bridge.

Tears spilled over his face. Small, salty rivers that pooled in the lines on his cheeks as he continued to edge backwards.

"John, listen to me," Hitchins began.

"It's all over!" Jessop cut across her, adopting the kind of aggressive stance he thought would help him get ahead in life. "Give yourself up, man!"

But he wasn't listening to either of them. He watched a seagull weave through the metal struts overhead with an elegant flap of wings, then dive towards the water somewhere below.

"...*John Edward Dobbs, I am arresting you on suspicion of murder. You do not have to say anything. But it may harm your defence if you do not mention when questioned something which you later rely on in court. Anything you do say may be given in evidence.*"

As they surged forward to restrain him, Dobbs grasped the thick safety rail on the edge of the bridge. Drawing on the last drop of strength he had left, he heaved himself over the barrier and clung to the top, his knuckles glowing white as he held tight. He pressed his cheek against the cold metal and closed his eyes, mouthing a silent prayer.

"John, come down from the railing," he heard one of them say.

"Stay back!" he muttered, and opened his eyes. Far below, the river glistened diamond-bright in the early afternoon sunshine as it undulated gently towards the sea.

"John!" Hitchins' voice sounded urgent. "Don't do anything stupid. You don't want to do anything final."

But he knew she didn't care. She couldn't; not if he was a killer.

Another radio crackle.

Subject is volatile, there's a strong suicide risk. We need a crisis negotiator here, now!"

Slowly, Dobbs began to relax his grip on the metal railing.

"John, there's still time to come down and talk about things," the woman tried again, her voice wobbling.

How strange, he thought, that it was they who were frightened in the end.

He watched the river, mesmerised by the ebb and flow of the waves as the police continued to talk, to cajole, and finally to threaten. New officers came and went, more sirens and more noise while Dobbs retreated to the recesses of his own mind.

"John! Tell us why, John! At least tell us whether there are any more! You owe us that!"

In his last moments, he thought of his life, and of the people he had known. He couldn't recall ever feeling truly happy; there might have been flashes over the years, but they had been outweighed by crushing loneliness. He thought of all the stupid, desperate actions he had taken to quell it. He thought of the dead woman, and started to laugh through his tears, a hysterical, maniacal sound that jarred in the surrounding silence.

And then, sweet oblivion as the water rose up to meet him.

CHAPTER 2

Thirty miles further north, two men sat side by side on the grassy verge of a different riverbank deep in the heart of Northumberland. The sun had begun its gradual descent towards the horizon and cast long, hazy summer rays over the landscape, lending it the kind of vintage hue that could rarely be captured on film. There was a peaceful hush, broken only by the sound of summer insects in the brush and the distant thrum of civilisation at the Angler's Arms pub further upstream.

"Do you think we'll catch anything before I start drawing my old-age pension?"

Detective Sergeant Frank Phillips favoured his companion with a stern look.

"The trick is to be *patient*, lad. Let the fish come to you."

"We've been sitting here for nearly two hours and my arse is getting numb. Maybe the fish have migrated."

Phillips shuffled against the hard ground and wished he'd brought a foldaway chair.

"That's City-boy talk," he grumbled, for appearances' sake. "The trouble with your generation is you want everything to happen immediately."

Detective Chief Inspector Maxwell Finley-Ryan looked across at his sergeant with an indulgent expression.

"That explains it," he said, mildly.

"Explains what?"

"Why you haven't asked MacKenzie out to dinner yet. You're waiting for the fish to come to you, I take it."

Phillips' ruddy face flushed an even deeper shade of red.

"Don't know what you're gannin' on about," he muttered, hunching his shoulders defensively. It had been a full five years since his wife passed away—God rest her—and he had no intention of replacing her. But just lately it seemed that every time he turned a corner, he'd run into Detective Inspector Denise MacKenzie and find himself jabbering nonsense or, worse still, saying nothing at all while she looked at him with those laughing green eyes of hers.

Damn the woman.

"I'm too old for all that," he decided.

Ryan grinned and felt a tug on his fishing line.

"Yeah, I suppose you're getting a bit long in the tooth," he mused. "MacKenzie's a few years younger, probably has a lot more energy—"

Phillips swung around to face him, squaring his stocky shoulders and jutting out his chin in the manner of a bull preparing to charge.

"I'll have you know there's still plenty of—"

"Fish tugging on your line?" Ryan offered.

"*Aye*! And I'm not too old to catch them, neither."

"Just as well, because you've got some catching up to do," Ryan said, as he unfolded his long body and began to reel in an enormous brown trout. There was a tussle by the water's edge and sweat glistened against his forearms as he braced his legs and struggled to overpower the fish's will to survive.

Phillips abandoned his own rod and jumped to his feet.

"That's it, lad, you've got him now! Put your back into it!"

Ryan blew strands of dark hair from his eyes and hauled the protesting fish from the water, experiencing a quick surge of adrenaline followed swiftly by regret as he held its cold, quivering body in his hands. Quickly, he unhooked the fish and released it back into the shallows, heart thumping as he waited to see if it would recover.

"What're you doing?"

Ryan's shoulders relaxed as the trout flipped over and swam furiously towards the safety of deeper waters.

"I didn't feel like fish tonight after all."

Before Phillips could pass comment, a brassy rendition of the *Indiana Jones* theme tune sounded out across the quiet valley, disturbing a flock of birds nesting in the high reeds on the other side of the river. Ryan searched his pockets to find his mobile phone and, when he noted the caller ID, prepared to face death once again.

Northumbria Police Constabulary Headquarters nestled on the leafy western border of Newcastle upon Tyne, in a gentrified suburb far removed from the daily grind of the Criminal Investigation Department. Its boxy, sixties-style architecture stood out as a glaring anachronism but provided a welcome relief to the men and women tasked with investigating the worst that man could inflict upon his fellow being.

"Home sweet home," Phillips said, from the passenger seat of Ryan's car as they swung through the barriers and into the staff car park.

"Why is the car park so full—on a Sunday?" Ryan murmured, eyeing the rows of cars.

The two men exchanged a glance.

"Bugger," Phillips said. "There goes my carvery dinner."

Ryan nodded and made a mental note to cancel his plans for the evening. If he was any judge, they'd be in it for the duration.

"Come on," he said. "Let's go and see what all the fuss is about."

The office was a hive of activity as they strode along the dingy, carpet-tiled corridors of CID and made directly for the executive suite on the top floor. Telephones rang and printers hummed as they passed offices and conference rooms staffed with people working overtime. There was a lingering smell of damp permeating the air, made worse by an unpleasant odour wafting from the general direction of the gents toilets.

"Howay, man, that's criminal! Give it a courtesy flush, for pity's sake!"

Phillips called out the directive as they passed the doorway and chuckled to himself as a stream of abuse followed swiftly from somewhere within.

He was still grinning when he turned the corner and almost collided with Denise MacKenzie.

"Sorry," he muttered, drawing himself up to his full height.

She smiled slowly and folded her arms across her chest.

"Didn't expect to see you in the office today, Frank. You've heard, then?"

Phillips hastily pulled himself together.

"I'm just on m' way to see Gregson, now," he answered, striving for nonchalance. "How bad is it?"

She pulled an expressive face.

"Bad enough. Cooper lost a prime suspect today and the IPCC's already making noises about negligence. The Chief Constable's on the warpath."

Phillips cleared his throat.

"Well—"

"I should—"

"Right. Thanks for the heads up."

Phillips scurried away, trotting to keep up with Ryan who was standing a discreet distance away.

Before the man could pass comment, Phillips growled a warning.

"Not *one* word," he said.

Ryan held both hands up, smiling broadly.

"Wouldn't dream of it."

Their smiles faded as they approached a door bearing a shiny brass plaque. Phillips checked his tie—a jazzy little number in a shade of sunflower yellow—before rapping a knuckle against the wood.

"Come!"

They stepped inside the private domain of Detective Chief Superintendent Arthur Gregson and found the room brimming with senior police staff from at least two area command divisions. Conversations ended mid-flow as they entered the room and heads swivelled to greet the newcomers.

"Ryan, Phillips, come in," Gregson gestured them inside and closed the door behind them before returning to his desk. "Take a seat, if you can find one. The rest of you, clear out!"

While the room emptied, they remained standing like sentries to their general.

"Thanks for coming in on your day off," Gregson said, in the kind of tone that suggested he expected nothing less. "I suppose you've seen the news?"

He looked between their blank faces.

"Have you been hiding under a bloody rock? There's been a major incident," he told them, without preamble. "Less than an hour ago, our prime suspect in the Harris case ran around half of Newcastle while Hitchins and Jessop chased after him. He threw himself off the Tyne Bridge in full daylight, to a crowd of spectators who streamed the whole thing on social media. I've already had the IPCC on the blower wanting answers and the phones are ringing off the hook in the press office."

Ryan frowned.

"Cooper's the SIO on that one, sir. It's regrettable that the suspect has taken his own life, but I don't see that it qualifies as a major incident."

Gregson linked broad, workmanlike hands on the desktop and took a moment before answering. He was an imposing man with a shock of steel grey hair, a permanent golfer's tan and over thirty years on the force. A man in his position knew how to handle difficult situations and difficult people with detachment, but he could only admire the clinical way Ryan cut straight to the heart of the matter.

"John Dobbs isn't the problem, Ryan. It's Cooper."

Only then did they realise that their colleague, DCI Sharon Cooper, was nowhere to be seen. Ryan swung his gaze back to Gregson.

"Where is she?"

"Cooper's been uncontactable since around eleven this morning," Gregson replied. "She sent a message to say she needed to take an hour's personal and that's the last we heard. John Dobbs had been under surveillance for three days. Jessop and Hitchins were on shift this morning when he spotted them and took off along the Quayside. They tried radioing her for instructions but heard nothing. We sent a response team and a crisis negotiator to the bridge, but it was too late." He lifted his shoulders and let them fall again. "While Cooper was AWOL, Dobbs offed himself. They did their best in the circumstances but Hitchins and Jessop don't have the authority or the experience. They were expecting to watch the bloke and make an arrest if necessary, not talk him down after running the length and breadth of the city. God knows, it's not the outcome any of us wanted."

"Or what the Harris family might have wanted," Ryan added, thinking that it was a cowardly way out for a killer. "Where's Cooper now?"

It was unthinkable that the SIO tasked with commanding their most high-profile murder investigation in recent years was MIA. It wasn't just negligent, he thought, it was unforgivable.

But he kept his thoughts to himself, at least until he had spoken to his colleague.

"There'll be hell to pay once the media gets wind of it," Phillips put in.

"They already have," Gregson intoned. "I've got the media liaison managing that side of things, but I want to get ahead of the evening news before the next disaster unfolds."

Ryan felt a coldness begin to spread inside his chest, a creeping dread he recognised as the kind of sixth sense murder detectives develop after a while on the job. In the face of what looked like gross professional negligence, Gregson was displaying a surprising lack of enmity. It begged the question *why*.

"Where's Cooper, sir?"

Gregson sighed deeply.

"Her police tracker's still transmitting from her home in Tynemouth," he replied calmly. "There's a response team on their way there now. They're under orders not to force entry until a senior officer arrives. Ryan, I need somebody I can trust to be there on the ground before they go in, making sure everything's done by the book. I can't have a bunch of squaddies trampling over the place; Cooper's one of our own, after all."

When the full weight of that implication hit home, Phillips' eyebrows flew into his receding hairline.

"You think Dobbs got to her before he topped himself?"

Gregson sighed and leaned back in his chair.

"Too early to say, Frank. All we know is that Cooper's police tracker is still transmitting, the doors are locked and her car's parked outside."

Ryan shook his head slightly.

"It couldn't have been Dobbs, not if he was under police surveillance. His movements are accounted for."

The room fell silent for long seconds and the sound of traffic filtered through the cracks in the walls.

"Both of you get down there as quickly as you can," Gregson said heavily. "And keep it as *quiet* as you can. The people in this city think the danger has passed. Let them stay blissfully ignorant for as long as possible."

CHAPTER 3

Ryan raced across the city with a blithe disregard for the highway code while Phillips rode in the passenger seat bracing one hand against the dashboard in case of impact. They barrelled along the Coast Road towards the sea, past old factories converted into overpriced apartments and council estates badly in need of investment until they reached the pretty village of Tynemouth, where DCI Sharon Cooper lived. Ryan slowed to a crawl along its quaint high street, finding it alive with locals enjoying the last of the summer sunshine breaking through the clouds and warming the walls of the ancient priory, presiding over things from its craggy outcrop overlooking the beach.

"Dunno why newspaper isn't good enough, anymore," Phillips mumbled.

Ryan gave him a distracted glance.

"What?"

"Fish 'n' chips," his sergeant elaborated, nodding towards a fancy-looking restaurant. "In my day, you got a freshly battered fish and a mountain of chips soaked in salt 'n' vinegar, all wrapped in yesterday's newspaper. Nowadays, it's all artsy-fartsy paper from France wrapped in bleedin' ribbons and bows. Waste of money, if you ask me."

"Probably more hygienic," Ryan said fairly. "And too much salt is bad for your health."

Phillips made a sound like a raspberry and patted the middle-aged paunch that was just visible beneath his summer jacket.

"You need a bit of padding ahead of winter," he explained, eyeing Ryan's lithe physique with a trace of pity. "The lasses like to have something to hold on to, y' know."

Ryan couldn't help but smile. It wasn't lost on him that Frank had a habit of lightening the mood in times of stress, such as now.

"You could just wear a jumper," he said, executing a sharp left turn into one of the residential streets lined with smart Victorian terraces. Further conversation was forestalled when they spotted a line of police vehicles blocking the road and drawing the unwanted attention of Cooper's neighbours.

"So much for keeping things quiet," Phillips said.

Ryan yanked the handbrake with more force than was necessary and stalked across the road.

"You!" He pointed an accusing finger towards one of the first response officers. "What the hell do you call this?"

He spread an arm to encompass the crowd of onlookers.

"Sir, we were told to guard the scene."

"You were told to act with discretion and intercept anyone entering or leaving DCI Cooper's home. We don't know if there's any scene to guard, yet," Ryan snapped, with rare optimism. "Above all else, you were told not to create a circus, which is what this is starting to look like. Where's your sergeant?"

"Sorry, sir," one of them mumbled. "The DS was supposed to be here."

Ryan's mouth flattened ominously.

"What steps have been taken to manage the crowd?"

They looked between themselves for divine inspiration.

"We—well, we told them to go home but they're not listening."

Ryan swore softly, eyeing the throng with impatience. Beside him, Phillips reached for a packet of Superkings and considered whether he had time for a smoke while Ryan delivered a quick lesson on crowd management.

"Listen up!" Ryan began, in clipped, well-rounded tones. "You've already been told to move along. If you continue to disregard a police instruction, I will not hesitate to issue formal cautions to each and every one of you. They remain on your permanent record," he added, for good measure.

The crowd scattered like rats, muttering discontentedly about things being different in their day, whatever that meant. Phillips let out a small sigh and replaced the packet of cigarettes inside his breast pocket.

Maybe later.

Ryan turned back to the two constables standing on the pavement outside Cooper's postage-stamp front garden. Behind them, the curtains were drawn at the windows of the house and nothing stirred on the air except a summer breeze.

"Set up a cordon," he ordered. "Log every entry and exit. The official line is, 'no comment', in case anybody asks."

Two heads bobbed up and down.

"And you can tell your sergeant to piss off, if he ever deigns to turn up. We can take it from here."

"Right. Yes, sir," they gabbled.

He began to turn, then his head whipped back around again.

"One more thing. If—and only *if*—there has been an incident, DCI Cooper's home and person deserve our respect. That means no smart comments and no pictures. You stay put, you keep your eyes forward and note anybody sniffing around. If I find either of you has breathed a word, you'll be pulled up on a disciplinary. Is that understood?"

Ryan watched their faces turn pale and was satisfied that his threat had hit home. He gestured towards two other officers who were standing a short distance away carrying a small battering ram, affectionately known as the 'enforcer'. Above their heads, he caught sight of several pairs of curtains twitching in the houses across the street.

"Let's get it over with," he said, and pulled out bright blue protective shoe coverings and matching nitrile gloves.

You could never be too careful.

He led the short way along an encaustic-tiled pathway towards the front door and knocked loudly.

"DCI Cooper? It's DCI Ryan and DS Phillips. Open the door, please!"

No answer.

He tried again, louder this time, hammering his fist until the door rattled.

"DCI Cooper! We have reason to believe your life is in danger! Be advised we are about to force entry!"

Still no answer.

On the off-chance, Ryan tried the door knob but found it locked.

"Back door's locked too, sir," one of the constables told him.

"Alright, let's get it open."

Ryan stepped back to allow the two waiting constables forward. In one easy motion, they swung the ram and there came the sound of splintering wood as the door flew open, revealing a shadowed hallway beyond.

Ryan held up a hand to signal caution, then stepped inside.

They smelled the blood first.

The air was saturated with the tinny scent of it as Ryan and Phillips moved warily through the downstairs rooms, eyes watchful for any signs of life. They found the crusted remnants of a bowl of porridge beside the sink in the kitchen and the dregs of a glass of wine on the coffee table in the living room but not much else. There was a curious stillness, as if the walls were watching their progress through the house.

Waiting.

"Upstairs," Ryan said quietly and padded up the narrow staircase to the first floor. Phillips' heavier tread sounded behind him, familiar and comforting as they walked headlong into the unknown.

The air grew more stagnant as they emerged onto the landing, searching inside each room they passed until only one door remained.

"Get ready," Ryan muttered and grasped the handle.

Both men remained standing inside the doorway for long seconds while their bodies adjusted to the horror, struggling to control the urge to reject what they had seen.

"Dear God," Phillips managed, swiping the back of his hand across his mouth to repel the stench of human waste.

Ryan's face remained shuttered. Calm grey eyes swept over Sharon Cooper's bedroom, noting the tiny details that would later become the fabric of his nightmares.

The curtains were closed.

"Make a note for Faulkner," he said, referring to the Senior Crime Scene Investigator attached to CID. "Check the curtain fabric in here and in the living room downstairs. He might have forgotten to cover his hands."

Phillips nodded, breathing hard through his teeth.

"Is it definitely her?"

Amid the destruction, it was by no means obvious.

"I think so," Ryan replied, and forced himself to look again at the remains of what had once been a woman.

Sharon Cooper's body parts had been laid out on her bed like the components of a macabre jigsaw puzzle against a canvas of blood, which drenched the linen and oozed onto the floor in coagulated drops, forming puddles on the pale blue carpet. A few strands of matted blonde hair hung limply from her head, which had been placed atop a broderie anglaise scatter cushion like a ceremonial offering. The clothes she had chosen to wear that morning were folded neatly at the end of the bed and a single fly flew in circles above her left foot, tipped with pink polish.

"It's inhuman," Phillips breathed. "I've never—in twenty years, I've never seen anything like it."

And he had seen his fair share. From bodies found in rubbish bins to the kind of vengeful murder inflicted between the ruling gangs in the criminal underworld, he'd seen it all in his time.

But this was different.

"Whoever did this really enjoyed themselves," Ryan agreed, swallowing back rage as he thought of the woman's family and of the friends she left behind. He thought of all the memories she would never make, all the life left to live.

Nobody had the right to take it from her, and never with such brutality.

Nobody.

Ryan closed his eyes briefly, remembering the last time he'd seen Cooper alive. She'd been stressed and run-down, both of which were natural by-products of heading up an important investigation that had drawn national headlines.

"Stupid thing's on the blink again," she'd told him. *"All I want is a packet of ready salted. Is it too much to ask?"*

"Give it a good kick," he'd said. *"It's therapeutic."*

Meaningless, nonsense words, but he thought of how her eyes had crinkled when they'd shared a joke.

Now, those same eyes were filmed white and stared sightlessly up at the ceiling.

"No sign of a break-in," Phillips said, bringing him back to the present. "Could be a vengeance kill. Could be somebody she's put away over the years…could even be Dobbs."

"No," Ryan turned away. "It's not Dobbs. Look at her, Frank. She can't have been dead more than a few hours. There's no way he could have done this whilst under surveillance."

He let out a short, mirthless laugh and shook his head.

"Whoever killed her is still out there."

CHAPTER 4

The remainder of the afternoon was spent overseeing the transfer of Sharon Cooper's body to the mortuary, where the police pathologist had given up his day of rest to begin the painstaking process of understanding how she had come to die. The CSI team rustled around her house in their polypropylene overalls searching the minutiae for traces of her killer, unravelling the fabric of her life and laying it bare, while a team of local constables knocked at every door on the street and took preliminary statements from her neighbours. They were only too glad to cooperate since the threat of police caution remained uppermost in their minds but, unfortunately, none of them had seen Cooper that day nor any unusual visitors or strange vehicles parked on the road.

Whoever had killed 'that lovely policewoman at number seven' had managed to come and go like an apparition.

"It was always a long shot," Phillips said, leaning back against the side of Ryan's car. "It's a Sunday. You can't expect people to be peeping through their curtains jotting down registration plates at eleven o'clock in the morning."

Ryan grunted.

"I didn't notice any CCTV on the road," Phillips continued, "but we're not far from the high street. There might be something we can get hold of there."

Ryan nodded, considering the access points.

"Plenty of local businesses nearby. Let's check with them, too."

They watched the CSIs carry a large, industrial film light from their inconspicuous black van towards the tent they'd erected outside Cooper's front door. It was almost six o'clock and daylight was starting to fade.

"Check the bus routes and the metro," Ryan said. "It's only a five-minute walk to the station from here. Who knows? We might get lucky."

"Consider it done," Phillips said, and reached for his packet of cigarettes once again. The tobacco fizzed orange as he took a long drag, which should have gone some way to calming his nerves but had the opposite effect instead.

"I've been thinking," he began.

"A dangerous proposition," Ryan replied automatically.

"Aye, I know. I've been thinking about the style. It's the same—isn't it?"

Ryan didn't need to ask what he meant. The dismemberment of their colleague bore a marked resemblance to the state in which Isobel Harris's body had been discovered, two weeks earlier.

The implications were terrifying.

"We need the pathologist to confirm," Ryan said eventually. "We have to be as sure as we can before we head down that path."

He stuck his hands in his pockets and thought of what led a man to hurl himself from a great height. Fear? Desperation? Perhaps there was some guilt mixed in there, too.

"Cooper threw the full force of the law at John Dobbs," he thought aloud. "She believed with every fibre of her being that he was the one who'd killed Isobel Harris. The public still believe it. Half of them are congratulating us, while the other half vilify us for driving a man over the edge and denying a family their rightful day in court. But, most of all, they believe we got our man and they've started to relax again, to walk home alone again without being frightened about who might be following. We need to be one hundred per cent sure of ourselves before we come out and say that the person who killed Isobel Harris also waltzed into Sharon Cooper's home and did *that*"—he bobbed his head towards the house on the other side of the road—"because, if it is the same person, that means an innocent man threw himself off the bridge today, Frank."

Phillips took another drag of his cigarette.

"It could still be a copycat," he said, a bit desperately. He'd known Sharon Cooper for over ten years; she'd been friendly with his wife and brought flowers to the hospital before she died. "It could be some opportunist, or someone holding a grudge."

Ryan looked him squarely in the eye.

"You know as well as I do that the details of how we found Isobel Harris's body weren't made public. Yet somebody copied her killer's MO almost down to the letter. Look, nobody wants to damage Cooper's reputation, but we can't overlook the possibility that she made a mistake. It may have been the biggest mistake of her life."

A few seconds ticked by while Phillips took a final, long drag of his cigarette and then ground it out with the heel of his shoe.

"Howay, let's find the bastard," he said.

The city was pleasant on a summer's evening.

There seemed to be a new energy in the air, a sense of relief that was palpable now that John Dobbs, the 'killer on the bridge', was gone. People strolled through the streets with less urgency than before, now that his blight had been brought to an end and the precarious balance between good and evil had been restored.

Or so they told themselves.

He watched them walk along the park avenue like sheep, bleating about their mundane jobs and banal lives, and wondered what it would be like to be so completely ordinary. There would be a simplicity to life, he supposed. A kind of comfort in being so ignorant, so commonplace. He couldn't blame them for that. He could be generous and allow them a small concession because they did not ask to be part of the masses; it was the luck of the draw. It was the natural order of the world that some must be predators and others the prey.

Idly, he watched a woman enter the park on a pair of improbable cork wedges that were at least a half-size too small. He watched her glance across at him and flick back her hair, thrusting her chest forward in an age-old dance he recognised and had used many times to his advantage. He gave her a lazy smile, schooling his face into the appropriate lines as he considered her attributes like butcher's meat.

"Too short and too blonde, for starters," he mused. He preferred his women to be *au naturel*. "Chunky thighs, probably doesn't exercise. Under-developed arms, dry skin."

She was smiling now, he realised, one of those coy smiles intended to convey innocence and inveigle men.

The thought was nauseating.

Even if he could forgive her various physical imperfections, he could scarcely overlook her abominable taste in clothes. She wore an over-tight denim skirt designed for a much younger woman and a clingy vest top that left little to the imagination. Her breasts swung like udders and he began to think it was almost worth putting her down as a supreme act of kindness.

She mistook his regard and sauntered across to the bench, settling herself beside him before making a great show of crossing her legs. The action drew attention to the mottled cellulite covering her exposed skin and he began to shake, revulsion snaking its way over his skin.

"Anybody sitting here?"

"Just you, beautiful," he said, with a flirtatious wink.

She giggled, and he checked the time on his watch.

Nearly six-thirty.

"I think I've seen you here before, haven't I?"

There was a momentary clutch in his chest, a tightening of the intercostal muscles, before he remembered it was just the kind of inane small-talk that men and women exchanged.

"I'm sure I'd have remembered seeing you," he replied.

She flushed with pleasure and he began to feel tainted by her presence, the stench of her skin beginning to overpower him.

He must not lose control.

A gaggle of young women passed by the bench where they sat. He studied them critically, watching their animated faces, trying to imagine what their eyes might look like as they died.

It would be so easy.

His hands began to shake, nothing more than a tremor but it was enough to remind him to be careful. The temptation was not worth the risk and it wouldn't do to become greedy.

Besides, he'd know her when he saw her. She was due any moment now.

He checked the time again and smiled.

"—did you?"

He realised the ugly blonde woman was still sitting there talking to him. His patience was exhausted, and his mind was occupied elsewhere. A game of cat and mouse to pass the time no longer held any appeal.

Time for her to move on.

He turned to look at her, skimming his intense gaze over the planes of her face, noting every crack and flaw. She blossomed beneath such an appraisal and wondered if, this time, she had found a prince.

He leaned forward, confidentially.

"You know, darling, if you lost about half a stone and went to a decent hairdresser, somebody might be interested in you. It wouldn't hurt to have your teeth looked at, either, but I'm probably being pedantic." He watched her face fall into lines of confusion and hurt, all the fuel he needed.

"You can't have thought I'd be interested in you?" he asked, gently. "Did you really imagine I could look at you and feel anything but pity? Really, sweetheart, there's a pecking order in all things."

Her eyes filled, and he watched her bear down, willing herself not to cry as she snatched up her bag, almost tripping over her preposterous shoes in her haste to get away.

Once the amusement faded, he turned his attention back to the gates of the park.

"She's late," he breathed, tapping an angry forefinger against the side of the bench. "She's never late."

The anticipation was exquisite, almost painful, and he began to worry he'd missed her while he was entertaining himself with the blonde. Timing was critical.

If he'd missed his chance…

Just then, he spotted her. A quick flash of long, dark hair bundled in a high ponytail that swung from side to side as she walked past the entrance to the park. There was a natural spring in her step, an infectious *joie de vivre* that had caught his attention weeks ago.

She was alone, just as he expected she would be.

Casually, he stood up. He stretched out his back in an unhurried motion, rolling out his shoulders before strolling towards the gates. He didn't bother to keep his head down; that would look suspicious. Besides, there was no need.

The cameras hadn't worked in months.

Once he passed through the gates and onto the pavement lining the road parallel to the park, she had crossed over to the other side. He anticipated that and lengthened his stride a fraction to keep up, whistling beneath his breath. The next part was trickier. She lived on an exposed street, in a garden flat with its own front door, accessible via a short flight of stairs in full view of anyone happening to pass by. Luckily, the street was busy enough to be inconspicuous; the kind of place where people came and went without ever stopping to notice what was happening around them.

But there would be no need to worry about anybody witnessing anything unusual. By his reckoning, she was going to invite him in of her own accord and nobody would be any the wiser.

Swiftly, he crossed the street to intercept her.

"Hey, Nicola!"

She spun around, a smile already lighting up her face.

"Oh, hello!"

"I thought it was you," he said. "Heading home?"

She gave a light shrug.

"Yeah, I'm off on holiday for a week and I need to finish packing."

"Sounds great. Well, I won't hold you up. Nice to run into you." He began to step away and affected a self-conscious air she found endearing.

"Are you heading my way?"

He was so close now, so terribly close.

"Ah, I don't know. I'm heading along Claremont Road, a friend of mine's having a barbecue," he improvised.

"Sounds nice," she said as she fell into step beside him. "I live along that way, so we can keep each other company."

She was so trusting, so ready to think the best of him, he almost regretted what was about to happen.

That was a lie.

He could hardly wait.

He kept her chatting all the way. He made her smile, made her believe she was safe. That was the most important part of all, he had learned. They must never suspect what was coming. He must never alert them to the danger and risk a scene. He'd learned that lesson before and didn't care to exert himself unnecessarily.

"This is me," she said.

They stopped outside a three-storey converted terrace that had been painted white at one stage or another but was now a dirty grey. Somebody had planted a few perennials in the tiny garden at the front to cheer it up a bit and a fat ginger cat sat staring unblinkingly out of the ground floor window. A stone stairwell led down to a separate entrance on the basement level, out of view.

"Alright, well, nice chatting to you and I hope you have a lovely holiday," he said, flashing a quick smile. "Don't forget to take your sun cream."

She nodded and cast around for something intelligent to say to prolong their farewell.

"Enjoy the barbecue," she said. "Might see you after I'm back?"

"Oh, I'm sure you will," he said, and gave her a lingering look.

When she turned away and skipped downstairs, Nicola was smiling. Wasn't it funny how the world worked? She'd been wondering whether she'd done the right thing in getting rid of Stuart and had almost cracked the other night when he'd called by to pick up his stuff. Then, when she least expected it, somebody else came along. She could hardly believe it, but she was sure he'd been flirting with her…

With the key already in the lock, she heard a slight noise and almost jumped in shock.

He was standing less than a metre behind her.

"I forgot something."

Even as the tiger opened its jaws, she failed to recognise the danger.

"What's that?" she said, dreaming of holding hands along the riverbank. All the things she hoped for, longed for.

All the things he would never be able to give.

He moved like lightning, one strong hand clamping across her mouth while the other stabbed the pressure syringe into her neck. Her eyes flew wide with shock as she felt the sharp stab of a needle but there was no time to struggle, no time to scream before the drug took effect. Her body began to sway, and she buckled, rapidly losing feeling in her arms and legs. He propped her against the door with one strong arm while the other turned the key in the lock, freezing as he heard footsteps passing by on the pavement above.

A moment later, they were gone.

"Come on, sleepy-head," he said. "Let's get you inside."

He shut the door softly behind him.

CHAPTER 5

Tom Faulkner watched the sun begin to disappear behind the rooftops from the driver's seat of his van, where he sat quietly sipping a bottle of lukewarm Irn-Bru. The Senior Crime Scene Investigator was a mild-mannered man of around forty whose face wore a constant hangdog expression of anxiety that belied his passion and flair for forensic science. Polypropylene overalls hung at his waist to reveal a faded *X-Files* t-shirt that had seen better days and his mousy brown hair was matted with sweat.

"Got a minute?"

Ryan poked his head through the half-open window and Faulkner scrubbed a tired hand over his face.

"Yeah." He looked back to see the tented entranceway and thought of what had lain beyond the innocuous front door. "Let's walk and talk. I need to shake it off."

"Bad business in there," Phillips sympathised, as they ambled down the street towards the village.

"Yeah. About as bad as it gets."

It came to something when a CSI laid claim to that.

"What can you tell us?" Ryan asked, never a man to beat around the bush. "Did they leave anything behind?"

"They always leave something." Faulkner took another sip of his drink and replaced the cap, swilling the sugary liquid around his mouth as if to rinse out the taste of death. "But it'll be a miracle if we have any clean samples after wading through everything. It'll take days before I know."

Ryan watched a woman cross the street clutching the hand of a boy of three or four and felt his stomach twist.

"We don't have days, Tom," he said quietly. "What happened to Cooper is a clear escalation. They won't wait long for the next one."

Faulkner hissed out a frustrated breath, weighing things up. His choice to forego dinner with his wife's family and come into work had caused a vicious argument, something that was becoming more and more frequent these days. It troubled him, but not half as much as it should have done; not half as much as the prospect of being excluded from the investigation.

"I'll do what I can," he conceded.

Phillips slapped a manly hand on Faulkner's shoulder.

"Good lad," he said.

"You're the best there is," Ryan said, without rancour. He made no effort to flatter the man, merely stated the fact.

"That remains to be seen," Faulkner muttered. "So far, I can't tell you very much. You already know the front and back doors to the house were locked. Well, it turns out we have a considerate killer because they posted the door keys back through the letterbox. We found them lying on the floor."

"Cocky bastard," Phillips spat. "Any prints?"

"Plenty, but I'll bet they all belong to Sharon. No way he'd have left them unless he was sure there'd be no risk."

The three men fell silent as they rounded the corner onto the high street. The village slumbered again now that the locals and visitors had returned to their homes and they could hear the faint sound of waves crashing against the shore, somewhere in the twilight.

"What about weapons? Did he leave anything behind?"

By mutual accord, they headed in the direction of the sea wall.

"I've bagged everything that could possibly have been used but frankly I'm not holding out much hope," Faulkner replied, with a trace of apology. "The kind of implement he'd need to get through...well, to saw through the bones, that would take a hacksaw or something similar. We didn't find anything that fits the bill."

"He could have dumped it somewhere," Phillips put in. "We've got the local team rifling through bins, just in case."

"He's meticulous," Ryan overrode him. "He's not averse to spending time researching his victims' lives, finding out where they live, when they leave home, whether they live alone... He probably prefers to use his own tools, in which case he brought what he needed and took them away again. We won't find anything in a bin."

He looked across to find both men watching him strangely. It was an occupational advantage but a personal hazard, the uncanny knack of being able to step inside the mind of a killer.

"We never found a murder weapon after Isobel Harris, either," he reminded them.

Phillips grunted.

"One thing we did have from the scene at the Harris place was trace DNA," Faulkner said. "Once we've had a chance to analyse the samples we've taken today, we'll see if any of them match up. We still don't have a name but it's better than nothing."

"We have John Dobbs," Ryan put in. "We can compare his DNA and it'll bring us one stage closer to ruling him out of the Harris murder—or not, as the case may be."

It was becoming increasingly unlikely that Dobbs had taken the girl's life, but they couldn't discount the possibility. Not yet.

"I'll make it a priority," Faulkner agreed.

They reached the sea wall and Ryan leaned forward, resting his forearms on the top to stare out to sea as the tide rolled in. The wind had picked up, buffeting against them as night drew in and he shivered, imagining what it had taken for a man to plunge himself into the water.

Abruptly, he turned away.

"There was one other thing we found," Faulkner broke the silence, fiddling with the plastic bottle he still held in his hands, not looking at either of them.

"What's that?"

"He left a calling card."

"You mean a note?"

"No, it's a gentleman's calling card, like something from another era."

"What did it say?"

Faulkner shook his head.

"It was so blood-stained, I've sent it back to the lab to have it cleaned up, so we can read what it said."

"The minute you do, call me," Ryan told him and, to their surprise, broke into a wide grin.

"Dunno what you've got to smile about," Phillips blurted out. "We've got two brutal murders on our hands, a pack of ravenous reporters yappin' at our heels and the wrath of the Superintendent to contend with when we get back to HQ. And there you are, grinning like a muppet."

Ryan laughed richly.

"Don't you see, Frank? Whoever killed Cooper broke their own rules by leaving that card. They were so careful, so controlled. But leaving that card? That's loss of control because they needed the challenge and the chase. They want us to come after them."

"There won't be any DNA on the card," Faulkner promised him.

"There doesn't need to be," Ryan shot back. "It's an insight into their mind, the type of person we're hunting."

"And what kind of person is that?" Faulkner enquired. Behind his head, the priory was illuminated as night fell rapidly and cast his face into shadow.

Ryan narrowed his eyes.

"They want to be superhuman but they're not," Ryan said flatly. "Our killer's just an average, garden-variety psychopath. They're two a penny down on the psych ward."

"Oh, that's all right then," Phillips mumbled. "I'll sleep better tonight, knowing that."

"You think he's challenging you?" Faulkner ignored the interruption.

Ryan's face transformed into hard, serious lines.

"They think they're invincible, beyond the law. I'll not only *accept* the challenge, I'll make it my mission in life. I won't stop until they're behind bars and neither will you."

His words hung on the air like a prophecy.

"Be careful," Phillips cautioned him and there was concern reflected in his eyes. "These ones, they have a way of worming their way inside your head. Make sure you keep yours clear."

News of DCI Cooper's murder spread through Police Headquarters like wildfire. Too afraid to speak the words aloud, analysts and technicians, telephone operatives and kitchen staff spoke in whispers, as if that would somehow make it bearable. A late briefing had been scheduled for eight-thirty and when Ryan stepped through the doorway of Conference Room A, it seemed every member of staff employed by Northumbria CID was in attendance and awaiting instructions from their new Senior Investigating

Officer. Their faces were sombre and their eyes bloodshot, whether from tears or a lack of sleep, he couldn't tell. While he waited for them to settle themselves in the ubiquitous plastic chairs that came with any government-owned establishment, he walked over to exchange a word with Phillips, who was chatting to one of CID's newest recruits near the front of the room.

"Phillips." He accepted a polystyrene cup filled with brown sludge and raised a single black eyebrow. "What the hell is this?"

"Vending machine calls it a double macchiato," Phillips told him. "Tastes more like paint stripper."

Ryan took a dubious sip, decided it wasn't going to kill him, then turned to the younger man.

"You did good work on the Khan case."

It was hardly glowing praise, but Detective Constable Jack Lowerson couldn't quite hold back the grin. He'd spent every one of his formative years as a lowly police constable looking up to the tall man who was now, miraculously, his boss. Ryan had plucked him from obscurity and given him a chance to shine. He was doing his best each day never to make him regret it.

"Thank you, sir."

Ryan was momentarily distracted by the glare bouncing off Lowerson's freshly-whitened teeth and found himself wondering whether that amount of bleach was even legal.

"You've got the right attitude, Jack. Just carry on doing what you're doing."

With that, he raised his cup and walked across to the long whiteboard covering the entire length of one wall, flanked by a flip-board and a desk set up with a laptop and projector. Ryan ignored the computer and dropped a heavy cardboard folder he had tucked under his arm onto the cheap Formica desk. While the room slowly fell silent, he retrieved four large photographs from inside its folds and began sticking them onto the whiteboard.

Over his shoulder, he heard gasps from around the room.

"I can't believe it," they said.

He tacked up the last image and stepped away again.

"Believe it," he said, not bothering with any of the usual pleasantries. "Most of you will have heard the news about DCI Sharon Cooper but, for those who haven't, allow me to bring you up to speed. Her dismembered body was discovered by DS Phillips and myself at approximately two o'clock this afternoon. Her team reported her as uncommunicative after eleven o'clock this morning."

The room was silent.

"I see some of you looking at the floor." He watched their heads snap up again. "I want you to *look* at her," he ground out, demanding their attention. "I want you to feel outrage, disgust, all the normal things you should feel. I want you to remember the woman we all knew and admired, who gave her life to the pursuit of justice and public service. And then I want you to feel angry. *Really* angry that somebody snatched it away from her."

He pointed at the images on the wall showing Isobel Harris and Sharon Cooper in life beside blown-up images of them in death.

"Remember these women when you're tired and hungry and begging for sleep. Remember that they'll never feel anything ever again, but their families will. Their loved ones will feel that loss every day for the rest of their lives while we carry on. Never forget we're the lucky ones."

This time, when Ryan looked across the sea of faces, he found every one of them riveted on the wall.

He leaned back against the edge of the desk and crossed his ankles.

"I know most of you were assigned to the Harris investigation over the past two weeks and I want to thank you for your diligence and hard work. I know that DCI Cooper would have wanted to thank you, too." He paused to let that sink in. "But what I need from you now is honesty."

They looked at each other in surprise.

"I want you to ask yourselves whether you can come back tomorrow morning and give me everything you've got. Nobody will think any less of you for taking the time you need to grieve and recover. In fact, it's a direct order. I need strong, healthy people working on my task force because we've got a mountain to climb. If you can't take the pace, go home now and come back when you're ready."

There was a two-thirds split of those who sat up a little straighter in their chairs and those who slumped, defeated.

But nobody left the room, which gave him hope.

Just then, the doors opened to admit a latecomer. DCS Gregson entered and moved to stand on the sidelines, causing a mass rustling of chairs.

Ryan spared him a glance, then clapped his hands to regain their attention.

"Alright, listen up! Before she was murdered, Cooper believed that circumstantial evidence pointed towards one man. That man was John Edward Dobbs, a forty-six-year-old hospital technician at the Royal Victoria Infirmary who committed suicide at around noon today."

There were a couple of unsympathetic snorts. Ryan made a mental note of their names then pushed away from the desk to add another face to the board, set apart from the others. Looking into Dobbs' myopic brown eyes in blurry Technicolour, he felt a tug somewhere low in his belly he recognised as guilt. He hadn't known the man, nor worked on building the case against him, but there was no denying the possibility that his department had driven Dobbs to take his own life.

It was more than possible, he amended swiftly. It was downright probable.

He stepped away, putting a physical and emotional distance between himself and the sad, milky-faced man whose bloated body now lay on an impersonal gurney down at the mortuary.

"Reading through DCI Cooper's notes, I can see there were several good reasons why Dobbs was her prime suspect. First"—he ticked them off on his fingers—"the injuries sustained by Isobel Harris displayed a level of clinical precision and anatomical knowledge suggestive of a healthcare professional or someone working within that field. The investigation ran to veterinary surgeons and local butchers but, ultimately, came to focus on hospitals and GP surgeries after other facts came to light. John Dobbs worked as a hospital technician at the RVI, which isn't the same as being a world-leading surgeon but it's a start. Secondly," he said, tapping his middle finger, "Isobel Harris was a member of an online dating community known as LoveLife. Data released by the company included a list of men she had dated over the course of her membership, which ran to four months in total. John Dobbs was one of them."

He paused to check they were still paying attention before continuing.

"Finally, and perhaps most damning, CCTV footage from Fenwick's department store showed an altercation between John Dobbs and Isobel Harris at the perfume counter where she worked, two days after their date on 17th June. Messages retrieved from her mobile phone provider and other social media sites tell us the date did not go well and she left early, apparently because Dobbs had not been honest in his online dating profile and because he was, in her own words, 'old and weird'. She was twenty-two, he was a man in his late forties but passed himself off as being ten years younger and a senior consultant. Taken together with the criminal profile created by our forensic psychologist, the working theory was that Dobbs couldn't stand to be rejected by Harris and so tortured and killed her in retribution."

His eyes fell on the pretty, smiling face of Isobel Harris and he was silent for a long moment.

"But?"

Phillips' voice interrupted his reverie.

"But what?"

"You were about to tell us why that theory was all wrong," Phillips supplied, reaching for the emergency Kit Kat he had stowed in one of his pockets. "Unless you think Dobbs killed Harris after all?"

Ryan resisted the terrible urge to laugh.

"Until we hear from the pathologist and the CSI team, we only have initial observations to rely on. *But*," he enunciated the word for Phillips' benefit, "there's a striking resemblance in the manner we found both women, and not just physically. Look at the behaviour leading up to their deaths: each time, their killer did his research to make sure they lived alone. The last thing he would have wanted is an interruption. That must have involved days or weeks of surveillance ahead of killing them, which suggests very high levels of *control*. That's mirrored in the way each woman was killed. He took his time, he was methodical, he planned ahead and, unless we find a murder weapon, it looks like he brought his own tools and cleaned up after himself on both occasions."

"But with Harris, the process was much longer," MacKenzie said. "He kept her alive for almost fifteen hours before finishing her. It was a marathon."

Ryan heard the wobble in her voice and chose to ignore it, not because he deemed it unworthy but because he knew MacKenzie was strong enough to handle herself.

"That's true, which suggests Cooper didn't interest him except as a vessel. At this point, it's still possible that Dobbs murdered Harris, if not Cooper. Why else did he have such an extreme reaction? Why run like he did? If there was nothing to hide, he could have come in for questioning without any fuss."

"Dobbs had a history of depression and anxiety," Phillips put in. "That may explain the overreaction."

"Maybe," Ryan conceded, but was not convinced. "In light of what we discovered today, we can't ignore the possibility that Dobbs didn't kill either woman and that some other reason exists to explain why he ran."

"Sir?"

Ryan searched the room for the source of the interruption and found Lowerson's eager face.

"If Dobbs wasn't responsible, does that mean we've got a serial on our hands?"

It was on the tip of Ryan's tongue to say 'no' and play down the possibility that a new serial killer had been born so they could deceive themselves about the level of threat they were facing.

But that was not his way.

"Yes, Jack. I think we should assume we're dealing with a methodical, experienced killer who has taken more than one life."

"Otherwise known as a fruitcake, son," Phillips put in, from the row behind.

Ryan rolled his eyes.

"The alternative definition," he said dryly. "From Professor Frank Phillips, MD…"

"Well, he mustn't be a full shilling. Normal people don't flit about like they're Jack the Ripper."

"What makes you think we're looking for a man?" DI MacKenzie queried, from her position a few chairs along.

Phillips opened his mouth and then snapped it shut again.

"Well, i-it fits the bill, doesn't it?" he stuttered, much to his irritation. "Normally, it's men who kill violently. Women don't like to get their hands dirty, do they?"

"Oh, believe me, Frank. Women can be just as deadly," MacKenzie shifted in her seat to pin him with the kind of direct stare that would have terrified a lesser man. "And, as I'm sure you're aware, the toxicology report on Isobel Harris's body showed abnormally high levels of sedative and adrenaline in her system; enough to disable her. It creates a level playing field when physicality isn't an issue, wouldn't you agree?"

"Look, love," Phillips began, and failed to see MacKenzie's eyes flash dangerously. "There's no way a woman could have dragged Cooper's sedated body up a flight of stairs and along to her bedroom. She would have been a dead weight. Same goes for Isobel Harris."

"Look, *sweetheart*, it may interest you to learn that, since being liberated from the kitchen, women tend not to sit around growing fat and playing X-Box," she hit back, touching a raw nerve. "I'll be happy to demonstrate just how strong we can be, just name a time and place."

Phillips turned a dangerous shade of puce, imagining all kinds of scenarios with Denise MacKenzie proving her feminine strength.

Ryan rubbed the side of his nose to hide a smile but decided it was time to step in before his sergeant went off the boil.

"MacKenzie makes an excellent point," he said briskly. "The presence of lorazepam swimming around Isobel's system was another black mark against John Dobbs. Working at the hospital makes for easy access to drugs, doesn't it?"

There were nods around the room.

"But the fact remains, unless he was Houdini, Dobbs couldn't have killed DCI Cooper because the pathologist has already confirmed that she had been dead no more than seven hours by the time we found her. That puts her death somewhere after seven this morning, during which time Dobbs was under full police surveillance at his home. It'll be a couple of days before the tox report comes back but, once it does, we'll know for sure whether we have a copycat or the real thing."

"And if it's the same person?" Lowerson asked. "What happens then?"

There was an infinitesimal pause.

"Then we go back to the start, Jack. We re-interview witnesses, chase the source of the drugs, think about who had the skill and the cold-blooded inclination to kill and carve up those women like they were pieces of meat. We look at every element of Isobel Harris and Sharon Cooper's lives to build up a picture until we find the missing piece we didn't see before. We don't just look at Isobel's love life, we look at her daily routine and every person she came into contact with during her final days, then we do the same for Cooper. That includes police personnel," he added, and almost felt their backs stiffen.

"Nobody said this job would be easy," he bit out. "We look at *everybody*. Is that understood?"

There were reluctant nods around the room, and he reached for the cup of cold, forgotten coffee, downing it in three long gulps.

"Alright, let's get to work."

CHAPTER 6

"Did you miss me, sweetheart?"

Confusion clouded her foggy brain. The words seemed to come from very far away, as if she was swimming underwater and a voice was calling her back to the surface. She remembered a time when she was very young, when her mother had walked into the bathroom to find her holding her breath beneath the bathwater to see how long she could stay there. She'd never forget the look of panic as she'd been snatched from the water and into her mother's soft, loving arms.

But it was not her mother calling to her now.

Fear raced across her cold skin and her eyes flew open. The first thing she saw was his face rising above her, blotting out the light from the hallway.

She shrank back against the covers of the bed that were damp with sweat and urine, shivering uncontrollably.

"There she is," he murmured.

She wanted to scream but the terror was so acute she found she couldn't do much more than stare limply into his eyes, half concealed beneath a paper mask and goggles.

His terrible eyes.

"I hate to tell you this, darling, but it's getting a bit stale in here," he said, conversationally. "Very unladylike, you know."

She said nothing. She couldn't speak, anyway.

"I thought you'd have more of a fighting spirit," he said. "Why do you think I chose you?"

He leaned forward and pulled her eyelids with a gloved forefinger and thumb.

"Shock," he told her, straightening up again. "A bit sooner than I thought but it's different for everyone, I suppose."

She continued to stare up at him from her inert position on the bed, wondering what he wanted from her. Perhaps she could bargain with him. If it was…if he wanted *that,* then she'd submit to it if he'd only let her go after he was done.

Tears leaked from the corners of her eyes.

"Wha— d' you—"

She tried to formulate the words to offer a bargain, but the muscles of her mouth would not cooperate.

"What's that?" He cocked a hand to his ear. "I didn't quite catch it."

She closed her eyes again, feeling her own tears run down the side of her neck.

"Now, now," he crooned, tapping a finger against her nose with nauseating intimacy. "Don't wear yourself out.

I don't want you passing out too quickly because there's still a long way to go. We have plenty of time to get acquainted."

He reached across and stuffed a scrap of material into her mouth, taping it securely in place. She was heavily sedated, and her faculties were so impaired there was little chance of her crying out for help, but you could never be too sure. Her nostrils flared widely as she struggled to draw air into her lungs, retching against the material and swallowing her own vomit.

"No, you don't," he said, slapping her face hard. "Pay attention."

Her vision blurred, and her head lolled against the pillow.

"Perhaps you need something to wake you up," he mused. "They say there's nothing quite like pain to remind you that you're alive."

Her chest rose and fell rapidly. In her mind, she thrashed and kicked, struggled to escape. But when she caught sight of her left arm, she realised it was lying immobile in the same position as before.

It hadn't moved.

She couldn't move.

Her mind had conjured up an alternate reality, one where she was able to fight and claw, to tear away the skin of his face. But she could do none of those things, not now.

The scream bubbled up in her throat and came out as a low, keening wail against the gag as she choked against the saliva pooling in her mouth.

He watched the passing emotions on her face with a look of supreme indifference, as if she were a lab rat, something to be studied and dissected.

He leaned over again, scenting her fear and inhaling deeply.

"Cheer up, Nicola. You're on holiday, remember? Right now, you're enjoying the sunny climes of Fuerteventura. That's what everybody thinks and that's why nobody's going to be calling around to see where you are. You don't need to worry about a thing because I've taken care of everything."

He reached for a mobile phone tucked away inside the bag he'd brought.

"Now, then, what have we here? Oh, yes. Your mum says she hopes you have a lovely time and she's very jealous. She also says she hopes you managed to find a new bikini and with any luck you might find a bit of holiday romance. She wants to hear all about it when you get back," he looked up at that, wriggling his eyebrows suggestively. "There's another message from Jacqui, who wants to know if you'll swap shifts with her when you come back to work next week. Sorry to disappoint you, Jacqui," he laughed, chucking the phone back into his bag now the novelty had worn off.

"Not very popular, are you, Nic? It's been hours and you've only received two messages. Maybe it's best all round that I'm going to kill you," he said, gently. "You're hardly lighting up the world, are you?"

His eyes were black chasms and she had been so mesmerised she didn't see the knife until it was almost touching her.

Its blade caught the light and her mind became curiously detached, numbing itself to the inevitable. She willed herself to die, willed her heart to stop beating of its own accord before he had the satisfaction of taking it for himself.

"You should be flattered," he was saying, while he went about the business of slicing away her remaining clothes. "I'm very selective about who I choose. Only the very best will do."

He whistled to himself, a muffled, cheerful sound as he prepared his canvas.

"There," he declared. "Now, we can make a start."

Ryan awoke suddenly.

It took him a moment to orientate himself after the nightmare, to realise that the shadowy room was his bedroom and that he was alone. There was no ghoulish, decapitated figure lying beside him and it was his own sweat soaking the covers, not pints of wasted blood.

"Jesus," he muttered, rubbing a hand over his eyes before reaching across to check the time.

Four-thirty.

He lay there for another minute or two, willing himself to sleep again, but it would not come. It had been a long briefing the previous evening and, by the time he'd divvied up responsibilities to key members of his task force, it had been almost midnight before he'd walked back through his own front door. Longer still until he'd been able to sleep and, even then, he owed a measly three hours' rest to two large glasses of Rioja drunk in swift succession. That would explain the mild headache thumping around his skull, but it was better than the alternative.

They thought he didn't care.

He hadn't shouted, hadn't made false promises or given a tearful speech about fallen soldiers, so they assumed that he didn't *feel*, that none of it mattered to him. He'd heard them muttering about it as they left the conference room, heartsore and world-weary.

"He's been waiting for a chance like this. Sharon's murdered and instead of choosing one of us, Gregson picks his little Southern pet to be SIO. Bloody stinks!"

Ryan watched the shadows shifting against the ceiling.

It was only one or two of them, he thought. Not enough to cause any real dissent. He'd taken over their investigation and shaken things up, told them that Cooper had been wrong. That rubbed some of them up the wrong way, those who were resistant to change.

And he didn't care, so long as they got the job done the way he wanted it done.

He rolled off the bed and padded barefoot to stand beside the long, floor-to-ceiling window of his apartment, leaning his long body against the edge of the frame. It had panoramic views of the river and the quayside where John Dobbs had fled the day before. The arches of the bridge were just visible against the awakening sky and Ryan watched its colour change from deep mauve to palest lilac while his mind wandered back to murder.

He reached for his mobile again, considered the time, then dialled.

"Mfffh?"

"Phillips?"

There was a scuffle as Phillips dropped his phone and found it again.

"Ryan? For the love of God. It's—what time is it?"

"Morning."

"Only just. Has there been another one?"

"No," Ryan said, hoping it was true. "But I think there will be, very soon."

There was a short pause while Phillips decided whether there was any point in trying to bargain for another hour's sleep.

Curiosity won out.

"How d' you mean?"

"If it's the same person, I have to ask myself why he'd target the DCI in charge of the investigation. What criminal in his right mind would draw attention to himself in such an obvious way?"

"Aye, but you're forgetting, he's not in his right mind."

"But if he'd left things well alone, Isobel Harris's murder would have been attributed to John Dobbs," Ryan argued. "Now, we can't be sure about Dobbs and we know for certain somebody else killed Cooper, so the investigation is ongoing."

Phillips sat up straighter in bed and scratched the stubble on his chin.

"Who knows what drives these lunatics? Maybe he just couldn't help himself."

Ryan rolled the idea around his mind and then frowned.

"I don't think so. I don't think he's a lunatic at all. These murders weren't frenzied; they were highly organised. With killers like that, there's usually a reason behind it, a motivator that drives them other than base need, although there'll be that too."

"Maybe he thought killing Cooper would end the investigation?"

"By killing her in the same way as Harris, causing us to draw direct comparisons? No. I think he killed her because he's proud, Frank, and he didn't want Dobbs taking the credit for his handiwork."

"If that's the case, killing Cooper wasn't personal, was it?"

Ryan shook his head grimly and watched the action reflected in the window in front of him.

"With Harris, he killed her slowly and thoroughly, sating himself on the act. But with Cooper, it's more than that. It isn't just killing the woman, it's trying to kill everything she stood for, everything we still stand for. He's attacking the law itself."

Phillips considered the implications of that.

"If he didn't baulk at killing a murder detective, that makes him fearless."

"Yeah," Ryan agreed. "He's not afraid of us and he wanted us to know it. He even left us a card to prove it. What's his next move, Frank? That's what I can't figure out. We need to stay ahead but we haven't got a hope in hell, at this rate."

There was another rustle as Phillips threw back the covers.

"I'll see you at the office in twenty minutes."

CHAPTER 7

Monday 7ᵗʰ July

The mortuary in the basement of the Royal Victoria Infirmary was the province of Doctor Jeffrey Pinter, the Chief Pathologist attached to Northumbria CID and the man whose unfortunate job it was to pore over the remains of Isobel Harris and Sharon Cooper. Never one to volunteer for overtime, he had nonetheless foregone his regular Sunday afternoon listening to Radio 4 from the comfort of his living room, and had streamed it through the in-built mortuary speakers instead. Thanks to an omnibus edition of *The Archers*, he was able to provide the police with his preliminary observations in record time.

As soon as they received his call, Ryan and Phillips left the clear, crisp air of a late northern summer and descended into the bowels of the hospital. They made their way through a network of stuffy, white-washed corridors lined with powerful air conditioning vents until they came to a set of wide double doors.

"Stifling in here," Phillips complained.

"Not for long," Ryan replied, keying in the security code.

As he had predicted, an ice-cold blast awaited them when the doors buzzed open and they stepped inside. The mortuary was just as they remembered; a bank of metal drawers covered one side of the room and a row of gurneys stood in the centre, one of which was occupied and receiving the ministrations of a couple of mortuary technicians. They looked up from behind surgical masks and their hair, hands and bodies were covered in protective clothing, so they became impersonal, asexual, just like the body they tended.

Ryan reached for one of the lab coats hanging on a peg beside the door and scribbled their names in the log book.

"Ryan, Phillips?"

Pinter covered the room at speed, his lanky frame calling to mind visions of a giraffe ambling over the plains of Africa.

He extended a hand in greeting and, after a moment's inspection, Ryan took it.

"Jeff," he said. "Thanks for getting around to this so quickly."

Pinter waved it away.

"It's the least I could do," he said. "Sharon was a good police officer. I'd known her for years, so I won't pretend it was an easy task. Terrible, what happened to her. Just terrible."

Ryan nodded. He would have liked to assign her post-mortem to somebody unconnected to the department, but over the course of her twenty-year career, Cooper had worked with every decent pathologist within a three-hundred-mile radius. That precluded the possibility of finding someone without a measure of personal bias, but he had to trust that Pinter could set his emotions aside and focus on the facts.

"What can you tell us?"

Pinter sucked in a long breath and then puffed it out again in the slightly pompous manner they had come to expect.

"Best if I show you, really."

Phillips made a show of straightening the lab coat that had been designed for a much taller, slimmer man than himself.

"No need for that, Jeff. You could just give us a summary—"

Ryan rolled his eyes inwardly. It was no secret that Phillips couldn't stand the sight of a cadaver.

"We need to see whether the MO is the same," he said decisively.

Pinter nodded and led the way through the main workspace to a smaller corridor with a series of anterooms leading off it. The lemony stench of chemicals used to pickle the bodies accompanied the three men and, beneath it, a subtle scent of decay that permeated their clothes and clung inside their nostrils.

"This way."

Pinter unlocked the door to one of the examination rooms and turned on the main light. A life spent mainly indoors had reduced Pinter's skin to a chalky pallor that was accentuated by the unflattering fluorescent lighting, giving the unfortunate impression he was one of the dead he cared for.

"Do you want to view the images on the computer first? That might be easier."

Phillips cast a wary eye over the shrunken, silent figure lying in state atop a central gurney and opened his mouth to agree.

"We can handle it," Ryan said, and nodded towards the gurney. "We need to understand what happened to her, Jeff."

Pinter nodded gravely.

"Are you ready?"

They could never be ready, but Ryan and Phillips steeled themselves as best they could before the pathologist whipped away the papery shroud.

Anger mingled with grief all over again. Somewhere over his shoulder, he heard Phillips' sharp intake of breath.

"When did she die?" Ryan asked.

"My initial estimate as to post-mortem interval when I attended the scene was no more than five to seven hours and I'll stand by that," Pinter said. "Taking into account her core temperature and other environmental factors, it's highly unlikely she'd been dead any longer."

"What about defensive injuries?" Phillips asked, keeping his eyes fixed to the clock on the far wall.

"None whatsoever," Pinter replied. "And I suspect this is the reason why."

He produced a retractable pointer and indicated an ugly bruise on the skin of Sharon's neck. In its centre was a puncture mark.

Both detectives leaned forward to get a better look.

"Pressure syringe?" Ryan looked up for confirmation and Pinter gave a short nod.

"Aye, that'd do it," Phillips said, clearing his throat loudly. "Same bloke as before, then?"

"It's looking a lot like it," Pinter replied.

"Not exactly the same," Ryan argued. "In the case of Isobel Harris, there were multiple puncture marks found on her body, not just one."

"Maybe he ran out of time," Phillips suggested.

"It's possible," Ryan agreed. "Or maybe she served a different purpose, a different kind of motivation."

"I'll leave the 'whys' and 'hows' to you," Pinter told them. "But I can tell you Sharon was blood type A positive and she enjoyed a bowl of porridge for breakfast after a liquid diet on Saturday night. Bruising and blood loss would indicate she was alive while the less serious injuries were incurred—removal of the ears and so forth—but once the major arteries in her legs and arms were severed, she would have died very quickly. The official cause of death is major cardiac arrest."

They thought back to the river of blood they'd seen in Sharon's bedroom.

"He didn't stop then," Pinter continued. "The hands and feet were removed post mortem, as was the upper part of her sternum and, of course, her head."

This last observation was delivered with a degree of clinical detachment that took their breath away.

"He would have needed the right tools," Ryan murmured. "What kind of implement would you say?"

"Undoubtedly, he used a series of different knives and a small saw. It's the only way to get through the bone, you see."

"The CSIs bagged up the kitchen knives and any other sharp tools in Cooper's home," Phillips said. "We still haven't found a murder weapon for Isobel Harris either."

Pinter shrugged his bony shoulders.

"It would make sense to remove the evidence and sterilise off-site."

Ryan looked up from his inspection of Sharon's hands, which had been bagged separately to preserve evidence.

"Has the tox report come back yet?" he asked.

"Not yet," Pinter said. "Neither has the histology report but they're doing an express service and I've told them to ring you as soon as the results come through."

Ryan paced a couple of steps around to the other side of the gurney, looking at the body from all angles.

"Is there nothing else you can tell us?"

Pinter bristled.

"I'm going as quickly as I can," he said. "There was no blood or other secretions found on her person, other than her own, of course. That makes things harder for the forensic team…and for you, of course. The only thing we can say with any level of certainty is that the method of execution is the same."

"With Isobel Harris, you said whoever did it had an exceptional level of skill," Phillips said. "Would you say the same about whoever did this?"

Pinter raised a hand to smooth his crop of thinning hair and stopped himself just in time.

"Yes, I would. Look at the incision here," he remarked, pointing towards the clean separation of Sharon's right knee from the rest of her leg. "And here," he pointed towards the neat separation of each of her finger joints. "It takes knowledge and skill to produce such a result and he consistently works from anterior to posterior, above the joint. With an everyday, run-of-the-mill job, you'd expect somebody to have hacked away willy-nilly but that's not the case here at all."

"Sharon Cooper has still been hacked apart," Ryan said coldly. "However it was achieved, her killer is an animal and needs to be put down."

Pinter flushed.

"I'm simply telling you that an amateur couldn't have done this," he argued. "And, while we're at it, I might as well tell you I never believed John Dobbs could have killed Isobel Harris. There might have been slightly less finesse in her case, but the facts remain that a healthcare assistant couldn't hope to emulate the mastery of an experienced clinician."

There was a long, pregnant silence broken only by the sound of the clock ticking loudly on the wall.

"Mastery?" Ryan queried, softly.

"Well, you know what I mean," Pinter said.

Ryan smiled but it didn't quite reach his eyes.

"Perhaps we're looking at this the wrong way. Here I've been searching for a psychopath whereas I should have appreciated the kind of superior intellect I'm dealing with. Is that about it?"

Pinter nodded.

"I'd have thought that was obvious."

Ryan gave him a long, level look.

"I'll bear it in mind."

They stayed for another hour discussing the intricacies of Cooper's death, then Ryan and Phillips retraced their steps, exiting the mortuary via the service entrance that led them back out into the late morning sunshine. They raised their faces to the wind, breathing in the exhaust fumes from the car park and the dual carriageway just over the perimeter wall but still finding the atmosphere preferable to the noxious fumes circulating around the mortuary.

"Bit tense in there," Phillips remarked, reaching for his cigarettes to clear the tension riding on his own shoulders. "This one's getting on top of everyone. You can feel it."

Ryan didn't answer at first but turned as one of the junior doctors stepped outside to join them beneath the plastic canopy. She moved off to the far end where she slid down to the floor in one exhausted motion, leaning back against the outer wall while she retrieved her own packet of cigarettes. There was hypocrisy in there somewhere, Ryan thought, but he couldn't blame her for not practising what she preached. Her fixed, glazed expression spoke of interminable double shifts dealing with emergencies and the general public. If nicotine helped, who was he to judge?

"Need a light, love?" Phillips called out.

She shook her head and waggled her lighter, sending them both a small smile of thanks before slumping back against the wall to stare off into the distance, puffing rhythmically.

Ryan picked up the thread of their conversation but kept his voice low.

"Did you hear the way Pinter was talking in there, Frank? It was…" He paused, searching for the right word. "Reverent."

"That's just Jeff. The bloke's a nerd when it comes to anatomy and bodies and all that. He doesn't mean anything by it. It's the same reason he can't get a girlfriend. He scares them off with all his shop talk."

"Does he have an alibi for yesterday morning?" Ryan wondered aloud, ignoring Phillips' attempt at levity. "I told you, Frank, I'm looking at everybody. Nine times out of ten, a victim's killer is already known to them."

"By God, you're a cold bastard, sometimes."

Ryan turned to him with fierce eyes.

"If that's what it takes," he snapped. "Whoever's out there killing those women doesn't give a damn about the sanctity of life, doesn't care about shattering families. I don't have time to worry about whether I've offended Pinter's sensibilities—or yours, for that matter. I only care about finding this scumbag before he takes another one."

Even now, the clock was ticking.

"Aye, but you can't go around suspecting everyone who wears a white coat."

"Why not?" Ryan demanded, jabbing a finger towards the hospital. "Everyone inside there is a suspect until proven otherwise and the same applies to everybody who can wield a scalpel from Land's End to John o' Groats. Until we narrow the field, we need to stay vigilant."

He paused, watching the junior doctor re-enter the hospital building, sending him a quiet smile as she went.

"You know what they say about high-functioning psychopaths, Frank? They tend to work in professions like the police, or as doctors and nurses. What if they could combine both and stay ahead of the game? They'd be unstoppable. We can't let our loyalties get in the way of basic facts."

Phillips thought of the pathologist, the CSIs, the various counsellors and psychologists attached to their constabulary and felt the tiny hairs on the back of his neck stand on end.

CHAPTER 8

On his return to Police Headquarters, Ryan had barely entered the foyer when he was accosted by the Duty Sergeant, who told him that Eileen Spruce and her grandson, Will, were waiting for him in the family room and had refused to budge for the past forty minutes.

Shit.

"Tell them I'll be there in a minute."

He jogged down to the staff locker room where he kept an emergency jacket and tie reserved for occasions such as these. After a quick change, he took another minute to splash a handful of tepid water on his face, to finger-comb his black hair into some semblance of order and decided that would have to do. Rehearsed speeches and training ran through his mind and, by the time he reached the door marked, 'OCCUPIED', he was already congratulating himself on the calm and collected way in which he would handle a grieving family.

But when he entered the room, thoughts of planned speeches flew out of his mind as he came face to face with Sharon Cooper's mother, who seemed to have aged overnight. He happened to know that Eileen Spruce had recently seen her eighty-fifth birthday and, until hearing the news of her daughter's death, had been an active woman who walked at least two miles a day and attended a Zumba class with a group of chatty fifty-somethings on Friday afternoons. But now, she looked every one of her years. She was seated on one of the cheap foam loungers arranged around a low coffee table littered with leaflets and pamphlets advertising grief counselling and victim support. Her eyes were red-rimmed, ravaged by a night spent contemplating the unthinkable.

Her daughter was dead.

It wasn't the natural course of things for a mother to outlive her child. Despite all the years spent worrying about Sharon and the inherent dangers in her chosen career, Eileen had imagined that longevity and good fortune meant the danger had passed. Willingly, she had believed the rhetoric that maniacs didn't attack older, divorced women with children; only young, beautiful ones the papers preferred to write about.

How wrong she had been.

Across the room, Will Cooper stood at the window dressed in a smart suit that made him look years older. Had he not made it his business to research Sharon's personal history, Ryan might have believed her son to be over thirty and not a tender twenty-four-year-old dentistry student. It was more than the clothes; he had a conservative, standoffish quality that was so unlike his mother. He didn't sit beside his grandmother or hold her hand, preferring to keep his distance from the raw grief that she made no effort to hide. He didn't even bother to turn around when Ryan entered the room.

"Mrs Spruce?"

Eileen watched a tall, good-looking man in his mid-thirties enter and close the door softly behind him.

"Are you the detective—are you looking after Sharon?"

Such simple words to convey the enormity of his task, Ryan thought.

"Yes, Mrs Spruce. I'm the Senior Investigating Officer in charge of your daughter's case. My name is Detective Chief Inspector Ryan." He paused to seek out the third member of their party. "Mr Cooper? Would you like to come and join us, please?"

Saying nothing, Will walked to the coffee table and selected a chair as far away from the other two as possible. He was a slight man and moved with an unhurried gait, as if he hadn't a care in the world.

Ryan gave him a level look.

"Can I offer you some coffee or tea?"

"She's really gone, isn't she?" Eileen whispered, ignoring his question while tears fell silently down her face.

"Yes. I'm so sorry."

She began to sob, a deep, gut-wrenching sound that tore at the insides.

"Gran…" Will started to speak and then fell silent again, his only concession being to push a box of tissues across the coffee table in her direction.

Ryan held them out to her.

"They told me, the people who came to the house, they told me Sharon had been murdered," Eileen said, the words falling out of her mouth in a sudden rush. "They told me somebody had killed her, but they didn't tell me *how*, or *why*. I need to know what happened. How did this *happen*?"

Tears began to fall again but Ryan continued to meet her eyes, fighting the urge to look away.

"Mrs Spruce—"

"Was it one of those awful gangsters?" she asked, and leaned forward to clamp a thin hand around Ryan's wrist, her eyes almost wild. "Sharon told me about some of them. I know about the kind of things they do to the police who put their family away. Was it one of them? Was that it?"

Ryan looked down at the woman's hand and covered it with his own in a gesture of solidarity.

"I'm terribly sorry for your loss, Mrs Spruce, Mr Cooper," he said quietly. "I admired Sharon very much and she will be missed by everyone here at the Constabulary."

They were trite words, but that didn't make them any less true. As he held her fragile hand, he felt it tremble as she fought to remain lucid, to face a reality that was every mother's nightmare.

In contrast, her grandson hadn't uttered a word and remained outwardly unmoved by the gravity of the situation.

"I can't tell you who killed your daughter, or why, but I will seek out the answers, Mrs Spruce, I promise you that. I won't rest until whoever killed your daughter is behind bars."

Eileen searched his face and whatever she found there seemed to satisfy her.

"We've been trying to get hold of Mr Cooper," Ryan began. It was always awkward, contacting a former spouse but, more often than not, they grieved just the same for the person they had once loved. No matter the reason for their marital breakdown, rarely does a person genuinely wish the other to be brutally murdered, regardless of what might be said in the heat of anger.

"He's with wife number three," Will said bluntly. "They're cruising around the Med and won't be back for another few days."

"Do you have the details of the cruise line? We can contact the ship directly."

"Haven't got a clue."

"I'll—I'll see if I can find out," Eileen said, overriding her grandson.

"That would be very helpful. You can contact me on this number at any time," Ryan said, fishing out one of his business cards.

"You'll never find him," Will said softly.

Ryan frowned at him.

"Your father?"

Will's lips twisted.

"No, you can find him sniffing around the cabaret girls somewhere between Cyprus and Rhodes," he said nastily. "I'm talking about whoever killed my mother. You'll never find him."

"What makes you say that?"

"They're saying on the news that it's the same guy who killed that woman a few weeks ago. It's the one my mother was looking for," he said, with a slight shrug. "It was all she could talk about, last time I saw her."

"And when was that?" Ryan asked, smooth as you like.

"A couple of weeks ago, maybe?" He shrugged again. "I can't remember."

"Will," his grandmother chided him. "You need to remember. We need to do everything we can to help this young man find out who…" She took a shuddering breath and swiped a hand over her eyes. "We need to help him find who killed your mother."

"That's what I'm trying to tell you, Gran. Mum thought it was the bloke who fell off the bridge yesterday, but it couldn't have been him who killed her, could it?"

Ryan watched the old woman's face begin to crumple and cut in quickly.

"We don't know anything for certain, Will. As soon as we do, we'll be in touch."

The young man actually laughed at that, his lip curling in contempt.

"My mother was the same as you, remember? I've heard all the standard lines, but the fact is, you don't have a bloody clue who killed her. Do you?"

There was an arrogance beneath the outburst that Ryan didn't like but he reminded himself that those who were left behind didn't always cry. Sometimes they grew angry and lashed out, the last bastion of denial before reality set in.

"Killers always leave a trace," he said. "Even the ones who plan everything down to the finest detail overlook something small, some factor they couldn't control. I'm doing everything in my power to find it, Will, but it takes time."

"What if this one thought of everything? What if there's nothing to find?"

This time, it was Ryan's turn to smile.

"It's just a matter of knowing where to look."

―――――

Will Cooper took off without a thought for his grandmother, so Ryan commandeered a squad car to transport Eileen Spruce safely back to her sheltered housing bungalow. It had been an eye-opening experience meeting the man of whom Sharon had spoken so often and so proudly, her loving son and star pupil who was fast becoming the best dental surgeon in his graduating class.

After a moment's thought, Ryan went in search of DC Lowerson and found him bent over a stack of papers at his desk. As reader-receiver, he had been entrusted with the dubious responsibility of sifting through all the telephone calls and statements compiled during their investigation and sorting the wheat from the chaff. It was critical, important work.

It was also mind-numbingly boring.

"Jack?"

He looked up in surprise.

"Yes, guv?"

"You ready to chew your own arm off, yet?"

Lowerson made a strangled sound and gestured vaguely to the mountain of different accounts from eyewitnesses on the Tyne Bridge the previous day.

"You could say that. We've had a hundred and forty people ringing the emergency number, all of them claiming responsibility for Sharon's murder."

"Any of them sound legit?"

"Not unless you count the one who claims to have killed Cooper from his cell in HMP Frankland through the power of the mind alone."

"Mind over matter." Ryan huffed out a laugh. "I've got another task for you, if you can manage it."

"'Course. What d' you need?"

"I need you to do a thorough background check on William Andrew Cooper, aged twenty-four, DOB first of March 1990."

He waited for the penny to drop, which it did. And quickly.

"*Will Cooper*?" Lowerson said, in a ridiculous stage whisper. "You don't think her own son could have done it?"

To a man like Lowerson, the very thought was abhorrent. He was devoted to his mother and never missed one of their regular Wednesday night dinners if he could possibly help it.

"Matricide is pretty common, Jack, and we know next to nothing about Sharon's relationship with her son. We only know what she chose to tell us; the rose-tinted version she was willing to share. That could've been all wrong, especially after meeting him today."

"You didn't like him?"

"Let's just say he didn't make me feel all warm and fuzzy inside."

"Yeah, but even if he wasn't close to his mum, how could he have known how Isobel Harris—"

Lowerson broke off as the penny dropped again.

"How Isobel Harris died?" Ryan finished for him. "Intimate details weren't reported but Sharon wouldn't be the first police officer to break the rules and share details of an investigation with her nearest and dearest," he said. "Added to which, he's a dental student. It's enough for him to have a decent knowledge of anatomy and rudimentary skill with the scalpel."

There was a short silence while Lowerson fiddled with a chewed biro.

"I'll get onto it straight away."

"You do that. And Jack? Keep it under your hat for now."

CHAPTER 9

"Nicola?"

"Dad?"

"Wake up, Nicola."

"Don't want to. Can't."

"Come on, sleepy-head. Time to get up."

"I'm scared to, Daddy."

Soft laughter and the touch of his hand caressing her face.

Except his fingers felt strange and rubbery. Not like the hand she remembered clutching when he'd slipped away, two years ago.

Her eyelids were so heavy, it was an effort to open them and, when she managed it, her first thought was that heaven looked just like her bedroom. Death was no different to life and there were no archangels, no guardians to protect her passage to the other side.

"Well, hello, sweetheart. I was worried for a minute you weren't going to come around."

Her body began to tremble violently at the sound of his voice and her heart stuttered against her chest in sheer animal panic.

At her bedside, he drank it in, savouring the power like an addict, tipping his head back in ecstasy.

"See?" he said thickly. "I'll bet you never thought you'd see me again, did you? You surprised both of us, darling."

He adjusted the makeshift drip at her bedside, surveyed the wounds inflicted the previous day, and then perched on the edge of a chair. He was covered in a plastic boiler suit and didn't worry about leaving any part of himself behind.

Nicola heard him rustling somewhere nearby and her fingers clutched at the bedclothes, trying to find purchase. Pain was beginning to bloom all over her body, from the innumerable slashing cuts he'd inflicted the day before. They traced the route he would later take to remove her limbs and torso but, for now, they were a road map of shallow red lines that stung whenever she moved.

"Now, I don't want you to worry about infection," he was saying. "I've taken the liberty of administering a little cocktail that will keep you fighting fit for as long as I need you. The fact is, Nicola, I have another woman in mind, but I'll have to wait a few days."

He sighed, affecting an air of regret.

"Now, don't be jealous. We've had a wonderful time together, but I've never been a one-woman kind of guy."

Quick as a flash, he leaned forward—so close she could feel his breath against her skin, could see his pupils dilate at the prospect of ending her then and there.

"Women love a bad boy, don't they?" he growled. "Want me to show you how bad I can be, Nicola?"

Tears leaked from the corners of her eyes and her bowels loosened.

"Tut, tut," he said. "Do you expect me to clean that up? There's very little point in changing the bed linen, considering you won't be with us very much longer."

"Please," she gasped, feeling her throat burn with the effort. "Please don't—"

She fell into a coughing fit and he watched impassively, settling back against the chair and crossing his legs to make himself comfortable.

"I know what you're thinking and what you're feeling, Nicola. You're wondering, 'why me?' and, 'what did I do to deserve this?' "

Her chest rose and fell as she tried to regulate her breathing.

"Well, I'll tell you, Nicola," he said, conversationally. "You didn't do a thing except exist. You're just unlucky. In a parallel world, you'd have gone on to live a long and healthy life, probably marry a doctor and have a couple of kids." He heaved a self-effacing sigh. "Unfortunately, I'd much rather see what your insides look like and I'm unable to do that without killing you in the process. It's a pity but I've always been a selfish creature, really. That's what the agony aunts say, isn't it? You can't change a man; he can only change himself. How right they are."

He heaved himself up again, rising above her like a towering demon.

"I can't stay long, this time," he whispered, reaching for his bag and the scrap of vomit-soaked material he'd used to gag her the previous day.

"N-no," she gargled.

"I'll have to make do with a quickie."

At four o'clock, Ryan's team re-assembled. Most of his workforce had mustered enough strength to stay for the duration, so the Incident Room hummed with a sense of renewed purpose. Strategic teams huddled in groups while telephone operatives occupied a corner fielding a constant stream of prank and nuisance calls from the public. Crime analysts requisitioned four tables at the back of the room and were seated in silence, eyes trained on their computer screens as they scrolled through pages of data. Lowerson and MacKenzie had stationed themselves in the centre of the room and sifted through an avalanche of paperwork, learning all there was to know about Isobel Harris and Sharon Cooper. Phillips had taken a seat as far away from them as possible—no doubt an act of self-preservation—while he harassed other law enforcement and government agencies for the information they held.

In the corner of the room, a wall-mounted television had been tuned to the local news channel with its sound muted and subtitles enabled. News of another murder had taken the city by storm and reignited a state of panic, causing ordinary people to imagine a killer lurking in every shadow and behind every door. Even if they had wanted to, there was little the press could do to subdue an increasingly restless mood. After all, if the police could not protect themselves, what hope did they have of protecting the rest of them?

These sobering thoughts had been echoed by the Chief Constable and Superintendent, who had issued Ryan with a stark reminder of the consequences they faced as a constabulary if justice was not seen to be done.

Having extricated himself from the stuffy confines of Gregson's office for the second time in as many days, Ryan now stood in the doorway surveying the activity in the Incident Room. He was pleased to see anger harnessed into productivity but considerably less pleased to see another sensational news report rolling across the television screen. With growing resentment, he watched a reporter walk down the street where Isobel Harris had lived, gesticulating towards the solitary constable whose unfortunate job it was to remain and protect the scene from intrusion. The camera zoomed in on his bored face and Ryan rolled his eyes heavenward, making a mental note to schedule a mandatory session on media training once it was all over. The segment moved on to another reporter, this time stationed outside Police Headquarters capturing footage of DCS Gregson dishing out a few soundbites earlier in the day.

"I want to reassure the public that we are sparing no resource in our efforts to bring to justice whoever is responsible for the deaths of Isobel Harris and Sharon Cooper—"

"So, you believe they are one and the same, Superintendent?" one of the reporters shouted. "We were led to believe that John Dobbs killed Isobel Harris. Are you saying an innocent man committed suicide? Have you heard from his family, Superintendent? Will there be an investigation?"

"Dropped the ball there, Arthur," Ryan murmured, folding his arms across his chest.

"I cannot confirm or deny anything that would prejudice an ongoing investigation," Gregson said, back-peddling furiously. "That's all I have to say for now."

"Superintendent! Who has taken over the investigation?"

"Detective Chief Inspector Ryan will be leading a joint investigation. Anyone with relevant information should contact the Incident Room number. That's all I have to say."

Across the room, Phillips slammed his phone down with alacrity.

"Bloody, buggering hell!" he roared.

Ryan decided it was an apt description for the train-wreck he'd just witnessed on television but presumed the outburst related to something other than shoddy public relations.

"Another ambulance-chaser trying to flog you OAP life insurance?"

Phillips snorted.

"I should be so lucky. I've just had some trumped-up, pen-pushing moron from Cooper's bank telling me they can't release her accounts information without a warrant. Same shit as usual."

"Privacy laws," Ryan commiserated.

"If I ever find the jobsworth who drafted the Data Protection Act, I swear, I'll wring their scrawny neck for them and consider it a public service."

"So, what's the upshot? They won't release her information without a rubber stamp from the magistrate?"

"Aye, that's about the long and short of it. I'll get the paperwork signed off this afternoon and get things moving."

"Alright. Money doesn't look like the motivation here, but it's usually involved somewhere."

"Money talks," Phillips agreed. "Cooper wasn't rolling in it, but she did alright for herself."

"It's enough for some people," Ryan said, then broke off the conversation as Tom Faulkner, the Senior CSI, stuck his head around the door and gave Ryan the 'thumbs up' sign.

"Alright, listen up!"

Ryan hitched a hip onto the edge of his desk and waited until he had their full attention.

"It's been over twenty-four hours since Sharon's body was discovered. What have we got to show for it?" He let the question hang in the air. "Let's start with the basics. Sharon was a forty-nine-year-old woman in the prime of her life. She went through an acrimonious divorce six years ago but there's no evidence to suggest her former husband is involved; he's sailing around the Mediterranean with his new wife, happy as Larry."

"Alright for some," Phillips remarked.

"Sharon had one child from that marriage. William, a twenty-four-year-old dentistry student."

Ryan nodded towards the image of Will Cooper he'd tacked onto the murder board. On the outer edge, perhaps, but still firmly on the board.

"As far as we know, there's no suggestion of a new man in Sharon's life. She'd dated over the years and used several online sites including LoveLife, but not recently. In summary, she was a woman devoted to her work and her son."

There were murmurs of assent around the room.

"The statements taken from her friends and neighbours corroborate that, sir," Lowerson chimed in. "Nobody recalls seeing a man visiting the house, except her son."

"Which was a couple of weeks ago, in any event."

Lowerson shook his head, rifling through his file with quick fingers.

"No, sir. Her neighbour at Number Five says she saw Will Cooper arriving the night before Sharon died."

Ryan looked up sharply, thinking back to his discussion with the man only a few hours before. He was a grieving son, some might say. He was entitled to forget things, to make mistakes. On the other hand, there were some things you just didn't forget and that included the last time you'd seen your mother alive.

Without a word, he slipped off the edge of the desk and moved the photograph of William Cooper closer to the smiling picture of his mother in her dress uniform. While the room watched the action with dawning comprehension, he rapped out the next order.

"Phillips? Light a fire up the magistrate's arse. I need to know if Will Cooper had a motive. Easy enough for somebody to replicate an MO, if he was privy to that kind of information."

"On it, boss."

Phillips shrugged off the sense of betrayal, the uneasy knowledge that Sharon would have hated her son being implicated, and reminded himself that she was not here to defend anybody. If there was ever a time to be objective, this was it.

"Alright, let's piece together what we know about Sharon's last movements. Working backwards, we entered her home at around two o'clock yesterday afternoon, shortly after a response team was called out to the property. John Dobbs committed suicide an hour before that and Cooper was uncontactable throughout that time. Just after eleven o'clock, DCS Gregson received an e-mail sent from Cooper's mobile phone, triangulated to her home address and copied to DC Hitchins and DI MacKenzie, telling them that she needed to take a couple of hours' personal time and to continue with the surveillance until further orders—"

"Aye, and that was weird," MacKenzie interjected. "I knew Sharon, but I wasn't assigned to her investigation. I don't know why she would have sent me an e-mail like that."

"The pathologist thinks Sharon died no earlier than seven o'clock yesterday morning, no later than nine," Ryan answered. "That being the case, it's likely her killer sent that e-mail and selected recipients from her contacts list."

MacKenzie cast her mind back.

"I sent Sharon an e-mail asking how she was faring and whether she wanted to have a quick drink after work if she could spare the time," she murmured. "He must have seen it and assumed we were working together."

Ryan nodded.

"You had no way of knowing," Phillips murmured, surprising them both. "There's nothing you could have done to prevent what happened."

MacKenzie looked into his warm, button-brown eyes and wondered: had her emotions been clear for all to see, or was Phillips more perceptive than she had imagined?

"I—thanks, Frank."

He shuffled in his chair, clearly embarrassed by his own insight.

"I'd say the same to anybody," he replied.

MacKenzie turned away to resume the discussion with Ryan.

"So, if Cooper didn't send those messages and the pathologist puts her death between seven and nine, we have to assume her killer gained access to her home around that time or even sometime before?"

Ryan nodded, bracing his hands against the desk while he skim-read the pathologist's notes.

"Pinter thinks she was tortured for over an hour and she didn't die until her arteries were severed, which would have brought on a severe cardiac arrest. It's possible her killer accessed the house as early as five or six yesterday morning.

We've already had it confirmed that Cooper made two outgoing phone calls yesterday morning. One was to her voicemail service, presumably to check messages, at five-fifteen. The other one was to DC Hitchins to check on the surveillance at around five-forty. Hitchins tells us Cooper sounded fine, if not a bit tired. She was planning to head into the office soon after. That narrows down the timescale."

"Sir?"

Lowerson had his hand up again and Ryan reminded himself to have a word with him about it. They weren't in a classroom, for pity's sake.

"Jack, you don't need to call me 'sir' all the time," he went so far as to say. "Just…speak."

"Thank you, s—" Lowerson swallowed the rest of that sentence and tried again. "Um, I was wondering how he managed to enter DCI Cooper's home. She was an experienced officer—I don't know how he could have managed it."

Ryan laughed shortly.

"If I knew the answer to that, we'd all be out of a job," he said. "Let's start by considering the puncture mark on her neck."

"Just one puncture wound?" MacKenzie queried.

Ryan nodded and thought, not for the first time, that she was a quick study.

"There were six or seven found on Isobel Harris's body," he said, pre-empting her next question. "What do you think that tells us?"

"He needed more sedative to take her out or maybe he misjudged the dosage?" Lowerson offered.

"Both plausible," Ryan said. "But it could be simpler than that. What if Cooper didn't interest him enough to prolong the execution? We don't have the toxicology report back yet, but I'll hazard a guess it will contain plenty of lorazepam but no adrenaline, unlike what we found in Isobel Harris's bloodstream."

"He had no interest in keeping Cooper alive for longer than the time it would take to set the scene," MacKenzie concluded.

"Why?" Lowerson asked. "Why is the adrenaline important?"

Ryan ran a hand over the back of his neck and stood up to ease out the kinks.

"He gave Isobel Harris a shot of adrenaline whenever she was about to go into cardiac arrest," he said. "It meant he could play with her for longer."

Lowerson fell silent, struggling to comprehend the kind of deviant mentality they were searching for. Ryan wished he could tell Jack Lowerson the world consisted of good people who sometimes did bad things.

But he couldn't.

Evil walked in human form. It hid in plain sight, walked amongst them, talked to them, deceiving them all. The sooner Lowerson came to terms with it, the better.

"It ties in with our theory about Cooper being a trophy kill, used to send a message," Phillips was saying.

"That doesn't help us to figure out who he, or *she*," he added swiftly, feeling MacKenzie's eyes boring into the side of his head, "is going to target next."

There was no question of whether there would be another target or of how they would die; only a question of when and who.

Ryan looked across the room to Tom Faulkner, who nodded awkwardly and stood up to face the crowd.

"Ah, well. Actually, it's likely that you are looking for a man," he told them. "We already had a partial DNA profile from the samples we picked up from Isobel Harris. As of this afternoon, we isolated a match from a similar sample we found at DCI Cooper's house yesterday. There's no match on the DNA database but I can tell you it's definitely male."

"Where'd he slip up?" Phillips asked. "Was it the curtains?"

"Nope, it was the gate at the end of the pathway leading up to her front door. It's possible he forgot to wear gloves on the way in, or he peeled them off after posting the door keys back through her letterbox and then forgot about the gate as he headed out. Easy mistake to make."

"It's not exactly a smoking gun," Ryan said. "A decent defence barrister would have a field day ripping it to shreds, but beggars can't be choosers. The chances of isolating the same DNA profile at the scene of two murders has to be off the chart and, besides, it's all we've got."

He headed over to the murder board, took a marker pen and drew a single black line through the centre of it. Then, he drew another one right beneath it.

"Ah, y' know, there are computer programs that can do all the charts for you," Phillips pointed out.

"Uh huh," Ryan said, and continued scribbling pertinent events on the timeline for each woman.

Phillips pursed his lips but privately agreed there was no substitute for the visual impact of a murder board.

After a minute, Ryan replaced the cap on his pen and considered the graffiti-covered wall in front of him.

"If we assume we're looking for one man and that his motivations for murdering Isobel Harris and Sharon Cooper were different, I think we'll learn much more by understanding his reasons for killing Harris." He looked at each person in the room, lingering on those he had identified as being potentially difficult. "Most of you worked on the case under Cooper, so you think you know all there is to know about Isobel Harris."

He saw the complacent looks, heard a couple of muffled laughs from the back of the room and came to an instant decision.

"The fact is, we need fresh eyes on this," he said. "We need to go back over everything, right back to the start. It's impossible for some of you to do that without being influenced by what has gone before. That being the case, Hitchins, Jessop, Clayton, Adowu, Umber and Lee will be re-assigned. Thank you for all your work so far, please go home and get some rest."

He reached down for a stack of papers, preparing himself for the backlash.

He didn't have to wait long.

"Are you kidding me?" Jessop burst out, his voice clattering around the room like old tin. "If you think I'm going to let you swan in here like King Dick and tell me where to get off—"

"Lower your voice and moderate your language." Ryan's voice cracked like a whip. "If you have any objections to raise about how I choose to manage this investigation, you can use the appropriate channels."

"You're not fobbing me off! I deserve to stay on the team, and I want my name on the charge sheet when we bring him in."

And that, Ryan thought, was the man's biggest mistake. It wasn't a question of who got the collar, it was a question of teamwork.

"You want to do this here, in front of all these people?" Ryan inclined his head. "Alright, we'll have this out now in front of a roomful of witnesses. Let the record show I advised PC Jessop to follow HR procedures, which he declined."

"Duly noted," Phillips said.

Ryan moved around to the front of his desk and spoke directly to the gym-hardened man who stood a few feet away with aggression etched into every line of his body.

"You say you deserve to be on this team," Ryan growled. "I say that's bollocks. I've heard reports that you failed time and again to follow orders from your superiors and encouraged Dobbs to take his own life, thereby failing in your first duty to protect and serve the public."

Jessop's face lost some colour.

"That's rubbish! Tell him, Hitchins!"

His partner's silence spoke volumes. She looked away, remembering the words he had used on the bridge, how he'd told Dobbs there was nothing to live for.

Just as Ryan had suspected.

"Furthermore, ever since I took over the investigation, your behaviour has been obstructive. You have sought to undermine my position as SIO and created division in the team you seem so keen to be a part of. Why?"

Jessop's lip curled.

"You're nothing," he spat. "You went to a fancy school and have a fancy name. That's why you're a DCI while I'm still a pissin' constable. I'm twice the man you are!"

"I'm your superior officer," Ryan shot back. "And you are relieved of active duties pending a full investigation, effective immediately. Now, get out."

Ryan watched the man's face and saw it coming, even before Jessop's fist swung out. He dodged and had Jessop's arms pinned behind his back in one smooth motion.

"Get off us!" Jessop shouted.

"You've just added attempted assault to your list of misdemeanours," Ryan said.

Phillips and MacKenzie jumped to their feet to give him a hand but Ryan shook his head. The others in the room watched without batting an eyelid as he strong-armed Jessop out of the room and thrust him down the corridor, only just restraining himself from planting his boot in the man's backside.

"Go home and cool off," he ordered. "If I don't have a written apology on my desk by nine a.m. tomorrow, I'll be straight down to the Super's office. Think about it."

When he returned to the Incident Room, twenty-three faces looked up at Ryan in a kind of wonder.

"It's always the quiet ones," Phillips told Lowerson, sagely.

Ryan appeared completely unruffled as he stalked back to the front of the room.

"Where were we?"

"Fresh eyes," Phillips supplied, folding his hands comfortably across his paunch. "You were saying we need to look at things afresh."

Ryan blinked a couple of times and thought that he could use some eye drops to clear his own hazy vision, thanks to a spate of sleepless nights.

"Right. I want us to re-examine everything we have on Isobel Harris. She's the key to working out what drives him."

"We managed to decipher the card he left on Cooper's body," Faulkner spoke up. "It said, 'CATCH ME IF YOU CAN' and was written in ordinary black biro on thick cream card stock, available from any stationery retailer in the land."

"Any prints?" Ryan asked.

Faulkner shook his head.

"No such luck, I'm afraid. Anything that might have been on there has been obscured by Sharon's own bodily fluids. It was a hard enough job recovering the message, let alone anything else."

"Alright," Ryan said. "It's still useful because it confirms what we already know: the man's a peacock. He wants our attention, our praise, and he likes the thrill of the chase. Why else leave such a juvenile message?"

"It's all a game to him," MacKenzie said, looking at her friend's face hanging on the wall. "If nothing and nobody matters to him, he needs to create his own sport, doesn't he?"

There was a short silence as her words rang true.

"Thanks, Tom," Ryan said eventually. "We appreciate you working around the clock on this and I need you to keep at it, for as long as possible. We need the answers."

"Happy to."

Ryan turned to the others.

"Phillips, Lowerson? Go back over the statements with a fine-toothed comb and re-interview anyone you need to. Look again at the CCTV. I want you to flag anything that strikes a chord with the Cooper investigation, anything that might connect the victims and give us a new line of enquiry. MacKenzie? You're with me."

Phillips watched them walk out of the room with an odd, sinking feeling in his belly. Ryan and MacKenzie were just a couple of colleagues working together, he told himself. Nothing to get riled up about. But the small, petty part of his brain whispered that they were the 'beautiful ones'. She, with her mane of red hair that shone beneath the shabby industrial lighting, and Ryan, who looked like he'd just stepped off the front cover of *GQ* magazine.

He'd hate him for it, if he didn't happen to like the bloke so much.

And what was he? An over-the-hill detective sergeant with a penchant for bacon stotties. What did he have to offer a vibrant woman like Denise MacKenzie? For starters, she was in her early-forties and he was ten years older. These things mattered to some people. He smoked, always had done, and it was common knowledge she couldn't stand the filthy habit.

They were obviously incompatible.

"—Frank?"

He jerked in his chair and was surprised to find Lowerson looking at him expectantly.

"Shall we get started?"

"Aye, lad. Sorry, I was miles away."

Lowerson stuck his tongue in his cheek.

"MacKenzie's a nice woman, isn't she?"

"You noticed, eh?"

"So did you, by the looks of it."

"Watch it, bonny lad. My interest in DI MacKenzie is purely professional."

"I believe you. Millions wouldn't."

"Oh," Phillips blustered. "Haddaway and shite."

CHAPTER 10

Fenwick's department store was a local institution housed in a grand, stately-looking building in the centre of Newcastle's shopping district. The perfume department where Isobel Harris had worked was located on the ground floor, accessible via a set of elegant brass doors leading directly into a gleaming hall. Bright spotlights illuminated acres of white marble and glossy display stands containing rows of colourful potions and powders in every conceivable shade. As they stepped over the threshold, Ryan surveyed it all with a hint of panic.

"*Minx Red,*" he said, picking up one of the lipsticks at random. "Do people really wear all this gunk? There must be thirty or forty different brands in here and they all sell red lipstick. What's the difference between them? How d' you know which one will really make you a minx?"

MacKenzie chuckled as he turned to her with an expression of dazed confusion.

"Depends on the person you're wearing it for," she replied, and was irritated to find herself wondering whether Phillips preferred a woman who wore lipstick. What did she care?

Maybe his wife had worn red.

Oh, stop it.

"Personally, I save the Minx Red for special occasions," she said.

"Me too," Ryan replied, deadpan.

MacKenzie grinned.

"Where's the *Lola* counter?" He turned a full circle, searching for Isobel's former workplace. "I can't see the wood for the trees in this place. They should put an epilepsy warning outside the main doors—this lighting is enough to give anyone a migraine."

"Come on," MacKenzie said, ushering him in the direction of a counter in the far corner of the beauty hall with sleek black countertops. It was manned by two reed-thin women dressed entirely in black, sporting flawlessly made-up faces and beaming white smiles.

"Can I help you today?" One of them stepped forward as they approached, assessing their faces with a practised eye. "Are you looking for anything in particular?"

"We'd like to speak to Amaya, if she's around?"

The girl's eyes turned cool and she gestured her colleague over, imagining she'd lost a commission.

"Amaya? This lady and gentleman would like you to serve them," she said.

A woman of around twenty greeted them, eyes widening as she took in the tall, dark-haired man with arresting grey eyes.

"Yes? How can I help?"

Ryan studiously ignored her reaction and retrieved his warrant card, holding it up for her to inspect.

"DCI Ryan and DI MacKenzie, from Northumbria CID. Do you have time for a quick chat?"

Her face fell into immediate lines of concern.

"I—yes, hang on a minute. Lydia! I'm just taking a quick break."

She led them away from the counter and made for the upmarket food hall next door, where Ryan's superior nose detected the sweet smell of freshly brewed coffee emanating from an artisan coffee stall.

"Is it okay to talk here?" Amaya twisted her hands nervously and MacKenzie stepped into the breach.

"Of course." She placed a gentle hand on the woman's back and nudged her towards a table. "You're not in trouble, Amaya. Would you like a drink?"

"Um, okay. Can I have a flat white, please?"

Ryan ordered three coffees and they settled down to talk while they warmed themselves from the inside out.

"I guess you're here about Isobel," she said, wrapping her fingers around the coffee cup. "I told the other detectives everything I could remember, I swear."

"We appreciate it," Ryan assured her, trying not to feel irritated as she stared at him over the rim of her coffee cup.

This was becoming awkward.

As though she had read his thoughts, MacKenzie stepped in once again and spoke in a motherly tone she reserved for skittish witnesses and those under the influence of excess hormones.

"We're grateful for all your help so far," she reiterated. "And we understand it can be frustrating to have to repeat yourself over and over, but it's really vital that you try. All we want to do is make sure we have everything very clear in our minds, so we can try to find the person who hurt your friend."

Amaya's big, kohl-rimmed eyes filled with tears, but she held herself together.

"I don't mind telling you again," she said softly. "I just don't know whether it'll help. I don't really know anything."

"Even the tiniest details can be important," Ryan put in, and she flushed.

"Why don't you start by telling us how long you'd known Isobel?" MacKenzie interjected swiftly.

Amaya sipped her coffee and nodded.

"Okay, yeah. It was just over a year. I remember, because Isobel started working on the *Lola* counter in May last year. We hit it off straight away because she was just so—so nice." Her voice wobbled, and she took another gulp of coffee.

"You're doing really well," Ryan told her. "Try remembering some of the good things about Isobel. Did you go out together, after work?"

Amaya cast her mind back to happier times and smiled.

"Yeah, we went out on Thursday nights, usually. We were both knackered on Fridays, so we went out mid-week instead. They have 2-for-1 cocktails on Thursday nights, too," she explained.

They murmured their understanding.

"Anyway," she shrugged a slim shoulder. "Isobel was kind of quiet, but she loved music. I guess she didn't have much money because she was always worrying about it, but she'd treat herself every now and then."

"What about when you would go out," Ryan prodded. "Did Isobel get a lot of attention?"

Amaya nodded.

"Oh, yeah. I mean, she was beautiful, wasn't she?"

They both nodded. Isobel Harris had been a stunner, and her killer a connoisseur.

"Was there anyone in particular? Anyone who upset or worried her?"

Amaya made a face.

"Not really. She went on a few dates, but she wasn't into anything casual. She was old-fashioned that way. I think she wanted to meet someone special and have a proper family. She never really had that growing up."

Ryan and MacKenzie thought of the background information they had about the late Isobel Harris and mourned the loss of a life that had barely begun. She'd grown up in care, moving through a series of foster homes until she'd turned sixteen and moved into her own supervised housing. By the time she'd celebrated her twenty-fourth birthday, Isobel had worked her way up to being a team leader and had bought her own little house in Jarrow. She'd set up a cottage business as a wedding make-up artist on the side and life was on the up.

That was before somebody decided to cut it short.

"Is that why Isobel joined LoveLife?" MacKenzie asked. "She was looking for someone special?"

"Yeah, she said she could vet them before she agreed to go out with them," Amaya said. "Not that they always told the truth. That's what happened with the bloke who killed himself the other day—John Dobbs, or whatever his name was. He was the only one who wouldn't leave her alone. He really pestered her."

"Tell us about it," Ryan asked, leaning back in his chair.

Her eyes watched the action and he sighed inwardly.

"Ah, yeah, well, she said she'd met this really fit guy online. He was thirty-five, *really* good-looking, and he worked as a consultant something-or-other in A&E. She was so excited to meet him. She made a real effort and everything. I did her eye-shadow," she muttered, glumly.

"And this was John Dobbs?"

"Yeah, that was him, but when she turned up at the restaurant, he was totally different to his profile online. He looked nothing like his picture, and it turned out he'd lied about everything. Isobel felt a bit sorry for him, so she stayed a little while and then made an excuse to leave. She must have told him where she worked because he turned up the next day, and the day after that. The second time, she told him to piss off and we had to call security to get rid of him."

Ryan thought of the CCTV footage they'd already seen.

"It's funny," Amaya murmured. "She'd only been in A&E a couple of weeks earlier and she said there'd been this really hot doctor. I think she hoped it would be him."

Their ears pricked up immediately.

"Isobel was in hospital? What for?" MacKenzie asked, leaning forward urgently.

Amaya looked between them.

"Ah, it was nothing really. She came over a bit dizzy one day and it's company policy to send us straight to A&E if one of us gets dizzy, just in case it's something serious. Turns out she was fine; it was probably just anaemia or something."

"Do you remember the date this happened?" Ryan asked, working hard to keep the excitement from his voice.

"Sure," she nodded, feeling around the pocket of her tunic for her phone so she could check the calendar. "It was the same day I went to see *Mamma Mia!* at the theatre, so I should be able to find the date."

Amaya scrolled back a few weeks.

"Yeah, it was Saturday 7th June," she told them, then looked up with hopeful eyes. "Did I help?"

Ryan smiled warmly.

"You definitely did. You helped your friend today, Amaya. She was lucky to have you."

The girl beamed, then her eyes clouded with worry again.

"I thought—when I watched the news on Sunday, I thought it was all over. I thought he'd been the one who

107

killed her but then I heard about what happened to DCI Cooper. She was so lovely when she came around to ask questions…" The girl stopped, blinking furiously. "Do you think it's the same person who killed Isobel?"

Ryan and MacKenzie exchanged a look. It was on the tip of his tongue to fob the girl off with a stock answer, but he couldn't bring himself to do it.

"We think so, but we can't be sure, yet," Ryan said, truthfully.

Amaya took a final sip of her coffee and pushed it away, seeming to draw herself up before she asked the final question that had, to her shame, been occupying her mind even more than the loss of her friend.

"Do you think he'll come back? I mean, do you think he'd come after me too?"

Another tricky question, Ryan thought.

"It's unlikely," he said. "But it makes sense to be careful. Try not to go anywhere alone, if you can help it. We have no reason to believe he'd target you, Amaya, but don't take any unnecessary risks."

She took a deep breath and nodded.

"I'm so lucky to be alive," she whispered. "When Isobel is—"

"It's not your fault," Ryan assured her. "It's nobody's fault, except the person who killed her. Try to remember that."

Dusk had fallen when they emerged from the garish, artificial light of the beauty hall and stepped outside. Ahead of them, a tall monument to Earl Grey rose up over a hundred feet into the pearl-grey sky. It stood as an island amid the pedestrianised zone around Grainger Town, the historic heart of the city which boasted classical Georgian architecture and wide avenues leading down to the river. Ryan looked up at the column and wondered what its figurehead had seen over the past two hundred years. How many people had passed beneath Grey's unmoving eyes, never to return?

"Ask Lowerson to check the hospital records for 7th June," he said, as MacKenzie came to stand next to him. "It could be nothing. On the other hand—"

"It could be something," she agreed.

"Yeah. Cooper assumed Isobel Harris met her killer via the online dating community. What if she met him on his own turf, at the hospital?"

"I'll chase up all the CCTV we can get our hands on," MacKenzie promised him.

Ryan nodded, and they turned towards the Metro station beside the monument and the next stop on their whistle-stop tour of Isobel Harris's last movements.

"The staff exit is around the side of the building," he remarked. "There's a camera on the door and we have her leaving work on Friday 20th June at twenty past eight. She would have walked from there straight to the entrance to the metro, over here. It can't be more than fifty feet away."

They stood at the top of the stone steps leading down into the station, below street level. The tunnel glowed yellow and they followed the stream of people down towards the ticket hall. There were machines dotted around, a few stalls, and a small supermarket designed for commuters needing a quick fix.

"CCTV shows that she entered the supermarket at eight twenty-four and came back out again at eight twenty-nine with one bag containing a carton of milk, a packet of sliced ham and a loaf of bread. CSIs found the bag sitting on her kitchen countertop," Ryan added.

MacKenzie felt a tightening in her chest because she recognised so much of herself in that description. How many times had she stopped by the supermarket next to Police Headquarters on her way home to pick up a carton of milk? Had she ever considered who might be watching her, following her?

"You just don't think about it," she murmured. "After work, you're eager to get home, put the kettle on and kick your shoes off. You don't even think about the danger. All you think about is home."

Ryan nodded.

"It's normal life," he reminded her. "You have a right to go about your business without living in fear. Isobel Harris had that right, too."

MacKenzie tore her eyes away from the supermarket entrance, where she'd just seen a young woman walking out with a single bag of shopping.

"She had a Metro pass," MacKenzie continued, "so she had no need to get a ticket from the machine. Metro scanners logged her entrance at eight thirty-one."

They showed their warrant cards to the ticket inspectors and passed through the turnstiles. Before they continued their journey, Ryan paused to look at the other entrances leading into Monument station. There was one connected to Fenwick's via the lower-ground floor and another one leading up onto Grey Street.

"Why didn't she use the internal entrance?" he wondered.

"Quicker to just step outside from the beauty hall exit," MacKenzie replied. "It would take longer if she went down a level and walked around."

"What about the Grey Street entrance?" Ryan left no stone unturned. "Do we have the camera footage for that entrance?"

MacKenzie frowned.

"Come to think of it, I don't think we were able to get hold of that footage because the camera covering those stairs had blown."

Ryan turned.

"What a coincidence," he said. "When did it break?"

"I can find out. It'd be interesting if it happened to go around the same time Isobel Harris went to A&E."

"Wouldn't it just?"

They followed the escalator down to the platform level.

"Isobel took the Metro south towards South Shields. Her stop was Jarrow."

"Cameras caught her on the way down to the platform," MacKenzie said, watching passing advertisements on the wall for *Cirque du Soleil* and local solicitors' firms. "It's a fair bet that he followed her down here and the camera would have caught him, too."

Ryan considered the habits of the creature they hunted.

"Not necessarily on the same day," he said. "But he may have followed her on other days, learning her routine, finding out where she lived and—most importantly for him—whether she lived alone. He might not have needed to follow her home from work on the day he finally took her if he knew her movements well enough. He could go directly to Jarrow and wait for her there."

MacKenzie shivered as she imagined the kind of cunning involved.

"He has to have a certain level of freedom," she said. "What if his own work allows him to come and go at set times? Unless he doesn't work."

"That's something we'll find out," Ryan said, watching the faces of those who passed by on the escalator heading up to the ticket hall level.

"Here we go," MacKenzie murmured, stepping off to follow a line of people towards the southbound platform. "Another camera right there, working fine," she told him.

They entered the platform and found themselves looking at a draughty tunnel with enormous billboards showing out-of-date Christmas albums and photographs of gap-toothed kids wielding microscopes to advertise local schools. The electronic sign on the wall told them they had another six minutes to wait until the next train bound for South Shields and they walked along to the other end, dodging their fellow passengers who waited at intervals along the platform.

"She got on the train near the front," Ryan kept up his narrative and looked around the area. "Cameras cover this platform at both ends and I presume they're still working. What about that one?"

He pointed towards a short corridor leading to a lift that was rarely used.

"I'm not sure," MacKenzie said thoughtfully. "I'll find that out when I'm asking about the cameras in the ticket hall."

"Yeah, because if he took out the camera at the Grey Street entrance and then took the lift down to the platform level, he could shield himself from prying eyes whilst staying close to his victim."

"Not all the cameras on the trains are working," she warned him.

"Typical. But we have some?"

"Yeah, they're still collating the footage, but the train operator has been co-operative so far."

"Good. Here's our train."

They felt the ground rumble beneath their feet as a train rattled through the tunnel towards them, coming to a jerky stop before its doors buzzed open with an alert telling people to, "MIND THE GAP" in an electronic drone.

"After you," Ryan said, letting MacKenzie go first. He was all for feminist principles and he didn't happen to believe chivalry was incompatible with any of them. It was a simple matter of putting others before himself.

The Metro wasn't too crowded, and they found a seat near the front of the train where they could talk quietly without fear of being overheard.

The train doors buzzed shut again.

"Something's been bothering me, ever since our chat with Amaya Golzari."

"Could be the fact that she was making moon eyes at you," MacKenzie teased him. "I feel sorry for the poor kid; she was used to dealing with Cooper and Jessop, then you waltz in and she probably wished she'd worn her *Minx Red* to work, after all."

Ryan's lips twitched.

"Actually, it made me wonder—why didn't Harris or Cooper show any defensive wounds? Sure, the drugs disabled them pretty quickly but why didn't they at least try?" He shook his head, trying to imagine what it would take. "I have to wonder whether he managed to put them at their ease, so they never saw it coming."

"He must be charismatic," MacKenzie agreed. "But he'd be taking a huge risk to rely on his own personal charms."

Ryan considered that, then shook his head.

"I don't think we should underestimate just how arrogant this guy is. I think he really believes he can get away with all this and that he's committed two perfect murders. A person like that doesn't underplay his own charisma, he uses it ruthlessly to his advantage."

They fell silent as the train sped through the dark tunnels beneath the city, and wondered whether there was another woman out there falling prey to the specious charms of a killer.

"Nicola."

She moaned, an animal sound of torment.

"Nicola, I won't ask again."

She heard his voice somewhere in the distant corners of her mind and shrank away from it, twitching on the bed as her body remembered.

His face.

His eyes.

Pain. Such pain.

The sedative was wearing off again and the feeling of nausea returned as her body battled with shock. She was sweating, shaking so hard that her teeth chattered. Her lips were dry and cracked, bloodied from his slaps and where the skin had torn around the filthy gag he used while she was awake.

"You're not going to be with us for much longer, are you, darling?"

He affected an air of sadness even as he wondered how much more he could do while she was still alive.

He checked the time and tutted.

"I was hoping to make some progress today, Nicola, but I really must be getting along. Time waits for no man, does it?"

He ran a gloved finger down her nose, as if she were a child.

"I don't suppose you'll be running off anytime soon, but I never like to get complacent. Let's give you a little top-up to make sure you don't go anywhere."

She didn't even feel the needle this time.

CHAPTER 11

Isobel Harris's house was a ten-minute walk away from Jarrow Metro station, on the south side of the River Tyne. It was a stone's throw from St Paul's Monastery, an ancient ruin that was the former home of Bede, an eighth-century scholar widely accepted as being the father of English history. More recently, the town was a major centre for shipbuilding and, as Ryan and MacKenzie cut through along the high street, the remnants of its proud history were there for all to see.

"Quiet here," MacKenzie remarked.

The night had grown dark and, although the weather was mild, she felt cold. It was embarrassing to admit she was glad to have somebody walking beside her, and she realised the case must be getting to her. She considered herself a strong, well-trained woman, capable of handling herself and, if a psycho killer made her his target, she liked to think she'd put up a fight.

She hoped it never came to that.

"You alright, Mac?"

She looked up at Ryan's profile and wondered if he knew how much she appreciated those three little words. At a time when her friend and colleague had been brutally murdered, it was hard to go home to an empty house where she jumped at every little sound. She'd hardly slept the past few nights and it was getting harder to convince herself that she was self-sufficient, that she didn't feel terribly, crushingly lonely.

Just to know that somebody cared meant all the world and, just for a moment, she found herself wondering if she'd feel differently towards the strong, quiet man walking alongside her if she were ten years younger, or he ten years older. It was an odd thought to have towards her boss, but she harboured no resentment about the fact he was her superior officer, at least on paper. It hadn't gone unnoticed that he made sure to include her in every high-profile investigation and he entrusted her with her own team, rarely needing to micro-manage. She appreciated his management style and she hoped that he appreciated the results she produced because of it.

"Yeah, I'm okay," she said, and meant it. "It's hard imagining Isobel Harris walking home alone through these streets in the dark, not having anybody to come home to or any family to look out for her. It seems so unfair."

"If there's one thing we can be sure of, it's that life is seldom fair," he replied.

She opened her mouth to argue but couldn't think of a thing to say.

They rounded the corner onto St Paul's Road and spotted the unmarked police car assigned to watch Harris's property. It was a well-established fact that killers often returned to the scenes of their crimes to re-live the glory and feed off the power all over again, and they couldn't risk missing their chance to intercept him.

Ryan stopped at the head of the street and looked at a line of two-up, two-down, red-bricked 1930s houses. Above their heads, the moon shone an eerie white glow across the rooftops, but the street was otherwise cloaked in darkness.

Nothing stirred, not even the wind.

"Street lighting is pretty bad around here," Ryan said, taking a wide survey. "Easy enough to hide behind one of the cars, or even to park further down the street without being noticed. Nobody's looking out of their window at this time of night."

MacKenzie looked at the other houses on the street and nodded.

"The curtains are closed at most of the windows and some of them look vacant," she said. "It must have been so easy for him."

It was a joy to feel angry again, she realised. Anger was so much better than fear.

"Shall we look inside?"

It wasn't really a question, but he asked all the same.

"We have to," she told him, and led the way towards Harris's front door.

When nobody approached to intercept them, Ryan marched across to the unmarked car supposedly on duty and hammered on the driver's side window. He took some small satisfaction in seeing two police constables rear up in shock, hastily shutting down their smartphones and scrambling out of the car.

"Sorry, are we interrupting you?"

"No, sir. Sorry, I was—I was responding to—"

Ryan held up a hand.

"Did you happen to catch the news while you were surfing your phone?"

"Um—yes. No. I mean, no."

Ryan smiled thinly.

"There's only one news story of the day: we have a killer running loose in our city. Does that worry you at all?"

"Of course, sir. It's awful."

"Good. Then listen to me when I tell you that the job you do is *important*. I know it gets boring and the hours are long," he surprised them by admitting. "Don't think I've forgotten what it's like on the beat. It's a thankless job, most of the time, but Isobel Harris would thank you if she could."

They said nothing, but their eyes skittered away, embarrassed.

"She had nobody to care for her in life," he continued softly. "Don't you think it's fitting she has people to care for her in death?"

"Yes, sir."

"I'm so glad we agree."

Ryan left them to think it over and followed MacKenzie up to Isobel's front door. They covered their hands and feet, broke the police seal and entered the silent house.

"The notes in the file say the needle came from behind."

MacKenzie tried the light switch but the electricity had been turned off days ago. The darkness was complete, thick with the lingering scent of violent death and food gone bad.

Ryan stood just behind her and the hairs on the back of her neck stood on end.

"Have you got a torch?" he asked.

MacKenzie started to say 'no'.

"Here, take mine," he offered. "Or would you rather I do a walk-through while you wait here? It's pretty close quarters in there."

She smiled in the darkness and added 'gentleman' to his growing list of likeable qualities.

"No, I'm okay."

"There was no blood spatter in the hallway here," Ryan began. "There was nothing to suggest she fought him."

"Must have taken her by surprise."

"Something struck me as odd," Ryan said, and brushed past her to peer inside the tiny living room. In the dim light, they could see the outline of a two-seater sofa and a coffee table. There was a bistro table and two chairs in the corner with a television resting on top of a unit beside them. "On the floor there, by the sofa, there was a stain on the carpet. Faulkner says it was fresh and the tests confirmed it was white wine. There was a bottle open in the fridge, too."

Ryan entered the room and MacKenzie saw his shadowy outline moving around the room, getting a feel for the space.

"What if he didn't need to stalk her?" he said, suddenly.

MacKenzie stepped back from the doorway to allow him to pass, then followed him up the narrow staircase towards the room where Isobel had died.

"What do you mean? You think he just snatched her on the fly?"

Ryan coughed as they reached the landing and his nostrils were assailed by the ripe scent of crusted blood and bodily waste emanating from the largest bedroom.

"No," he replied. "That isn't his style. It looks opportunistic, but it isn't. He wouldn't risk being discovered so soon. I was thinking somebody could have found out her home address from hospital records, or struck up an acquaintance."

"That's an extreme level of control," she replied, shining the torch light along the landing to guide their way. The little white circle of light shook, bobbing across the wall. "Amaya didn't mention Isobel having met anybody and she was her closest friend. Surely Isobel would have told her if she'd met somebody new?"

"He's manipulative," Ryan said darkly, and reached for the door handle.

There was a half world, somewhere between life and death, where the senses no longer worked as they should.

There was nothing to taste, nothing to touch, to smell or to see.

But you could still hear.

You could hear the small sounds of skin tearing and heavy breathing that might not be your own. You could hear the man whistling, everything from show tunes to classical arias.

And there was his voice, muffled behind the paper mask he always wore.

"Still with us? That's good."

More time passed and more confusion until nothing was certain anymore.

Was she dead?

Was this what happened when you died?

It was a slow, endless process. Like an elastic band stretching to breaking point. Only, she hadn't broken.

Not yet.

Her eyelids flickered, and she saw a splinter of light, thought she heard a bell ringing. She gasped for the breath to speak, to shout for help, then the darkness came again.

No more pain.

Ryan and MacKenzie stood at the foot of the bed where Isobel Harris had been found. The light from the torch moved over the small details of the room: framed photographs of Isobel and Amaya, of Isobel as a child standing beside an older woman who might have been her grandmother or a foster parent. An enormous silver make-up case had pride of place on the shelf she'd used as a dressing table with a small stool tucked beneath. Stuffed toys sat on the window ledge, some of them worn with age.

The bed had been stripped of its mattress and bedding for forensic testing but the carpet beneath it remained, crusted with dried blood.

"Just like Sharon," Ryan murmured. "He doesn't like to sully his own doorstep or risk killing them out in the open. He likes to take his time and do it on their own turf."

"Adds insult to injury," MacKenzie said. "He invades every element of their lives."

"What drives him?" Ryan thought aloud. "Where does this level of hatred come from?"

MacKenzie looked across at him in the inky blue darkness.

"Hatred would imply a strong emotion," she reminded him. "It's possible that the person we're looking for doesn't experience any normal human emotion. He may see them simply as bodies."

Ryan heaved a deep sigh.

"Come on," he said. "We've seen enough."

Ryan knew something was wrong the instant he entered his apartment.

It was after eleven by the time he'd collected his car from CID Headquarters and driven home through the quiet streets.

He'd taken a longer route along the river so he could stop and look at the bridges lit up against the night sky and clear his head. Phillips had been right when he'd issued his warning about self-protection; stepping into the mind of a killer was like suffering from a kind of cancer that could strike without warning and make a home in your heart, festering there until there was nothing good and pure anymore. He'd felt the shadow of Isobel Harris's killer crawling against his skin when he'd entered her home. It had been an almost tangible thing, as if he'd been standing in the room beside them.

Every step they took brought them closer, and the greater his understanding, the more likely it was that Ryan would recognise him when the time came. That wasn't policing. It was pure instinct.

Just like the instinct warning him that he was not alone.

Quietly, Ryan set down his briefcase and reached across for a heavy ornamental bowl sitting on the console table in his hallway. He moved softly across the wooden floor and almost swore when one of the boards creaked.

He froze, listening for any sound of movement behind his living room door and, beyond it, the bedrooms.

Nothing.

But he knew he was not alone. His body was on high alert as he prepared to defend himself.

He stepped into the living room and came to a halt as the scene unfolded.

Long, tanned legs stretched out on his sofa in striped pyjama shorts. The woman they belonged to was fast asleep and snuggled into one of his sports sweaters with a faded tick on the front. Her face was bare of make-up and her long hair was still wet at the ends from the shower. She had the face of an angel and was even more beautiful in repose.

Ryan let the air in and out of his lungs in one long breath and set the bowl back on the table before walking across to sit on the coffee table beside her.

"Natalie?"

She stirred, then rolled over.

Ryan let out a short laugh and wondered if her timing could possibly be any worse. It was neither safe nor convenient for his sister to be there, but it seemed the decision had been taken out of his hands. That would teach him in future not to go handing out keys, willy-nilly.

His mother was behind it somewhere, he was sure of it. She'd been making noises recently about him spending too much time alone and not seeing enough of his family. He'd tried telling her that he was caught up in a murder investigation, but his protests fell on deaf ears.

"Come on, sleepy-head," he said, unconsciously echoing a killer. "Time for bed."

"Mm."

"I see you helped yourself," he muttered, eyeing the carnage she'd left in his kitchen with long-suffering acceptance. "When did you arrive?"

"Couple of hours ago," she yawned, leaning against him comfortably as he led her through to the spare bedroom. "You've run out of milk. And chocolate."

"I don't keep a ready supply in my chocolate cupboard," he replied.

"That's why you're so grumpy all the time."

He moved across to switch on the bedside lamp and ran an awkward hand through his hair.

"Natalie, look. You know, it's great to see you but now is a really bad time. There's a lot going on—"

"You always have a lot going on," she pointed out, and settled herself under the covers. "You need to relax more."

"Not right now," he said. "I'm in the middle of a major murder investigation. I can't have any distractions."

"I get that," she said, yawning widely. "But I've been given strict instructions to make sure you eat properly and get a bit of sleep. Oh, and I'm supposed to make you laugh, if I can."

"Mother."

"Yes, Mother," she replied. "Otherwise known as, She Who Must Be Obeyed."

"Let's talk about it in the morning," he said. His eyes were so tired he could hardly see, let alone think straight.

"You'll hardly know I'm here," Natalie said, with an imperious wave of her hand.

"Right. Like a hole in the head."

"Switch the light off, will you?"

"I live to serve."

CHAPTER 12

Tuesday 8ᵗʰ July

A new day dawned dull and misty, curling its way in from the sea in thick white clouds so the river was barely visible. Ryan watched the city awaken as he polished off a piece of toast and warred with himself over what to do with Natalie.

His sister was almost ten years younger than him and most of their childhood had been spent apart at separate boarding schools. He loved his parents, respected them, but would make a different choice when the time came to educate his own children.

If the time ever came, he corrected.

At present, his work was all-consuming. Even if he did find somebody patient enough to put up with the antisocial hours his work dictated, how could he expect them to share the burden of what he carried home each night? When you saw first-hand the violence that one person could do to another, it was hard to shrug it off and speak of other things.

It was easier to remain alone.

"You look thoughtful."

He turned to see Natalie enter the lounge area, rumpled from sleep.

"I am. I was thinking you should go back home today. I can't look after you," he said, as gently as he could.

"I don't need you to look after me," she said, testily. "As it happens, I'm between jobs so I came here to look after *you*, for a change."

He didn't know what to say.

"Thanks, but I don't need anything."

"Bollocks," she said, heading across to switch the kettle on. "You need a shave, for a start. There's designer stubble and then there's whatever you've got on your chin."

Ryan raised a hand to his face and found it alarmingly bristled.

"I have more important things to worry about," he muttered.

"Temper, temper," she warned. "You've got bags under your eyes so big they could carry shopping and I've seen the state of your fridge. Why don't you let me help for a few days? I can feed you some steak and consider my sisterly duty discharged."

Ryan checked the time on his watch and shoved the last of his toast in his mouth.

"Fine," he mumbled. "Just don't start scattering any cushions about the place."

According to Sharon Cooper's neighbour, her son, Will, had been the last person to see her alive. However, Will Cooper's recollection of events was very different and so it fell upon Phillips and Lowerson to find out whose version was correct.

"The thing is, son, you can't go in guns blazing," Phillips said, as they made their way towards the main entrance of the Dental Hospital, where Will was a student. "The last thing we want is for him to clam up. We need young Will Cooper to tell us as much as possible about his relationship with his mum and he won't do that if he thinks we're against him."

Lowerson nodded vigorously.

"D' you want to be good cop or bad cop?"

Phillips barked out a laugh.

"Let's not run before we can walk, eh? We're not interviewing Al Capone."

Lowerson was mildly disappointed but recovered quickly.

"He says he was at home on Saturday night, studying, and hadn't seen his mum for a couple of weeks."

"And what do you make of that?"

They paused outside the main doors to the Dental Hospital while Lowerson considered the question.

"Cooper's bank accounts haven't flagged any unusual activity and no large sums were paid out to anybody, including her son. She wasn't minted, she got by the same as the rest of us, so there's no obvious financial motive that I can see for Will Cooper wanting to off his own mother.

On the other hand, her neighbour seems adamant it was Will she saw entering his mum's home on Saturday night, around eight o'clock. I don't see what possible reason the neighbour would have to lie."

"My thoughts exactly," Phillips said, and clapped an arm around the younger man's shoulder. "You're growing more cynical and suspicious every day and it's enough to warm the cockles of m' old heart. Howay, let's go and find out whether Will Cooper has any reason to lie."

Ryan had been ambushed.

He realised that he should have seen it coming when Gregson rang him twice in the space of half an hour to make sure he was running on time for their supposed progress meeting. He also should have seen it coming when Gregson told him to wear a tie.

And yet, when he entered his superintendent's office to find the constabulary's media liaison officer and two of the city's leading journalists already seated with half-drunk cups of coffee, he was taken aback.

"Sorry, sir, I thought we said ten o'clock."

"We did, Ryan. Pull yourself together and close the door."

Ryan did as he was told but remained standing beside the door, in case an emergency exit was required.

Gregson was not fooled.

"Come in and meet Tayo Jackson and Jacqueline Beard, from the BBC and ITV News, respectively."

"We've met before," Ryan replied. Innate good manners compelled him to shake their outstretched hands.

Two pairs of probing eyes watched him, stripping him bare.

"Sir? I'm sorry to hurry things along but we have quite a busy morning ahead of us."

Gregson steepled his hands and smiled genially. He recognised the ploy and had used it many times himself.

"It's time we spoke to the public," he said, in his usual forthright manner. "It's necessary, for us and for them. There's a lot of unease on the streets and it's time we put their minds at rest."

"Sir, if I can speak freely?"

Gregson glanced meaningfully at their guests, who listened with unconcealed delight.

"By all means," he said mildly, but his voice held a warning.

"The public interest is better served by letting our team do its work. Without interruption," Ryan said. "There's been enough news coverage of the murders and it's only inciting more panic."

"That's where you come in," the woman spoke up. "They want to hear from the person leading the investigation. It's important they see you and connect with you, so they know somebody is fighting to protect them. Otherwise, you're just another faceless name and rank."

"This isn't up for debate," Gregson put in, before Ryan could argue. "Jacqueline and Tayo have some questions they'd like to ask ahead of a press conference which has been scheduled for eleven. I trust you'll be able to allay any concerns they might have."

Ryan stood for one fulminating second, irritation radiating from his body and transmitting itself across the room. But duty and professionalism won out, as they always did.

"Yes, sir."

The Dental Hospital in Newcastle resembled any other clinical facility across the land, built sometime in the eighties and with the laissez-faire attitude towards inspiring architecture that characterised the era. It was located next door to the Royal Victoria Infirmary and the university medical school, forming a triangle of buildings within a two-minute walk of each other.

After some time spent navigating a series of badly signposted corridors, Phillips and Lowerson made their way to the Undergraduate Student Office with the intention of finding out Will Cooper's schedule. Unfortunately, that was not possible, since Will Cooper had been suspended from the university and was not scheduled on any shifts for the foreseeable future.

"Are you *sure*?"

The administrator glared at them.

"I'm sure," she said, tapping a long fingernail against her computer keyboard in a staccato rhythm. "He's been suspended. That's all I can tell you."

"Why was he suspended?" Lowerson asked.

She turned her withering gaze on the younger detective with the impressively gelled hair.

"I can't tell you that. It violates Data Protection, doesn't it?"

Phillips made a noise somewhere between a growl and a cry.

"We're from CID," he said. "It's information pertinent to our investigation."

"I don't care if you're from Mars," she retorted. "If you have the proper authority, then you won't mind putting it in writing, will you?"

Phillips knew when he was beaten.

"Have you got a manager?"

"I am the manager."

Phillips weighed up the likely success of waging a charm offensive and thought his chances were slim to none.

"We'll be in touch," he said.

Ryan stood outside Police Headquarters dressed once again in his emergency tie and jacket, feeling like a man about to face the gallows. It wasn't that he minded public speaking or that he disagreed with the general proposition that the public deserved peace of mind. He objected to the whole rigmarole simply because it was premature. There was nothing new to report and nothing he could say that wouldn't prejudice their investigation. He'd already proven that during the last hour spent answering tedious questions in an overheated room while time continued to march forward.

There was something else to consider, too.

The last person to address the cameras about the murder of Isobel Harris had been DCI Sharon Cooper, less than a week before she'd turned up dead herself. It was a strong possibility that their killer had watched the press conference on television and had taken it upon himself to lash out at the police with her as the figurehead.

As her successor, it was a sobering thought.

"Ryan? We'll be ready for you in a couple of minutes."

He nodded and watched the media liaison scurry away clutching a clipboard filled with questions she hoped he would avoid answering.

"How do you intend to play it?"

Gregson came to stand beside him while they watched the press gather themselves together, fiddling with microphones and earpieces.

Ryan frowned.

"I'm not playing at anything, sir. I'll answer any reasonable questions with a truthful response that takes account of the need to reassure the public of their safety and security."

Gregson nodded.

"Good. You're up. Oh, and Ryan? Try to look a little less forbidding and a bit more approachable, there's a good lad."

Ryan ignored that edict, stepping up to the freestanding microphone and simply waiting until he had their attention.

Gregson watched him with interest and thought the man was a chameleon. Ryan could cloak himself in a tailored suit that fit him like a second skin and, suddenly, it was as though the bloke in jeans and shirtsleeves had never existed. That was breeding, he supposed. He knew Ryan came from somewhere down south and suspected his family had a big pile of bricks down there. Probably owned horses and rode with the hunt, too. It had taken a good couple of years to figure out why he'd left his roots behind and chosen a new life in the north after living it up at the Met, in London, but he'd come to realise that the landscape suited his newest Chief Inspector. Ryan might have the airs and graces, and he might know the difference between a Petit Chablis and a Chardonnay, but he had the stomach for the kind of work they did and wasn't afraid to get his hands dirty. There was a core of pure ice beneath the pretty face the lasses seemed to love, and his temperament suited the climate.

Right on cue, a light drizzle began to fall.

"Thank you for coming," Ryan began, in a clear tone that carried across the crowd. "There has been a lot of press coverage over the past few weeks concerning the death of Isobel Harris and, more recently, of my colleague, Sharon Cooper. Before I say anything else, I'd like to start by offering my sincere condolences to their families and loved ones, and to assure them that we are doing everything in our power to bring the person or persons responsible to justice."

"Are you treating their deaths as linked? Was it the same person, Chief Inspector?"

Ryan turned to the reporter and pinned her with a stare.

"Unofficial reports of that nature have already been circulating in the press thanks to unscrupulous journalism. I have no intention of confirming or denying any element of our active investigation."

"Isn't it true that John Dobbs was the prime suspect in the late DCI Cooper's investigation? Isn't it true that Dobbs had been under police surveillance for days by the time he died?"

Ryan's eyes turned sharp as he sought out the reporter who had spoken. The police surveillance operation was strictly confidential and had not been given the green light for open discussion. He should know; he was the one dictating what could and could not be said.

He thought swiftly of all the weak links who might have blabbed, and one name stood out above all the rest.

PC Steve Jessop.

"No comment," Ryan said.

"Why has the Harris investigation been re-opened, Chief Inspector, if her killer is already dead?"

"The investigation has not been 're-opened'," Ryan replied. "It is ongoing."

"What about Dobbs? If he wasn't her killer, does that mean an innocent man died?"

There were very few innocent people in the world, Ryan thought, and did not answer.

"Chief Inspector! What about DCI Cooper? Was her death gang-related? Why have you been investigating her son?"

Ryan turned blazing eyes on the same reporter who had spoken earlier and had clearly been in receipt of confidential information.

"During the course of our investigation, we will be conducting full and thorough enquiries into *all* parties connected to either victim. It is usual procedure to eliminate family and friends from our enquiries, first."

"Chief Inspector, we understand both victims sustained brutal injuries including decapitation. Do you believe the person responsible is still at large?"

Ryan knew the party line, had been briefed to within an inch of his life and could almost feel Gregson's breath on the back of his neck. He was supposed to say they were close to making an arrest or otherwise to play down the fact they were nowhere near apprehending the killer.

But he owed a higher duty to the citizens of a city that was under attack. They deserved to know the level of threat they faced so they could adjust their lives accordingly.

"Yes," he said, very clearly. "I believe he is still at large."

There was a second's calm before a storm of questions descended.

"Is the Mayor going to impose a curfew, Chief Inspector?"

"Why aren't there more police on the streets?"

"Why hasn't more been done to safeguard the people of this city?"

Ryan didn't so much as flinch at the barrage of questions, most of which he'd heard many times before. This was no time to debate philosophy versus politics;

to talk about why the criminal justice system was almost at breaking point. He could have spoken of the sword and the shield, of the line he was asked to walk each day to protect and serve. He could have told them that the reason there weren't more bobbies on the beat was because there was no money for them and, even if there were, there was no evidence to suggest it would make a blind bit of difference in preventing crime.

All it would do is make the public *feel* better and, unfortunately, that didn't cut the mustard with The Powers That Be.

As for safeguarding, they were doing everything they could, above and beyond the hours they were contracted to work because every member of the team he had chosen was dedicated to the cause. Sharon Cooper had sacrificed her life in the pursuit of justice.

But the public didn't know that. Not yet.

"I want to urge everybody, and women in particular, to exercise extreme caution," he said. "Do not travel alone at night unless absolutely necessary. Carry an alarm and keep friends or family informed of your movements. Be aware of who is around you and avoid walking, running or cycling alone or with headphones. Be safe, not sorry."

Ryan remembered his audience and one viewer in particular. He chose his final words with care.

"To the person responsible, I say this: never doubt that we will find you. There will be no place for you to hide, because we *will* find you. Every day you continue to walk free, make sure to look over your shoulder because, one day, you'll find me standing there. That's all."

He watched the interview playing on the midday news, riveted by the new detective they'd put in charge of hunting him. There was an odd thrill to be able to put a face and a name to his mirror image; a man who not only bore a slight resemblance to himself but represented the other side of the coin. It was fascinating to watch him speak, to study the play of emotions crossing his face as he addressed the cameras. He amused himself for a moment and tried to imagine what it would be like if the tables were turned, if he were passionate about his fellow man and their wellbeing.

It was too fantastical to imagine.

"Oh, that's good news."

He almost jumped at the sound of his colleague's voice as they came to stand beside him in the staff room.

"What is?"

"I recognise that detective from a case last year. DCI Ryan or Brian or something. He's been in here before."

"As a patient?"

"No, it was to do with another case. A stabbing, I think. Anyway, they say he's brilliant. Always gets his man and all that."

He smiled thinly.

"Really? It seems to me he's being pretty slow in finding his man this time."

"You reckon it wasn't Dobbs, then?" the other asked, innocently. "Why else would he jump off the bridge? He must have killed her."

Careful, he told himself. *Careful.*

"Dobbs didn't have what it takes," he said. "You remember what he was like."

He shrugged.

"I hardly knew the bloke. Saw him on the wards sometimes but I wouldn't have been able to pick him out in a line-up. He seemed harmless enough. Then again, it's always the ones you least expect, isn't it?"

"It certainly is," he purred.

He returned the cheerful farewell, schooling his facial muscles into a smile, before letting them fall again into hard lines of anger as he caught the last lines of Ryan's interview.

"…make sure to look over your shoulder because, one day, you'll find me standing there."

He stood perfectly still, long after the news programme had finished and was replaced with a show dedicated to houses sold at auction.

"Perhaps you should take your own advice, Chief Inspector," he whispered.

CHAPTER 13

Will Cooper shared a smart student house in an upmarket area of Newcastle known as West Jesmond. It had a large student population and was within walking distance of the city centre and the dental hospital so, after bidding the undergraduate administrator a frosty farewell, Phillips and Lowerson decided to stretch their legs and cover the distance on foot.

Being far too proud to ask his younger colleague to slow down, Phillips puffed alongside Jack Lowerson and was forced to admit it might be time to start going to the gym. It wasn't a question of trying to buff up for any woman; he wanted that to be clear from the start. It was purely a matter of staying fit and healthy in the long term. And that went for the smoking, too. It was absolutely nothing at all to do with Denise MacKenzie.

"Wonder why Cooper was suspended?"

Phillips was afforded a temporary reprieve as they paused beside a set of traffic lights.

"That's what we're going to find out, lad. It's usually something to do with dishonesty, like cheating."

"Could be some kind of dental negligence, if there is such a thing."

"Aye, he might have pulled out the wrong tooth, I s'pose."

"Maybe he was too embarrassed to tell us before," Lowerson said.

Phillips turned to look at him.

"Embarrassed or not, he still lied in his statement. We don't take too kindly to that, down at CID. He's lucky we're the ones to pay him a visit and not The Big Man."

"Gregson?"

Phillips laughed; a rich, rumbling sound that disturbed a pigeon walking nearby.

"No, lad. I'm on about Ryan. It's either black or white to him. No shades of grey in between, y' nah what I mean?"

Lowerson nodded.

"Isn't that what it's all about? Good and bad?"

Phillips smiled a private smile as the lights changed and they stepped into the street.

"Jack, I was born and bred up here and I've lived here all my life. Wouldn't have it any other way, neither. There are lads I grew up with, scrapped with, knocked a ball about with, who took a wrong turn too many and ended up in prison, or worse. I've seen their wives and their sons, some of them who went the same way, and thought: that could have been me."

"But it wasn't."

"No, it wasn't," he agreed. "But I nicked a loaf of bread or two when I was a nipper. That's stealing, isn't it?"

"Yes," Lowerson agreed, carefully.

"Aye, and m' Da thrashed me for it, n'all," Phillips remembered, with fondness. "But the fact was, we had nowt to eat. There's kids on the streets with hungry bellies. It doesn't make it right by the law but are you telling me you'd rather see them starve?"

Lowerson was silent, watching the toes of his shiny shoes against the paving stones.

"Now, you take Ryan. He's a good, solid bloke," Phillips said, and meant it. "There's none better. He'll do owt for anyone and you'll never hear him complain. But he's from a different sort of world. He wouldn't know what it feels like to be really hungry or to wear shoes that're too small. He does the job and does it like a pro but, all the time, he's expecting better of people. He looks at people and expects them to do the right thing because he can't imagine why they wouldn't. That's what I mean when I say that there are no shades of grey for him."

Lowerson nodded his understanding.

"I wish I were more like that," he confessed. "It makes me want to be better at what I do."

"Aye, that's what makes him the best," Phillips mused. "That kind of raw idealism makes us all want to be better."

They were silent for a few beats, then a thought struck Lowerson forcefully.

"What if he doesn't catch this bloke—if it isn't Will Cooper, or anyone else we can find. What if it ends up being one of those we have to let go?"

A shadow crossed Phillips' face.

"I've never seen him so fixated," he said. "Tell you the truth, lad, I'm a bit worried. It's getting into his blood."

"It's been a couple of days, since the last one," Lowerson muttered.

"Aye," Phillips agreed. "There'll be another one soon."

———

Nicola regained consciousness slowly, her brain fighting its way valiantly through the mire of drug-induced stupor.

"Mm…Mmm…"

Her lips tried to form the word, to call for her mother or anyone who could help, but the sound could barely be heard above the patter of a light summer rain against the windowpanes.

Her body was a patchwork of cuts and scabs, of deeper wounds he'd left to fester and some he'd seen fit to patch up until the time came when he could let himself loose. The pain was acute, burning all over her skin unlike anything she had ever known. Her chest felt heavy and each breath was a gargantuan effort, wheezing air in and out of her broken body.

In the flat above her, she heard the sound of a television set.

"D— Do—"

Donna. Please, help me, Donna.

Her mind screamed for help and tears streamed from her eyes even as her body collapsed into unconsciousness again.

When Phillips rang the intercom at Will Cooper's house, nobody answered immediately. After buzzing several more times, the disembodied voice of a young woman crackled down the line.

"Yes?"

"This is DS Phillips and DC Lowerson from Northumbria CID. We'd like to speak to William Cooper, please."

There was a long pause, then her voice came back down the line.

"Um, sorry, he's not home."

"Where is he, love?"

"I don't know! Um, I have to go now!"

The line went dead and Lowerson shrugged.

"Guess he must be out," he said.

"Oh, ye of little faith," Phillips replied, and tried the front door which opened easily into a shared hallway. The large Victorian villa had been separated into four apartments, housing two or three students apiece.

"Um, shouldn't we wait for someone to let us in?" Lowerson squeaked.

"Always rely on a student landlord not to worry about basic safety measures," Phillips muttered. "As far as anybody knows, Cooper's neighbour held the door open for us."

"Mm."

"Shades of grey, Jack."

Lowerson rolled his eyes and followed Phillips across the bland hallway and up a single flight of stairs to Cooper's front door on the first floor.

Phillips knocked loudly and adopted a stern expression for anybody checking the peep-hole.

They heard feet shuffling behind the door.

"Howay, you might as well open up," Phillips called out. "Lying to the police is a serious matter, pet. It's not worth it."

A few seconds later, the door opened a crack to reveal the girl they'd spoken to on the intercom. She looked young, no more than eighteen or nineteen, and her hair had been dyed a bright electric blue that shone in a neon halo around her head.

"Did you say you were from the police?"

"Aye, but there's no need to worry. We just need to have a quick chat with Will."

Her eyes fell away to the left and Phillips imagined he was standing somewhere nearby. He pulled out his warrant card and held it up.

"You might have heard that Will's mum died the other day," he continued, gravely. "We're part of the team who're trying to find her killer. I'm sure you want to help us to do that, don't you?"

She swallowed, then nodded.

"I—Yes, it's awful what happened to Sharon."

"Are you one of Will's housemates?" Lowerson stuck his head over Phillips' shoulder and gave her a sunny smile that seemed to put her immediately at ease. There wasn't much not to like about Jack.

"Yeah, I'm Petra."

"Beautiful name," Phillips said. "Mind if we step inside for a moment, love? My throat's parched."

She seemed nervous but opened the door a bit wider to let them pass through.

"I—I only have a few minutes," she improvised. "I'm heading out soon."

Phillips looked down at her clothes—which looked suspiciously like pyjamas—and at the girl's bare feet, but said nothing.

"We won't take up much of your time. Could I trouble you for a glass of water, though?"

"Um, okay, sure. Just wait here."

She hurried into one of the rooms off the small hallway and presently they heard glasses clinking and water running.

"Notice anything unusual?" Phillips asked, under his breath.

"You mean, apart from the fact Will Cooper's hiding in his bedroom?"

Phillips beamed at him.

"See? You're catching on quick. But I was thinking more of the smell in this place."

Lowerson took an ostentatious sniff, just as their hostess returned.

"Here you go." She thrust the glass towards Phillips, who smiled gratefully and took it, but did not drink.

She crossed her arms defensively.

"So, what did you want to talk about?"

She hadn't offered them a seat, so they remained standing in the hallway.

"Well, like I was saying, Will's mum, Sharon, was a good friend of ours. Wasn't she, Jack?"

"Um, yes, very."

"And we're all heartbroken about what happened. She was a very fine police officer."

The girl was looking more crestfallen by the second.

"We know Will must be feeling equally devastated by the news and we want to do all we can to help...that's why we went to see him at the dental hospital today."

Her eyes were like windows into her soul, Phillips thought. She didn't need to tell him that she was already aware of the suspension because it was written all over her face.

Still, he kept up the pretence to put her at ease.

"The thing is, somebody at the hospital told us Will's been suspended. He didn't mention it and, to be honest, we can't understand why he'd lie to us at a time like this. It doesn't look good, does it?"

She looked between them, then at the door at the far end of the hallway.

"Do you—do you mean you're thinking he might be *involved*?"

Phillips sucked in a breath and shook his head sadly.

"We don't know what to think. Do we, Jack?"

"Um, no. We don't."

"If—If Will's been suspended, I'm sure it's got nothing to do with his mum," she said, the words rushing out in her haste to defend him. "He would never hurt anybody."

"Do you know where he is now?"

She opened her mouth as if to speak and Phillips held up a single finger.

"Let me stop you there and remind you that if you lie to us, we can charge you with perverting the course of justice. That's the kind of thing that can ruin your career prospects, just like…oh, something like drugs. I'm sure a smart lass like you has a long way to go in life and wouldn't want to get mixed up in anything like that."

Her eyes began to well up and she nodded.

"Will!"

She called out to him and, finally, his bedroom door opened. He stood there, fully dressed in chinos and a designer polo shirt, looking intensely displeased.

"I'm sorry," she sniffled. "I didn't know what to do."

He looked straight through her.

"Since you've already barged your way in, you might as well make yourselves at home," he said.

"Thanks," Phillips said brightly. "We thought you'd never ask."

CHAPTER 14

A late morning deluge had left clear, cornflower-blue skies in its wake. The sun beat down on Ryan's back through his office window at Police Headquarters and gave his hair a blue-black shine. The tie he'd worn earlier was draped across the back of his chair and he'd rolled his sleeves up to reveal lightly tanned arms, from Sunday morning spent down by the riverbank. It seemed a lifetime ago that he and Phillips had whiled away their time chatting about this and that, debating politics and arguing about the merits of football versus rugby as they soaked up the beauty of the countryside.

That was then.

Now, his eyes were trained on his computer screen as he watched the CCTV footage of John Dobbs' altercation with Isobel Harris at Fenwick's. He'd seen it several times before but found himself drawn to it again as he went back over the girl's movements leading up to her death. The footage was slightly grainy and in black and white, but he could make everything out clearly enough. At twelve-seventeen on

19th June, the CCTV captured a man of average height and build entering the beauty hall. He might have been anybody; a father, a brother, an estate agent or a civil servant. There was nothing to set him apart from the rest. John Dobbs didn't need to find his bearings; Ryan watched him move directly to the far corner where Isobel Harris worked on the *Lola* counter. He was clutching an enormous bouquet of flowers in his hands—red roses—and the overhead lights bounced off the top of his balding head.

Less than ten seconds later, another camera captured Dobbs' profile as he made his way down the aisle and, finally, a third camera trained above the *Lola* counter caught Dobbs full in the face as he shuffled up to greet the object of his desire.

Although there was no sound, Ryan could read the body language very easily.

It began innocently enough, with Dobbs smiling and presenting his bouquet to Isobel. The angle of the camera only captured the top of her dark head, but she shook it and held up her hands to wave him away, stepping back from the counter and turning to her friend, Amaya, presumably calling out for help to move Dobbs along.

Ryan's eyes narrowed on the screen as he watched Dobbs' face change from an unthreatening, middle-aged man to something else entirely. There was menace there, he thought, and Isobel had felt it.

Dobbs walked quickly around the counter to invade her space, this time forcing her to take the flowers. Ryan knew from the statements given by Amaya and the security guard that Dobbs had been wild, shouting at Isobel to take the flowers and be grateful.

"Ungrateful bitch! I came all the way here to give you these! You're just like all the rest!"

He'd made a grab for Isobel's arm and at that point, a security guard waded in. Ryan watched the burly man in a black suit appear at a run, speaking into his lapel, before clamping an arm around Dobbs and dragging him away. Another guard came from the opposite direction to help remove him.

The last of the footage showed Isobel in Amaya's arms. A couple of passing customers stopped to pat her back and congratulate themselves on witnessing the drama. It would make for something to talk about over the dinner table, wouldn't it?

Ryan sat back in his chair and thought again that there were very few innocent people in the world.

"Mac? Got a minute?"

"Sure. What's up?"

Ryan walked across to MacKenzie's desk and picked up a stray biro, fiddling with it as he spoke.

"I've just been reviewing the footage we have from Fenwick's again," he told her. "I know that Dobbs had a history of depression, a couple of pops on his sheet for drunk and disorderly, but I still don't understand why that would lead a man to suicide. If he was innocent, he would have defended himself rather than running like that. Wouldn't he?"

MacKenzie tapped a finger against her lips.

"Aye, right enough. To be honest, he was a bit of a sad case," she said. "The dating profile he set up is something else." She tapped a few buttons and brought up the file containing his LoveLife profile. "Check out the picture, for starters."

The image showed a man somewhere in his late thirties, movie-star handsome.

"Must be a stock image he found online," Ryan said. "Happens often enough."

"According to this, he's a surgeon," she continued. "'World-renowned cardiothoracic surgeon looking for brunettes who like an older man with means, for friendship, romance and maybe more.'"

MacKenzie pulled a face.

"Isobel probably read that and thought he was Prince Charming. Amaya said she'd actually met someone at A&E who fit the bill, or close enough. Poor kid."

Ryan said nothing, but thought of a lonely girl without a family and resolved to be more grateful for his own, even if they did turn up on his doorstep unannounced.

He reminded himself to let Natalie know he'd be late getting home and was irritated at the need to be answerable to anybody.

He shrugged it off.

"People see what they want to see," he murmured, then remembered that the dead man had a family too. "Who spoke to Dobbs' mother?"

"Gregson took care of it personally, in case she decided to start making noises about police harassment. Said she was a bit eccentric."

It was a cynical ploy but, apparently, it had worked. It was one of the many reasons why Gregson was ideally suited to his position and why Ryan would never aspire to it.

"It's time we paid Mrs Dobbs a visit," he decided.

"He's not our prime suspect any longer," MacKenzie said. "Shouldn't we concentrate on the others?"

"It's a loose end, Mac, and I don't like loose ends. Besides, if he's not a suspect, that makes him a victim. He worked at the hospital and there might be something she can tell us about that, or about the people he worked with. We owe his mother some time, if only to eliminate her son from our enquiries."

———

Across town, Phillips and Lowerson sat on the edge of a brown PVC leather sofa in Will Cooper's living room. His housemate and sometime girlfriend had retreated to her room and out of the firing line, having failed to perform her role as an effective decoy.

"Right, lad. Why don't you start by explaining why you've been telling porky pies and hiding in your bedroom?"

"I wasn't hiding," Cooper muttered. "I just didn't want to talk to anyone."

Phillips pursed his lips. Could be that the boy was grieving for his mother. Or could be he was hiding something.

"Alright, why don't you tell us why you've been suspended from the university?"

"That's none of your business."

"Look, son. We can do this the easy way or the hard way, under caution, down at the station. Which is it to be?"

"I know my rights."

"Good, glad to hear your mum rubbed off on you somewhere," Phillips shot back, deliberately reminding him why they were all there. "Now, you can sit here wasting time we don't have, or you can give us the answers we need so we can be on our way and find the bloke who really killed her. From where I'm sitting, it's hard not to draw what we might call 'adverse inferences' from the fact you keep telling us so many lies."

"I haven't lied."

"Oh, but you have," Phillips said. "How about the one where you told us you hadn't seen your mum in a couple of weeks? We've got an eyewitness who says otherwise. They say you visited your mum the very night before she died."

Cooper shifted in his seat but remained silent.

"Then, how about the one where you said you needed to hurry back to the university or you'd miss a lecture? You haven't set foot in the dental hospital for over a month. I'd like to know why."

"Like I said, it's none of your business."

Phillips pointed a stubby finger squarely at Cooper's face.

"Mind yourself, Will. We're not your enemies but you're going the right way about changing that."

Cooper sank back into his chair and crossed his legs, as if he hadn't a care in the world. Phillips gave him a genial smile.

"Jack, do me a favour, would you? Put a quick call through to DS Flynn in the Drugs Squad."

Cooper sat bolt upright.

"Tell him I've got a strong suspicion the occupant here is in possession of drugs. He should get a couple of his officers over here, pronto."

Lowerson pulled out his phone.

"Wait. You can't do that."

"Oh, no? Watch me," Lowerson said, and began keying in the number.

"Just a minute. Maybe—maybe we can talk."

There was a slight sheen of sweat on Cooper's forehead and a distinct edge of panic had crept into his voice.

Lowerson paused, waiting for Phillips to make the final call. When his sergeant gave a tiny shake of his head, he returned the phone to his pocket.

For now.

"Alright, Will. You want to tell us something?"

"I-I got into a bit of trouble at the hospital," he stammered, showing the first signs of stress either of them had seen. "They accused me of lifting drugs from the pharmacy and selling them on the campus. Nothing's been proven," he said, forcefully. "They're investigating it all now, speaking to people, I guess. Anyway, they rang my mum when it all kicked off."

"And she wasn't very happy about it?"

"Understatement of the century," Cooper said, running both hands through his hair in an agitated gesture. "Look, they don't have a leg to stand on. I didn't do it."

Phillips looked into the man's eyes and felt the same disappointment Sharon must have felt, because every instinct told him that Will Cooper was lying. Again.

"You're the injured party, then," Lowerson said, in bored tones. "Let's get back to your mum. Did you see her the night before she died?"

Cooper looked away and then back again.

"Yes. Alright, yes, I did. Look, there was a huge argument. All I wanted her to do was write a letter to my supervisor to say I'd been with her some of the times they're saying I was on campus. She wouldn't, and we had a few words about it. That's all."

"You mean, she refused to falsify a statement?"

"It wasn't like that," Cooper mumbled. "I'm her son. She should have helped me out."

"And now she's dead," Phillips said, laconically. "Don't you think that's more important?"

Cooper looked at his hands and then ran them through his hair again, looking lost.

"Of course it is," he said quietly. "It—I guess, it doesn't feel real, yet, y' know? I keep thinking she's going to call and tell me to get my act together."

Unexpectedly, his eyes filled with tears.

"The last thing I said to her… it was awful. Terrible. I can't get it out of my head."

"What was it?"

But Cooper only shook his head and used the sleeve of his shirt to swipe at his eyes.

"I go to sleep thinking about it, and I wake up thinking about it. I'll never forgive myself, knowing that she died thinking I hated her."

Phillips let him gather himself together again before asking another question.

"What time did you leave her house, Will?"

Cooper raised tired, tear-stained eyes.

"I don't know. Maybe around ten, ten-fifteen? I needed to get back here to—I just needed to get back."

"Okay, Will. We appreciate your time," Phillips stood up to leave and Lowerson followed suit. "I want you to think carefully about what you're doing, think about whether it would have made your mother proud. When you're ready to do the right thing, you know where we are."

Cooper sucked in a shaky breath and nodded, not looking at either of them.

"We'll let ourselves out. Thank Petra for the water."

CHAPTER 15

Frances Dobbs lived in the scenic commuter village of Wylam, ten miles west of Newcastle. Aside from its convenient location, the village laid claim to being the birthplace of George Stephenson, the nineteenth-century engineer known as the 'Father of Railways'.

"This is the place," MacKenzie said, as they pulled up alongside a large, stone-built cottage with trailing wisteria.

Ryan peered through the window. In cases such as these, he expected to find John Dobbs' ageing mother struggling to make ends meet, heavily reliant on her son. It would go some way to explaining Dobbs' inability to socialise with members of the opposite sex; it was all there, in the criminology textbooks.

When Frances opened the door, he found his suspicions partly confirmed. Dobbs' mother moved with extreme difficulty, leaning on a polished walking stick carved in the shape of a totem pole. She was hard of hearing and, they came to realise, in the early stages of dementia.

"*Who?*"

"DCI RYAN AND DI MACKENZIE, MRS DOBBS. FROM NORTHUMBRIA CID."

"Alright, alright. No need to shout at me," she muttered. "Come in."

They followed her slow progress along a dim passageway decorated in the style of thirty years ago, packed to the rafters with objets d'art and what Ryan's mother might have called 'collectibles'.

They found themselves in a room that smelled heavily of cats and spotted an overflowing litter tray tucked behind one of the frayed chesterfield sofas. Overall, it spoke of faded grandeur and the ravages of old age.

"Sit down, sit down," she said.

They perched on the extreme edge of a sofa.

"Mrs Dobbs, I understand one of my colleagues, DCS Gregson, has already been in touch—"

"What? Speak up a bit."

Ryan took a deep breath.

"DCS GREGSON HAS ALREADY BEEN IN TOUCH?"

"Yes, yes. Nice man, very smart-looking. Good with the cats."

Ryan looked away, stifling the urge to laugh.

"WE'RE VERY SORRY ABOUT JOHN," he began again.

Frances turned away to call one of the cats across to her.

"Here, Mabel. Here, sweetie."

A bundle of fur the size of a small horse bolted across the room. Its fur was matted, and Ryan didn't like to think when it had last seen a flea treatment.

"John didn't like the cats," Frances muttered, stroking its fur with one arthritic hand. "He never liked them."

"We understand John lived here with you," MacKenzie said.

"Yes, he always stayed. Never wanted to leave me alone. I don't suppose he'll be coming back now, though."

Ryan envied MacKenzie's ability to be heard without raising her voice but began to worry about Frances Dobbs' capacity to give a statement. There was more here than grief or shock, neither of which seemed very evident.

"No, Mrs Dobbs, he won't be coming back."

"What's that?"

Ryan took another deep breath.

"JOHN WON'T BE COMING BACK."

Her hand stilled on the cat's fur and then started up again as she cooed to it, murmuring endearments.

"Did John ever mention anybody special, Frances?" MacKenzie asked.

"How d' you mean, love?"

Once again, Ryan was agog.

"Like a girl, or maybe a special friend at work?"

"No. Well, he was a very busy man. My John worked very long hours, so he didn't have time to mess around with girls."

Ryan frowned. As far as he was aware, John Dobbs had worked part-time as a healthcare assistant, hardly the kind of hours she seemed to be suggesting.

MacKenzie had the same thought.

"Did John enjoy his work, Frances?"

"He used to tell me about all the patients who'd written to him, thanking him for saving their lives. He was a miracle worker, my son. A genius."

Ryan leaned forward, speaking clearly so she could lip-read.

"Remind me, Frances, what did John do for a living?"

"He was a surgeon," she said proudly. "Look at all those certificates."

She gestured to one of the walls and they looked up to find a wall full of fake certificates, all framed.

Ryan and MacKenzie looked at each other and nodded. They couldn't continue without another person present to look after Mrs Dobbs' interests, if not her mental wellbeing.

"Thank you very much, Frances. We'll come back and visit you another time, if we may."

"Any time, dear."

But as they were leaving, Ryan hesitated.

"Mrs Dobbs, would you mind if we looked at John's room?"

She began to fret.

"Oh, I don't think you want to do that. It's... it's not very—well, it's very untidy."

"We don't mind."

"No, you can't. I don't want you to see."

"See what, Mrs Dobbs?" MacKenzie asked, very gently.

The old woman clutched her stick and shook her head in agitation.

"All those women. All those women he's got up there."

Ryan looked at MacKenzie, who read the message in his eyes.

"Come on, Mrs Dobbs. Why don't we sit down and you can tell me what your cats are called?"

"Yes, alright, dear."

Ryan waited until they were back inside the living room before heading upstairs, taking the stairs two at a time. A quick search led him past a room full of bric-a-brac and an ancient bathroom until he found the room that had been John's domain.

It was like stepping into another world.

An expensive desktop computer dominated one wall, complete with cameras, microphones and other add-on devices. A heavy-duty printer was tucked beneath the desk alongside several unopened packets of paper.

Ryan spent a few minutes conducting a search and tried accessing the computer but found it password protected.

What did Frances mean? Where were, 'all those women'?

He returned to the living room and shook his head when MacKenzie looked across at him. Equally puzzled, she turned back to the woman who was sitting quietly beside her, talking to her animals as if they were human.

"There, Boxer. No, don't claw Mummy. That's not nice."

"Frances? What did you mean when you said John had women in his bedroom?"

"What, dear?" She looked up, then away again. "I got rid of them. Filthy, disgusting pictures. I won't have them in my house."

"Magazine pictures or real pictures?" Ryan asked.

When she didn't speak, he repeated the question a little louder.

"Real ones. Awful ones."

"Where are the pictures now, Mrs Dobbs?"

"I put them in the bin, dear, with the other rubbish."

They spent another half hour talking to Dobbs' mother and, by the time they bade her farewell, they could be reasonably certain of two things. The first was that Frances Dobbs was in the early stages of dementia or a similar illness, and the second was that she'd found indecent images of women and girls in her son's room, which she had subsequently destroyed. Neither fact gave them much pleasure.

"We knew there had to be some reason why he jumped," Ryan said, as they stood on the pavement outside. "He thought we were coming for him because of the pornography."

"What do you want to do about that?"

"I'll let Digital Forensics know," he said, referring to the specialist unit who investigated online sexual abuse. "Those women and girls are being harmed every day the images are still in circulation. They're out there, somewhere, thanks to Dobbs and whoever else he communicated with. Maybe they can get something from his computer that might help them track down others."

MacKenzie nodded.

"Interesting that he told his mother he was a surgeon and passed himself off as one on his dating profile, too."

"Clearly, he felt he'd missed his calling," Ryan said. "Or perhaps there was someone he identified with at work, someone he looked up to."

"Cooper was right when she said we're looking for someone with surgical skill," MacKenzie said. "She just set her sights on the wrong man."

Ryan felt his phone rumble and paused to answer it.

"Ryan."

MacKenzie watched his face adopt a fixed expression she recognised immediately as controlled anger. She could feel it, coming off him in waves.

"Are you sure it's the same person?" *Pause.* "Alright, thanks."

He ended the call and looked down at the phone he held in his hand, considering the new information he'd received.

"That was the office," he told her. "They've been going through the disclosure from LoveLife to see who else Isobel Harris went on dates with. They also looked at the disclosure about Sharon, since she went on a couple of dates through the site a few months ago."

"And?"

"They came across a name we all recognise," Ryan said. "Doctor Jeffrey Pinter, Chief Pathologist and the man with access to all the bodies."

"*Jeff*?" MacKenzie was shocked. "Why didn't he mention it?"

"That's a question I'd very much like to ask him myself."

CHAPTER 16

Ryan called an urgent briefing at four o'clock. He made a quick detour to the corner shop to buy a packet of paracetamol and a bottle of Lucozade, but ended up leaving with two carrier bags of crisps and chocolate to feed his team. It might not be healthy but, at times like these, lettuce leaves just didn't cut it.

"What've you got in there?"

As they fell upon the multi-coloured wrappers like a pack of hungry wolves, Ryan took the opportunity to have a quiet word with Phillips.

"Frank?"

His sergeant ambled across the room clutching a bag of beefy Hula Hoops.

"Pinter's name flagged up today," Ryan said. "He went on a date with Cooper six months ago. It's not recent, but—"

"He should have told us," Phillips said.

"Yeah. He knows the drill. There was a clear conflict of interest, over and above just knowing her like he knows any one of us. Going on a date with her rolls over into the personal side of life and, since Isobel Harris used the same dating site, it's bad whichever way you look at it."

"Pinter might not know Harris used LoveLife," Phillips reminded him. "But he still should have mentioned it. Hard not to wonder what else he might be keeping under his hat."

Ryan nodded, looking at the faces on the board and mentally adding another.

"Let's keep it quiet for now, at least until we know more. We need to be sure."

"Aye, we do. He's one of us, or as good as."

"Speaking of Pinter, he's sent the toxicology report through," Ryan said. "It's as we thought. High levels of sedative in Sharon's bloodstream but nil for any other alien chemicals and zero added adrenaline content. She had a bit of alcohol swimming around but nothing out of the ordinary."

"Enough to slow her down a bit."

"Yeah, enough to do that."

Phillips thought of where a killer might lay his hands on large quantities of medical-grade drugs and was troubled.

"We went to see Will Cooper today," he said. "He's been suspended from the dental hospital for over a month on suspicion of stealing drugs and possibly dealing."

"Why didn't we know about it?"

Phillips ran a hand over his chin and let it fall away again. Better to get it all off his chest.

"The university are still investigating but they're supposed to report it to the police. I couldn't find any report, but the university say they spoke to his mother and Sharon said she'd take care of it personally."

"You're thinking Sharon tried to look into things herself, to keep it quiet?"

"Yeah, I'm thinking that."

Ryan tried to imagine how he might act if put in the same position, and the answer was simple.

"She should have referred it to the Drugs Squad," he said.

Phillips gave him a lopsided smile.

"Black and white, eh?"

"Is there any other way? Let's go back to Will and find out who he's been selling to and where he gets his supply. I want to know if he's been buying or selling medical-grade sedative, adrenaline, or any of the paraphernalia."

Ryan didn't wait for an answer but headed to the front of the room, having allowed his team sufficient opportunity to tank themselves up on sugar.

"Alright, settle down! It's been two days since DCI Cooper was murdered," he said. "During that time, we've taken statements, handled hundreds of calls, isolated male DNA at both crime scenes and the same sedative compound has been found in both women's blood post-mortem. There was one difference between them: we found no excess adrenaline in Sharon's system. That wasn't the case for Isobel Harris."

He looked over at Lowerson and judged it was time to throw him some more responsibility.

"Jack, you've been looking into Sharon's son, Will. What has that thrown up?"

"He hasn't got any previous," Lowerson said. "But he's currently suspended from university, pending an investigation into alleged drug offences. His mother knew about it and he admits they argued the night before she died."

"So he's changed his statement?"

"Yeah. We believe his housemate may also be involved but that's more of a hunch."

"It'll probably be right," Ryan said. "Bring her in for questioning, if you think you'll get anything out of it."

Lowerson nodded. "The upshot is, Will Cooper doesn't have a reliable alibi for the time his mother died. Her neighbour remembers him arriving the previous night but doesn't recall when Cooper left. His housemate—or girlfriend and suspected business partner—claims he was in the house from eleven p.m. until the next day. She stuck to her story when we followed it up with her, but a cynic would say her evidence is unreliable."

Ryan's lips twitched.

"Alright. I want you to keep digging. There's no smoke without fire, so keep sweating him for information, speak to his supervisor and get hold of the documents relating to his suspension."

Lowerson took a hasty note.

"In the meantime, let's focus on CCTV," Ryan turned back to the room. "We need to ask ourselves: how did Sharon's killer know her home address or where to find her? If we assume he's a stranger, then the logical conclusion would be that he followed her home at some point prior to killing her or just before."

He looked at Phillips.

"Where are we with the CCTV around Tynemouth?"

Phillips swallowed the last Hula Hoop and licked the tip of his finger before answering.

"I'm still waiting for the footage from the Metro station," he said. "I've chased them up. We've got plenty from the cameras on the High Street but it's dark and patchy. If we give Will Cooper the benefit of the doubt and assume he's telling the truth when he says he left his mother's house around ten, that gives us a window of between ten p.m. on Saturday night and eleven a.m. the following morning to find our man."

"And are there any potentials?"

Phillips blew out a noisy breath.

"Plenty of people stumbling out o' the pubs," he said. "But it's the cars I'm interested in. Seems unlikely he would have walked along the High Street and risk being caught on camera. Much more likely he drove to her place, so I've got the team going through the footage now, logging every car in the vicinity within that timeframe. But it's going to take days, guv, unless we get lucky and something comes through from the Metro station."

Ryan felt his heart sink but kept a smile pasted on his face. Part of his job was to keep his team motivated, even when he could find little to motivate himself.

"That's great, Frank. Keep at it and maybe we'll get lucky. Compare any cars they find with the footage from Isobel Harris's place in Jarrow."

"Er, about that," Phillips began.

Ryan raised an eyebrow, already anticipating what was to come.

"Most of the cameras weren't working, so we've got next to nothing. Just the speed cameras and the Metro, but there's nothing to see on there."

Ryan looked away while he gathered his thoughts. It was a major blow and he had hoped they'd have a bit of luck. He wished there was more time, that he had more resources.

Well, if wishes were horses, beggars would ride.

Everything felt heavy.

Nicola lay with her eyes open, staring at the ceiling as she waited for Death to return. It seemed a long time since he'd last appeared, but she'd lost all sense of time. Was it hours, days, or weeks since she'd led him willingly into her home?

She thought of Lucy Westenra throwing open her bedroom window to Dracula, unwittingly letting in the demon that would kill her. She had made the same mistake and knew that his would be the last face she ever saw. That was her punishment.

Except, it would not be his face. He kept it covered at all times.

For a delirious moment, she imagined tearing away his mask and using his own knife against him, slicing away the layers of his face until his evil was gone from the world. She smiled through her pain.

Pain.

She hadn't really felt pain until now, she realised. Her body was racked with agony. Every inch of her throbbed and every nerve ending screamed.

Suddenly, she realised what that meant.

The drugs were wearing off.

She was still alive.

Having left instructions for his team, Ryan made his way back to the Royal Victoria Infirmary with Phillips in search of a second opinion. They had known Jeff Pinter for years and, until recently, had trusted him implicitly. But as Phillips had already observed, cases such as these bred mistrust and, when a person chose to lie by omission, it made matters worse. They owed a duty of care to the women who had died to ensure no stone was left unturned.

All roads seemed to lead back to the hospital.

With hospital parking at a premium, they used the nearby Claremont Road car park. The road itself was a long one, giving easy access to the city centre and Exhibition Park to the east and the university medical and dental schools and the hospital to the south. A long row of smart three and four-storey houses ran the length of the road to the west, split into small businesses and residential flats. As they waited for a gap in traffic at the pedestrian crossing, Phillips turned to look at them.

"Nice road, this. My wife used to volunteer at the cat and dog shelter down at the other end," he bobbed his head towards the shelter, four doors further down from Nicola Cassidy's garden flat. "Handy to live around here, if you work at the hospital."

Ryan was studying the enormous chimney rising over the rooftops directly ahead of them and realised it must be part of the hospital's furnace. Fire could erase a multitude of sins.

"How many more d' you reckon there are?" he thought aloud. "How many other women has he killed—the ones who wouldn't be missed, let alone discovered?"

Phillips shook his head, feeling sick at the thought.

"Everything about his MO speaks of experience, from the lack of trace evidence all the way to bringing his own equipment," Ryan continued. "You only perfect that kind of technique with practice, so there must have been others aside from Isobel Harris and Sharon Cooper. It stands to reason."

"Hey, hey, lad," Phillips put a hand on Ryan's shoulder in quiet support. "We can only do what we can, when we can. You're not superhuman and, God knows, neither am I."

But Ryan thought of a city full of people, every one of them a potential target.

"He won't wait for us to catch up with him. He'll kill again and again. He won't stop until we find him and, by then, who else will we have lost?"

Phillips said nothing but reached for a cigarette, only to change his mind at the last moment as he remembered a certain Irish redhead's disapproval. He thought of a killer watching her, waiting to strike, and curled his hands into fists.

"Howay," he said, heavily. "Let's flush him out."

There was a gap in traffic, and they crossed the street, cutting along a footpath that would lead them around to the hospital's main entrance. As they passed beneath the chimney, Ryan looked up at the smoke-stained brickwork with renewed anger.

"He's close, Frank. So close, I can almost smell him."

CHAPTER 17

The Management Team of the Royal Victoria Infirmary was comprised of four senior clinicians, one of whom was a close friend of their own DCS Gregson. He and the Medical Director had spent many a pleasant afternoon on the golf course while their wives spent an even more pleasant afternoon without them. Thankfully, since the Director was at a conference in America, there was no need for Ryan and Phillips to go through the usual bureaucratic process of back-slapping and hoop-jumping. Instead, they sought out the Director's next in command, Head of Emergency Medicine and reputed to be one of the UK's leading cardiothoracic surgeons, Sebastien Draycott.

They had been inside the Emergency Department many times before and, as they stepped through its automatic doors once again, they could see why it was one of the best performing in the land. There was no sense of chaos they might have associated with a Major Trauma Centre, only calmness and order. Difficult patients were handled swiftly and those who were truly in need were given priority, ushered through to the ward without fuss while those who must wait their turn did so with long, resigned faces.

"Excuse me, we're looking for Mr Draycott?"

The receptionist inspected his warrant card.

"I'll alert him," she said, holding up a finger to the next person in line. "You might have to wait a few minutes, mind. He had a suspected GBH come in not long ago."

That would explain the squad car they'd seen parked outside, Ryan thought. One of their colleagues must be attending, in case GBH became something worse.

"Thank you, we'll wait."

They stood around for twenty minutes in the large waiting area of A&E until, eventually, they spotted Sebastien Draycott striding across the floor with a general air of authority. He was an arresting man and considerably younger than they had imagined although, as Ryan knew from his own experience, age was not always commensurate with expertise.

"Chief Inspector Ryan? Sebastien Draycott. You wanted to speak to me?"

He ignored Phillips completely, as befitted his status.

"Yes," Ryan said. "Is there somewhere private we could talk?"

Draycott marched across the waiting room towards a side door marked, 'PRIVATE', with a sliding tab to denote whether the room was occupied or unoccupied. After a brief check to ensure it was free, they entered what was the hospital equivalent of a family room. Ryan recognised the counselling leaflets as being the same ones stacked on an identical table back at Police Headquarters.

"I'm afraid I haven't much time," Draycott said, straight off the bat. "I'm sure you appreciate this is a busy department."

"Yes, of course," Ryan replied. "We won't keep you long. I presume you're aware of the murders of Isobel Harris and DCI Sharon Cooper?"

"Yes."

He ventured no further comment, so Ryan continued.

"Frankly speaking, Doctor—"

"I'm a surgeon. The correct title is Mister."

Ryan studied him with growing interest.

"My apologies," he said. "We're looking for an expert opinion and your reputation precedes you. As you can imagine, we're somewhat limited—"

"I should have thought that would be a job for the police pathologist," Draycott said, cutting him off. "Without wishing to be rude, Chief Inspector, I hardly need to supplement my income providing expert opinions. I only tend to do so in the most unique cases, or those that interest me."

Ryan happened to believe every person was unique and the implication that the two women he represented were not worthy of this man's time angered him immediately.

But he merely smiled.

"I understand, Mr Draycott. The thing is, we're out of our depth," he said, slipping into the role of harried, slightly dim policeman with difficulty. "This is the *biggest* case of the year; the most urgent murder hunt going on in the country right now. We need someone with gravitas and experience to give us some specialist advice. The only person we could think of was you."

Phillips looked at Ryan as though he'd sprouted three heads. His SIO was rarely given to displays of flattery, or humility, come to that.

Still, it seemed to work because the mention of national coverage was enough to have the surgeon's ears pricking up.

"What exactly is it you want me to do?"

"We need you to look at the wounds," Phillips said, pulling out a file of photographs. "There are some close-up images here taken from both women. We'd like you to tell us what kind of level of skill we're looking for in the man who did this because it's not your bog-standard cut-and-run, that's for sure. It's a difficult question to ask but, do you know anyone who might be capable of this?"

Draycott sat down briefly on one of the easy chairs and studied each photograph with single-minded intensity. They waited while his long, artistic fingers turned over each page and listened to the sound of ambulance sirens outside, signalling an emergency was imminent.

"Amateurish," he concluded.

Ryan and Phillips stared at him. Draycott was the first person to claim the incisions were anything short of highly skilled and it was enough to grab their attention.

"How so? We were led to believe these wounds demonstrated a high level of surgical skill."

Draycott shuffled the photographs and thrust them back at Phillips.

"Those women have been hacked apart. As for knowing anybody capable of doing it?" He laughed shortly. "As far as I'm concerned, absolutely anybody could have achieved that sloppy job. If you want my honest opinion, you're barking up the wrong tree sniffing around the hospital when the person you're looking for is probably a bin man— or a butcher at best. Now, if you'll excuse me, I have to get back to my patients."

Ryan waited until the door clicked shut behind him before turning to Phillips.

"Funny, isn't it? He's the only one who seems to think our killer's nothing special."

"Downright peculiar, if y' ask me."

"He is the best," Ryan mused. "Could be that he has very high standards and anything less won't do. On the other hand—"

"He might not want us hanging around his department," Phillips finished. "Poking our noses in."

"Got it in one."

Less than a five-minute walk away, Nicola Cassidy was transfixed with fear.

What if he came back?

Her body was weakened by blood loss and severe dehydration, but her mind was clear.

She was still alive.

He had not killed her, not yet. She was still alive and there was a chance of escape, if only she could muster the strength to move.

Move!

Her fingers clutched at the sodden sheets and she tried to pull herself up. The action brought a cry of pain as the wounds on her belly oozed and wept, the muscles in her stomach ripping apart.

"*Hiiim, hiiiim,*" she panted against the gag at her mouth, her nostrils sucking in deep breaths of stagnant air.

The sounds she made were guttural as she fought to survive. He had left her alone, but he might return at any moment and that was more terrifying than anything else, even death. The drugs had worn off and this may be her only chance of escape. Her mind begged her to take it, to grasp at the life she had left, while her body wanted to collapse into unconsciousness again, to retreat from the horror of reality until he came back and finished what he had started.

She would not allow it.

His would not be the last face she saw; his would not be the last sound she ever heard as he sliced her skin again. She would love and grow old and die peacefully in her bed, not writhing in agony at the mercy of a sadistic killer.

She gathered her strength, gritting her teeth against the pain she knew would come, and pulled against the surgical tape at her wrists and ankles.

Her scream was muffled against the gag and her chest shuddered. For one horrible moment, she thought she would faint, or worse.

She tried again.

Then again.

She pulled at the tape until her wrists were bloody and torn but, eventually, she worked her left hand free, twisting her arm until it fell away like a dead weight, the circulation having left it hours ago. It fell against her bedside table, disturbing the lamp so it clattered to the floor.

Nicola froze, listening for any sound, any indication that he might be there.

He did that sometimes. He waited at the end of the bed where she could not raise her head to see him, watching her silently until she sensed his presence.

He liked those times the best, she thought. He liked to watch her come around, just enough to believe she could survive, then he would stand up and she would discover he had been waiting there all along.

Like a spider.

She twisted her head to look down at the arm that was now free and began to shake. Hysteria threatened to overwhelm her over when she saw he had taken three of her fingers. There was nothing left, only bloody, infected stumps of flesh. She started panting again, willing herself to stay strong, to endure.

In an enormous act of defiance, she ordered her broken arm to move, turning white with pain as she lifted it to her face. She used her remaining thumb to pick at the gag around her mouth, sucking great, gulping breaths of air into her body as it finally gave way.

Her lips were cracked and bone dry, but she didn't notice.

Black spots swam in front of her eyes again and she bore down, ordering herself to continue just a little longer.

The scream was little more than a croak at first but then she was howling, crying out because her life depended upon it. But her neighbours weren't at home and there were no convenient passers-by to come running.

"Help," she sobbed, brokenly. "Please. *Please.*"

Nobody came and, after minutes passed, she knew she could not wait around for a miracle. She must be her own saviour.

Greg Iveson steered his van along Claremont Road, humming along to Tina Turner telling him he was simply the best. He could have done without taking on another plastering job, but his wife fancied a new pair of boots and they were hoping to buy an old VW campervan and take it for a spin around Cornwall, so he was racking up as many hours as he could. His mind was pleasantly occupied with thoughts of surfing and shellfish suppers when he spotted something in his peripheral vision.

"Shit!"

He slammed his foot on the brake as a woman stumbled into the road, half-naked and covered with blood. The van skidded to a stop, swerving dangerously to the side but not quick enough to avoid clipping her as she ran blindly towards freedom.

"Oh my God!"

He punched the hazard lights on his van and clambered out, practically falling over in his haste to see if she was alright.

He found her collapsed beneath his headlights, gasping for breath.

"Oh, Jesus. Wait—wait there. Don't die. Please, don't die. I'm going to call for help."

But his hands were shaking so hard he dropped his phone.

There was so much blood.

And—oh, Jesus—parts of her were *missing.* His treacherous body wanted to retch, to pretend he hadn't seen this woman who was only half alive, but she was trying to say something. Her mouth was opening and closing but no sound was coming out. Her eyes started to roll back, and he realised there would be no time to wait for an ambulance.

He acted like lightning, bending down to lift her up into his arms.

"Stay with me," he begged her. "Please, stay with me."

He was crying now, big, shuddering tears as he felt her slipping away. She was only a stranger, a woman he'd never met, but already he grieved.

He lifted her into the passenger side of the van and strapped her in as best he could, draped his hoodie across her body for warmth, then hurried around to the driver's side. He willed himself to keep it together for just another few minutes.

"Come on. *Come on!*"

His hands were trembling so badly he couldn't turn the ignition key but, on the third try, the van roared into life. With a final look at the woman slumped against the window beside him, he put the engine into gear and pushed the accelerator to the floor.

CHAPTER 18

Ryan and Phillips were crossing the foyer at Accident and Emergency when they spotted the van's arrival at breakneck speed. Instinct had them surging forward through the automatic doors as a man in his mid-twenties leapt from the driver's side and raced around to retrieve his passenger.

"Help! Somebody, help!"

Ryan covered the tarmac in seconds, long legs eating up the ground. When he saw the woman's face and the wounds on her body, he understood the situation immediately.

Without a word, he helped to lift her from the car and held her close as they hurried back into the foyer, grateful to find Phillips had alerted the team of their new arrival. A group of men and women rushed forward with a gurney, taking her from him with gentle hands and wheeling her towards the resuscitation room. All around them, the waiting room forgot their burns and broken ankles, falling silent as they sensed the fear amongst medics and police alike.

Their faces became a blur as Ryan and Phillips watched their only witness disappear through a set of double doors.

"Adult trauma, call A&E resus department."

The tannoy sounded above their heads and they saw Sebastien Draycott run across the waiting room to join others from the Major Trauma Unit—nurses, junior doctors and hospital porters bearing blood products—to try to save the woman's life.

Ryan picked up his heels and ran after Draycott, who turned on him in anger.

"You can't be in here! Stay back!"

"That woman is a victim of crime. I have every right to be here," Ryan replied, flashing his warrant card and muscling aside the security guard who tried to stop him entering the resuscitation room. He followed the sound of urgent voices behind a half-veiled screen and waited to one side where he would not be in the way.

Phillips found him there.

"I'm praying for her," he said, quietly.

Ryan was not a religious man, never had been, but he would have prayed to Old Nick himself if it would help.

"The van driver found her on Claremont Road," he murmured. "Take down his statement while it's fresh and send a car down there to preserve any evidence. Tell Faulkner to get down there, too. She can't have run far by the time she was picked up."

Phillips was ashamed he hadn't thought of it himself.

"Aye, I'll do that now."

"Frank?" Ryan swallowed back a sudden constriction. "Find out her name. She has a name."

A team of medics surrounded Nicola Cassidy, from the most revered specialist to the lowliest of hospital porters. They fought to keep her alive while Ryan stood guard, silently watching their every move. His eyes followed them fitting an oxygen mask over the woman's face and an IV tube, hooking her up to a monitor so they could check her blood pressure and heart rate. He watched them arrange a sats probe to check the oxygen levels in her bloodstream, and then quickly administer fluids and begin a blood transfusion.

It all looked right.

But the woman was in cardiac arrest, Ryan realised. He heard the loud, ominous alarm sound on the heart monitor and knew they were losing her.

Everything moved in double speed.

He watched them prepare the woman's body and heard Draycott shout, "CLEAR!"

Her feet shuddered and her body reared up on the gurney in reaction to the defibrillator. She was missing several toes and the soles of her feet were dirty and scuffed from the road.

There was a deafening silence.

"Again!"

They went through the process again and more people arrived, responding to the fast bleep on their pagers. Ryan noted each of their faces and every action they took.

The woman's body reared up.

"How's she doing?"

Phillips hurried back and took stock of the situation immediately, falling silent as they waited.

And then, when they thought all hope had gone, the monitor began to beep slowly.

Beep…beep…beep.

Ryan closed his eyes and sent up a prayer of thanks to a God he didn't believe in.

When Nicola's eyes opened, there was a sea of white light.

Heaven.

Shapes began to emerge. The edge of the heart monitor, the line of the curtain, the shape of their heads. Faces came into view, so many faces, some in surgical masks. Doctors, nurses.

The hospital.

She blinked against the light and, suddenly, his face appeared.

She would have known his eyes anywhere.

"Hi-hi…" she gasped, her fingers twitching as she tried to point.

"She's going!"

Across the room, Ryan and Phillips heard the monitor flatline again as her body collapsed. Ryan ran forward, refusing to believe they'd lost her, only to be held back by Phillips as the medics performed manual CPR on her inert body.

"No, lad! Let them try. They have to try!"

They watched Draycott take charge, rapping out orders. They tried for long, painful minutes to revive her until he told them quietly to stop. One of the doctors was taking a turn to manually pump her chest and they could see the muscles of his arms contract as he continued to work on her, long after she was gone.

"Come on," he muttered. "*Come on*!"

"Edwards, it's too late. We've lost her."

"No, we haven't!"

"She's gone, Keir. She's gone," one of the older nurses said.

They saw Draycott step forward to pull the other man gently away in a rare show of compassion.

"You did everything you could," he told him. "Nature has taken its course."

Ryan and Phillips watched the other doctor stumble back and raise a forearm to wipe the sweat from his brow, looking down at the woman lying on the trolley with intense sadness.

"Whatever people say, you can't knock the NHS," Phillips said, with admiration. "They gave it everything they had."

"True," Ryan said. "But nature had nothing to do with what happened to that woman."

Phillips remained silent, watching them go through the motions of recording the time of death for the coroner, removing tubes. There was a moment of quiet in the room while the crowd came to terms with losing her, and one revelled in the thrill of it all.

The *brrrriiing* of a red telephone interrupted the silence.

A blue-light ambulance was on the way and the cycle needed to begin again. Several members of the crash team peeled away to prepare another resuscitation area for the next person in need, and it seemed Nicola Cassidy was already forgotten.

In the residual quiet, Ryan walked across to her body. He found Draycott standing beside the doctor who had performed CPR, and a nurse.

"I thought we had her," Draycott said, in the kind of unemotional tone that set Ryan's teeth on edge. "A pity."

"You did your best," one of the nurses murmured to the other doctor. "Nobody could have done more."

"What happened?" Ryan asked.

They looked up in surprise, seeming to notice him for the first time.

"Who're you? You shouldn't be in here," the nurse began heatedly, seeking out the security guard.

"This is DCI Ryan, from Northumbria CID." Draycott stopped her with calm authority and removed his glasses to polish them against the edge of his scrubs.

"Major cardiac arrest," the surgeon said, reaching across to cover her body. "She was resuscitated once but we couldn't do it again. She was too weak."

"Wait."

His hand paused on the blanket at Ryan's sharp command.

"We need to move her," he explained gently. "I'm afraid she can't stay here."

"I just need a minute," Ryan said.

The other doctor's pager beeped, and he gave them an apologetic half-smile before heading to the next emergency. Draycott gave him an absent pat on the shoulder as he left.

In his wake, Ryan stepped closer and forced himself to look down at the woman, at her bruised face and body which bore the evidence of days' worth of torture. Her skin was so pale it was almost translucent, and he had no way of knowing how many days she had survived without food or water. It was a miracle she'd made it this far and yet, he'd hoped. He'd hoped so very much that she would live.

Ryan fell back on training while his heart quietly shattered.

"You were here when they brought her in," he said, as the nurse moved around disconnecting tubes. "Can I have your name, please?"

"Me? I'm Joan Stephenson."

"And who was I just speaking to?" Ryan enquired, glancing over his shoulder in the direction the other doctor had taken.

"That was Doctor Edwards. He's one of our senior consultants here," Draycott told him. "You must excuse me, I'm needed elsewhere."

Ryan gave him a straight look.

"I'd appreciate it if you could make yourself available at the first opportunity. I'll also need you to set aside time for each of the attending members of staff here today."

For once, Draycott didn't argue.

"I'll see to it."

After he left, Ryan watched the nurse tuck the dead woman's hands beneath the blanket and give them a motherly pat.

"I can hardly believe it," she said. "Nicola was such a lovely girl."

Ryan gave her a searching look.

"You *knew* this woman?"

Joan was startled.

"Well, yes. I-I think so. I recognise her from a placement she did in the department last year. She's a student doctor. I'm sorry, I assumed you knew."

"Do you know her full name? Anything else about her?"

Joan looked down at the girl's face and her chest tightened.

"Yes, I think her name was Nicola Cassidy. I remember, because it reminded me of David Cassidy. You know, the singer?"

He made encouraging noises and signalled to Phillips, who was on his phone issuing a series of hushed commands to the team back at CID.

"As I say, she was a student doctor. I think she lived just around the corner. I'm sorry, I can't remember much else."

"Don't worry, you've been very helpful," he said. She had saved them precious time that was in short supply. "Tell me, who did Nicola work with while she was here? Do you happen to remember?"

She screwed up her face while she cast her mind back.

"Well, obviously, anyone who's been here a while would have worked with her, like me; we've had a bit of staff turnover in the past few months, so that's why I'm trying to think who would have been here. Mr Draycott, of course," she said, listing a few other names. "Doctor Chowdhury, one of our consultants, and most of the nurses. They've been permanent fixtures for a while. I couldn't tell you how many security guards we've had, or hospital porters and healthcare assistants. There was John—" She stopped abruptly, thinking of their former healthcare assistant. "But he's—he's gone now."

"How about Doctor Edwards?" Ryan asked.

"No, Keir only joined the department in the New Year. He's such a positive person to have around," she added. "Never complains, just does his job and usually a bit extra, too. He's just come off the back of a double shift and he was still the last one trying to save this poor lass."

She tutted, reaching out to place the palm of her gloved hand on Nicola's head.

"We see a lot come through these doors," she said. "And, you know, we do our best for everyone. But sometimes it gets you, right here."

She tapped her other hand against her chest.

"Yes," Ryan said, simply. "She didn't deserve this."

Joan turned, busying herself to hide the sheen of tears.

"Right. Time to get going," she said.

Soon after, the porter came to wheel Nicola away to the hospital mortuary and into Jeff Pinter's waiting hands.

Ryan stayed beside her all the way.

CHAPTER 19

With a curious kind of detachment, Ryan oversaw the transfer of Nicola Cassidy's body to the hospital mortuary and was there to witness Jeff Pinter's surprise when he uncovered her face.

"I think I know this girl," he said.

"Oh?"

Ryan's eyes never moved from the other man's face.

"Yes," Pinter said. "She's a student at the medical school. I've seen her quite a few times."

"Professionally?"

Pinter heard an odd tone in Ryan's voice and bristled.

"Yes, of course, professionally. What else?" He gave a nervous laugh. "She could almost be my daughter."

"But she's not your daughter," Ryan said. "Tell me, Jeff. Where were you on Saturday evening?"

"Wh—*Me*?" Pinter squealed. There was no other word for it. "I-I was at home. I don't have to answer that!"

"Think yourself lucky I'm asking you informally," Ryan snapped. "While we're at it, you can tell me why you didn't mention you knew Sharon Cooper personally. You went out on dinner dates, more than once, through the dating website used by both victims."

Something flickered in Pinter's eyes.

There, Ryan thought. *There it was.*

"I-I'm sorry."

"*Sorry?*" Ryan barked. "You know better than that, Jeff. Now, you put me in the position of having to ask you again: where were you on Saturday night?"

Pinter swallowed, and his Adam's apple bobbed precariously.

"I told you, I was at home. I, ah, I can give you the name of the woman I was with, if you need it."

"I need it."

Pinter nodded miserably, thinking that would be the end of that romance.

"I'm sorry, I know I should have mentioned it. I was— well, I was embarrassed," he said.

Ryan waited, not giving any quarter.

"Both of us knew it was a bad idea, really. Dating people at work? It rarely works out, does it?"

Pinter forced a laugh, which was not returned.

"Look, I made a mistake. I should have been upfront about my...my personal association with Sharon. It won't happen again."

Ryan stepped forward until they were almost toe to toe.

"You're damn right it won't happen again. I want the name and address of the woman you say you were with on Saturday night and, until I've checked it out, special measures apply." He nodded towards Nicola Cassidy, who had been taken into one of the private examination rooms. "You don't work on her alone. Make an excuse if you like, tell your staff it's a new protocol, but you don't work on her alone. I can't risk it, Jeff. Not for you and not for them."

Pinter gave a jerky nod.

"I—yes, alright. Ryan, I mean it. I sincerely regret not mentioning it and I understand it's made things difficult."

Ryan looked straight through him.

"Difficult? You don't understand, Jeff. It isn't just a case of making my job harder. Even if your story checks out, I'll always question the information you give me in future. I'll always wonder if you're holding something back."

To their mutual embarrassment, Pinter looked as though he would break down.

"What can I do?"

"Never, *ever*, lie to me again."

Pinter nodded.

"You have my word."

Ryan left the mortuary behind him and moved quickly through the corridors, following the signs for the gents toilets. He needed to splash some cold water on his face and clear his head, re-group and figure out where to begin managing three active murder investigations rolled into one. There was little hope of keeping the latest news out of the press, but he needed to call DCS Gregson to update him anyway; perhaps the man's infamous charm would help to buy them some time.

Ryan looked up and realised he'd taken a wrong turn somewhere in the rabbit warren.

"Lost?"

He turned from his inspection of the signs on the wall to face the doctor he'd met earlier.

"Doctor Edwards?"

"Yep."

He held out a hand, which Ryan shook briefly.

"I was looking for the gents."

"Use the one through here," Edwards suggested, leading him through to the staff room. The central area was taken up with cheap round tables and chairs. An assortment of nurses and doctors were sitting flicking through dog-eared magazines and watching the television fixed to the wall in the corner. To Ryan's mind, it could have easily been the staff area at CID Headquarters, minus the smell of shepherd's pie.

Beyond it, there was a small locker room lined with tall metal doors on either side.

"Straight through here and on the left," Edwards told him.

But Ryan lingered.

"Joan mentioned you'd only recently joined the team," he said, watching Edwards select a locker and retrieve the key which hung from an elasticated key band at his hip.

"I transferred back in January, so it's not all that recent. I was over at North Tyneside General before." He paused. "Mind if I get changed? I've been in these scrubs for hours."

"Sure," Ryan murmured. And then, "Have we met before?"

Edwards looked over his shoulder.

"I don't think so. Have we?"

"I thought we had. Perhaps I'm mistaken."

Suddenly, it came to him. Keir Edwards' face was the one John Dobbs had used for his online dating profile. They'd assumed it was a stock image, but Dobbs had lifted one from much closer to home.

"Did you have much to do with John Dobbs?"

Edwards shrugged into a fresh shirt.

"The guy who killed himself?"

"Yes, he was a healthcare assistant here."

"Oh, right, John. Yeah, we were all quite surprised when we heard what happened," Edwards said, and gave a jaw-cracking yawn. "Sorry. Long day."

"So, you knew him from on the wards?"

"Yes, although I hardly noticed him. That's an awful thing to say, considering the bloke killed himself," he added, pulling a face.

"But honest," Ryan murmured, watching him bend down to tie the shoelaces on a pair of running shoes. "How about Nicola Cassidy? Did you know the girl who died this afternoon?"

Edwards moved on to the other foot.

"Sort of. I recognise the name from one of my class lists," he said. "I teach a couple of classes at the university and I think she was in one of them. I'm afraid I didn't recognise her when she was brought in. It was only when Sebastien mentioned her name that I realised."

He paused, resting his forearms on his knees.

"As a doctor, I give my life to healing people, or trying to. It's the worst part of the job, having to walk away like I did today."

"What did you make of her injuries?"

Edwards scrubbed a hand through his hair and shrugged.

"Thorough. Practised."

He stood up and reached for his rucksack and car keys.

"Whoever did that to her really took his time. Is there anything else you need, Chief Inspector? I can stay a bit longer?"

"No, thanks. That's fine for now but we'll be in touch shortly. I'll need you to provide a formal statement."

Edwards nodded, then gestured towards Ryan's shirt.

"I'd offer you a change but—"

Ryan looked down and realised his hands and clothing were covered in Nicola Cassidy's blood.

"This will wash off," he said, raising his eyes again. "It won't be so easy for the man who killed her."

Edwards closed his locker and turned to face him.

"Whoever killed that girl probably sleeps like a baby." He flipped his car keys to his other hand and slung his rucksack over his shoulder, preparing to leave. "I hope you find who you're looking for, Chief Inspector."

Ryan smiled.

"Never doubt it."

CHAPTER 20

Phillips had busied himself in Ryan's absence tracing Nicola Cassidy's last known address and next of kin. He had taken preliminary statements from several of the staff who had worked to save her and, by the time Ryan re-joined him on the main floor, he was consoling the man who'd ferried her to safety.

"I-I can't believe she's dead," Greg Iveson was saying.

He held his head in his hands, elbows resting on his knees as he stared down at his scuffed work boots.

"There, lad," Phillips said. "You did what you could."

"One minute, I was driving along and then, the next—she just ran into the road. I swear, I tried to brake. I tried—"

He stared hard at the linoleum floor.

"I think—I need to tell you, I think I hit her."

He used the heels of his hands to stem the sudden flow of tears again.

"You told me," Phillips reminded him. "I've had a word with the doctor, and he says there was no major impact from your van. There isn't even a dent or a scratch on it and there would have been, if you'd hit her at any speed."

Iveson looked up at that.

"You're sure?"

Phillips nodded.

"She—she was so badly hurt…" Iveson swallowed. "At first, I thought all the blood was because of me. I thought I'd done that."

Phillips was silent, lending an ear.

"I'll never forget how she looked. Somebody had taken her fingers. And there were cuts all over her body. Who would do that?"

Ryan stepped forward.

"We're going to find out who," he said quietly, waving the man down when he would have stood up. "And we need your help, Greg. I know you need to talk about what happened, maybe speak to someone at home, but I'm going to ask you not to tell anyone about the kind of injuries you saw. It's important that we don't make that public right now. Alright?"

Iveson nodded.

"Aye, alright."

"There's something else I need to ask, and this is really vital."

Greg's eyes sharpened, a renewed sense of purpose distracting him from his shock.

"Of course. Anything."

Ryan came to sit beside him.

"Did she say anything to you, when you found her? Anything at all? Try to remember."

Iveson shook his head slowly.

"The only thing I remember is her *trying* to speak. She opened her mouth a few times, but she was gasping, and I couldn't make out any words. I thought, maybe, she was trying to say 'here, here', but then she passed out."

Ryan tried not to let his disappointment show.

"Thanks, anyway. You did the right thing today, Greg. Thanks to you, she had a chance."

The man's eyes were pools of sorrow.

"Can I go home now? I want—I need to go home and see my lass." *And hold her tight.*

Ryan exchanged a glance with Phillips to check he'd already given his statement, then nodded.

"Sure. And Greg?"

He waited until Iveson looked up.

"You aren't responsible for what happened today. Remember that."

"I'll try."

There was an army of police surrounding Nicola Cassidy's garden flat by the time they made the short, five-minute journey from the hospital on foot. They took the route they thought it most likely she would have taken each day from her current placement, which was on the paediatric wards in the main hospital building and the university dental and medical faculties. Small footpaths connected the main roads to the hospital from either side and it would have been an easy commute each day for the woman who wanted to work with children.

"Her supervisor says she wanted to qualify into paediatrics," Phillips said, as they passed by the dental and medical faculty buildings. "Says she was a solid student, popular with the patients and staff. They all seemed pretty cut up about it."

"We'll look at all of them," Ryan said shortly. "Anyone who ever knew her or worked with her."

"Already got Lowerson on the case," Phillips said, reaching for a cigarette. "But we're snowed under as it is. It'll take weeks."

"Everybody works overtime," Ryan said. "We can't afford to ease off, Frank. He's still escalating."

Phillips gave him a questioning look.

"With the first, he had his fun, but it was still a quick kill. Maybe a part of him was still worried about getting caught. But then, there was Sharon. With her, he hit out at the police, at justice. He was less cautious, but he was still in and out of her house in a few hours." Ryan paused as they stepped around a group of students. "With Nicola Cassidy, he didn't just spend hours, he devoted *days*. That's the next level."

Ryan slipped inside the mind of a killer, braving the darkness once more.

"He must be furious," he murmured. "She deprived him of the final kill."

"We got to her house pretty sharpish," Phillips said. "If he left anything behind, Faulkner'll find it. He didn't have time to clean up after himself, this time."

Ryan nodded.

"Here's hoping."

His body trembled, both in anger and ecstasy.

The police had been so close. He'd thought about striking out, about surprising them all and watching them goggle as he offloaded the shackles he wore each day and showed them the man beneath. How he would have laughed to see their astonished faces. It would have been interesting to see how many he could get through before he was overpowered. It might have been worth it, if only to be recognised, for once.

Above all else, he longed to be *recognised*.

It was exhausting, the skin he wore each day to blend in with the rest of them. Even more exhausting was the effort he made to socialise, to remember the right faces to make at the right time, and the right words to say at the appropriate moment.

It had been a shock when he'd seen Ryan at the hospital with his little sidekick in tow. Of course, he had expected them to turn up at some stage, but he'd still experienced a little jitter of excitement. It had been a supreme test, talking to them, playing the part, pretending to care whether the woman lived or died.

And that had been another shock, he admitted. He'd worried for a split-second whether it had shown on his face as they'd wheeled her in. Had anyone noticed?

They'd been too busy trying to save her and, ironically, so had he.

Of course, he'd have made sure something happened. It wouldn't have taken much to orchestrate an overdose or threaten to kill her mother if she talked before he could finish the job.

He'd have thought of something.

As it turned out, the mere sight of him had been enough to finish her off. That brought a smile to his face, followed swiftly by a snarl of anger.

How *dare* she leave?

How dare she leave *him*?

True, he'd known the risks of leaving her unattended for too long. The sedative was bound to wear off and with every passing hour he'd worried about the dosage. All the same, he'd never dreamed she would escape. That was a lesson, he supposed, to be tougher in future.

He'd know better, next time.

CHAPTER 21

When Ryan stepped inside Nicola Cassidy's garden flat, he could still sense her killer's presence. Beneath the human faeces and infected flesh, beneath the rotting food in her tiny kitchen, he could smell his essence following them from room to room like a spectre.

They found Tom Faulkner standing in the doorway of her bedroom holding a sketchbook and pencil in his gloved hand.

"No camera?"

His pencil stilled, then continued to fly across the page.

"Sometimes it helps to visualise what happened," Faulkner explained. "I've taken photographs, too."

He didn't bother to add that the process of drawing was cathartic. He was as human as the next man, and some days were harder than others.

Besides, there was the small matter of his wife leaving him. She had upped and left, clearing out her things sometime while he'd been at the lab helping to find a serial killer.

But they didn't want to know about that.

"Can you tell us anything yet?" Phillips asked, peering at the man's sketch with admiration. "Hey, Tom, you've got a good hand there, mind."

"I do a bit in my spare time," Faulkner said, tucking the sketchbook under his arm. "Usually more attractive scenes than this."

He bobbed his head in the direction of the front door.

"Let's start at the point of entry. I can walk you through what I think happened," he said, as they congregated in the narrow passageway. There were pictures on the wall of Nicola with a variety of friends; smiling, happy.

Alive.

"There's no sign of forced entry, so my bet is that he used her door keys to come and go," he said. "Unlike the last two, we haven't found them yet."

"He'll still have her keys, unless he's thrown them in the Tyne by now," Phillips said.

Ryan said nothing but thought privately that her killer might choose to keep them as a trophy. A small memento, to remind himself of the power he'd wielded.

Faulkner indicated a small yellow marker on the wall in the narrow hallway.

"We found some fluid here," he said. "There's a slight scuff mark, too. We don't know whether it belongs to Nicola or her killer yet; time will tell."

He turned and faced the flat's interior.

"Straight ahead, you can see one of the picture frames on that little console table has been disturbed at one time or another," he said, pointing to the next yellow marker. "If we presume the same pressure syringe was used on Nicola as the others, it's possible he knocked the picture while he moved her into the bedroom."

They said nothing, imagining the struggle.

"There's no sign that she was injured in any room other than the bedroom," Faulkner continued. "We found traces of semen on the living room sofa but it's old, embedded in the material. If the flat is a furnished rental, it might be older still."

"Test it anyway," Ryan said.

Faulkner nodded.

"There were trace fibres on the bedroom door frame. I've sent them for testing, too. There's usually a decent chance of finding some LCN DNA," he said, referring to Low Copy Number DNA, found on the tiniest samples of trace evidence. A feat of forensic science but notoriously unreliable in court.

"What about on the bed, or the frame?"

Ryan watched two CSIs dressed in white hooded suits rustling around the small bedroom Nicola had painted in a sunny yellow.

"We're looking now," Faulkner said. "It'll take hours, yet."

There was a long pause while they surveyed the evidence of Nicola's captivity with heavy hearts. Blood and other fluids matted the bedclothes, which had once been a pretty floral cotton. The curtains were closed at the single sash window overlooking the garden but the last of the day's rays filtered through the heavy linen and lent the room a sinister orange hue. Small, tightly wound circles of plastic hung from the slatted bedhead, coloured pink from Nicola's struggle to free herself.

"What's that?" Ryan asked.

"We think it's surgical tape," Faulkner said. "That's another deviation from the previous two, where he didn't need to tie them down at all."

"This one was a keeper," Ryan muttered, in disgust. "Can we get a line on the brand used?"

"It's possible," Faulkner said. "It'll take a few days."

Ryan thought of their stretched finances and of the politics, then overrode any potential objections. He'd put his hand in his own pocket, if need be.

"Draft in more contractors to cover the lab work," he said. "I'll approve the resources. Just get it done."

Faulkner nodded, thinking of his own staff workload and coming to the same conclusion as Ryan. Public safety overrode any other objections.

There was no sign of body parts having been left in the bedroom.

"She had digits missing," Ryan said, heavily. "Have you found them?"

Faulkner sighed and fiddled with his glasses.

"We found them in the freezer," he said. "We always check in there…just in case. Killers aren't all that original, I'm afraid, and the old methods are the best."

Neither Ryan nor Phillips bothered to ask why; they'd seen enough to understand the logic.

"I'm surprised he couldn't get his hands on some formaldehyde," Phillips said. "Seems more clinical."

"Even for someone working at the hospital, it's hard to get hold of," Faulkner explained. "It's a protected substance, so he'd need to fill out all kinds of forms. Harder to fly beneath the radar."

Unless you were a pathologist, Ryan thought suddenly.

"They keep a locked box on the wards, including A&E," he said. "One or two people have a key for it, depending who's on shift at a given time. If it's on rotation, it'd be easy enough to swipe a few vials here, a few vials there, whenever the opportunity arose."

The other two nodded in agreement.

"There's the hospital pharmacy, too. He's using lorazepam at a steady rate—he might need a bigger supply," Phillips put in.

"Or someone who could get their hands on it," Ryan said, then came to a decision. "Tell Lowerson to bring Will Cooper in for questioning. I want it official, all whistles and bells. He needs to feel afraid enough to tell us who his contacts are."

"The lad's been dying to play Bad Cop," Phillips chuckled. "Might be a good time for him to try."

Ryan was on the cusp of ruling it out; there was too much to lose and no room for error. On the other hand, Lowerson would never gain the experience he needed if he was never given the opportunity to try.

"Alright. Tell him to bring Cooper in. MacKenzie can brief him on a few pointers if we're not back in time."

Phillips nodded his agreement and stepped outside to put a call through to Lowerson. In the remaining silence, Ryan turned to Faulkner.

"It's a big ask, Tom, but I need you to work round the clock on this. Whatever it takes. He's not stopping now; he'll have the next one lined up already." He lifted a hand to encapsulate the room and let it fall again. "He planned all this, right down to his choice of victim. There are any number of women in this city but how many of them could he have vetted personally, spoken to and struck up an acquaintance?"

"Not only that," Faulkner said. "We're within walking distance of the hospital where she worked and came into contact with hundreds of people. It wouldn't take much to strike up conversation and find out that she lived nearby, then to follow her home one day to find out exactly where. If he works at the hospital or anywhere in the vicinity, he could pop back regularly to top up the drugs, so she was always doped up."

"Yes, he needed to strike a very careful balance. He couldn't risk an early overdose, or she might die before he had time to play. On the other hand, he had to give her enough so she'd be unresponsive while he was away. He couldn't risk her making an escape, as she did today."

"He made a mistake," Faulkner observed.

"Yes. That tells me he's either losing control, he was held up, or both." Ryan took one final, sweeping look around the room. "Whichever it is, it brings us one step closer to finding him. I only hope we can do it before he kills again."

"He wouldn't do it so quickly," Faulkner argued. "He has to know there's an army of police looking for him."

Ryan's mouth flattened into a hard line as he thought of Nicola's killer prowling around the city, his lust for blood unsated.

"It's the nature of the beast."

CHAPTER 22

Back at Police Headquarters, the sun blazed through Gregson's office window, setting the sky aglow in shades of ochre and cardinal blue but its splendour was lost on the two men who faced one another across the room.

"Ryan, take a seat."

"Thank you, sir. I'm fine standing."

"Suit yourself," Gregson muttered, feeling at a disadvantage. He rose from his chair and walked around to lean against his desk.

"Report," he said.

"Sir, since my last update, I can confirm we have completed the initial stages of securing the scene of crime at the victim's home. Nicola Cassidy was twenty-two years old and a medical student at the university, completing her training through the RVI. Her last rotation was spent in Paeds."

"What?"

"Paediatrics, sir."

Gregson grunted, and Ryan continued.

"We're in the process of interviewing her former colleagues in that department but our current focus is centred on A&E."

"Why?"

Gregson had never been a man to waste words.

"Isobel Harris attended the department within weeks of her death. If our working theory is that her killer works in A&E or is associated with the department, the timescale would have given him enough time to research her personal situation and plan his approach. DCI Cooper was known to the A&E department already given her professional duties and our most recent victim, Nicola Cassidy, completed a rotation in Emergency Medicine late last year. There's enough of an opportunity, sir, for somebody minded to kill."

"You're reaching, Ryan."

"It's the only thing that connects the three of them so far," Ryan argued.

"Cooper believed LoveLife connected them," Gregson said. "What makes you think she's wrong?"

"I don't think she was wrong. Cooper thought Harris's killer had clinical training and I happen to agree. In fact, everybody other than the Head of Emergency Medicine agrees with that working theory. The only difference is that Cooper focused on the dating site whereas I believe we should focus on the hospitals. The fact that two of our victims have associations with the RVI narrows down the search radius."

"What if you're wrong?"

Ryan had thought about that. He'd lain awake most of the previous night asking himself the same question, without any satisfactory answer.

"All I can do is my job," he said. "If I'm wrong, then I'll have more names on my conscience and I'll have to live with that."

Gregson's eyebrows drew together.

"You didn't kill those women," he said. "You needn't have them on your conscience."

Ryan said nothing, only continued to stare at the wall above Gregson's head until the older man let out a long sigh.

"Speaking of the Head of Emergency Medicine, I've had Draycott on the phone. He wants to make a formal complaint about how you barged into a protected area and threw your weight around, thereby obstructing the work of his team. Care to comment?"

"Utter bollocks," Ryan said, with such refinement that Gregson burst out laughing. "Phillips and I were both there to witness Nicola Cassidy's arrival at A&E. She was in a bad way, that much was obvious, and her injuries resembled those we'd seen on two dead women. I helped bring her in and she was wheeled into the resuscitation area. As the attending officer, it was my duty to observe at a distance— to see how events panned out."

He paused, the echo of the heart monitor ringing in his ears.

"Unfortunately, as you know, Nicola Cassidy didn't survive."

"Yes," Gregson cleared his throat. "Sad business. You said she came around and then they lost her a second time?"

"Yes," Ryan said, and a thought struck him like a bolt from the blue.

What if she'd seen her killer?

"—something we could do without."

Ryan tuned back into the conversation.

"I'm sorry, sir?"

"I said, a complaint from a senior member of the hospital's management committee is something we could do without. Particularly since it's the second complaint I've received today."

Ryan's face remained impassive.

"It's from PC Jessop," Gregson elaborated. "He's threatening to make a formal complaint about bullying, harassment and—ah—discrimination."

"Oh? On what grounds? Unless you count his stupidity as a formal disability."

Gregson laughed appreciatively.

"I've already asked around and heard the full story from MacKenzie," he continued. "Jessop's behaviour is already on record following his exploits with John Dobbs and it's no great secret that he resents your rank and background. It's an occupational hazard," Gregson shrugged. "But he took a swing at you and that crosses the line."

"I handled it."

"Yes, you did. But he's a liability to the team. I'm seeing to it."

Ryan thought of Jessop and his attitude.

"I offered him the chance to make an apology," he said. "Clearly, that was rejected in favour of making spurious complaints. I agree, he's a liability."

"Good. Now, what to do about Draycott? Have you seen the evening news?"

Ryan shook his head. There had been no time to surf the internet or tune in to the evening round-up, so Gregson walked around to his desktop computer and brought up a selection of articles.

The first headline screamed at him, in bold black capitals:

HACKER CLAIMS NEXT VICTIM
Northumbria Police have confirmed that a woman who has been named as Nicola Anne Cassidy (22), a medical student, died in hospital today from extensive knife injuries. Her death is being treated as murder and is being investigated alongside others believed to be perpetrated by the man people are now calling, 'The Hacker', after sources close to the hospital claim her body was 'hacked apart'.

Ryan read the remainder of the article and stepped away from the computer, swearing viciously.

"They've given him a name," he said. "It feeds into his ego and it'll spur him on. He'll feed off the attention. He craves it."

Gregson chose not to pass comment on how Ryan could possibly know that. He was used to the way he operated by now.

"It was bound to happen, sooner or later," he said. "A name like that is clickbait for the masses."

"*Sources at the hospital.* It had to be Draycott," Ryan said. "He was given clear instructions not to speak to the press. They all were. When we spoke to him earlier today, he said anybody could have hacked those women apart and he meant it as a professional slur. I think he knows it's one of his own."

Gregson sat down at his desk and tugged open one of the drawers, feeling around for the cigar box he kept hidden there. There were countless signs around the building reminding its occupants that smoking was strictly prohibited but he wasn't about to traipse all the way downstairs to the depressing Perspex smoking hut outside. For one thing, he couldn't be arsed. For another, he was the boss, and he hadn't spent thirty years clawing his way to the top only to be thrown in with the plebs.

Ryan watched him strike a match and eyed the smoke alarm above his head with mild concern.

"Sir—"

"If you're about to lecture me about my health, or yours, you can shove it up your jacksie."

"I was about to say, I need more resources. I've allocated work to everyone in the division with a minute to spare but I still need more eyes on this. We're drowning, just trawling through the CCTV, let alone anything else. I'd like your permission to set up a joint task force with Durham CID."

"He hasn't killed anyone within Durham's catchment... yet," Gregson amended.

"He's been north and south of the river," Ryan said. "Speaking frankly, sir, I think this has gone beyond lines on a map. We need all the help we can get, and we need it yesterday."

Gregson breathed deeply of the pungent smoke and eyed him through the developing haze.

"If you're wrong about the hospital, it'll be your head on a block."

Ryan's eyes turned icy at the poor choice of words.

"No, sir. It'll be some other poor soul's head we failed to save."

Gregson raised his cigar in the parody of a toast.

"Alright, Ryan. You've made your point. Take the resources you need. As long as you keep your end up, I'll take care of mine."

But when the door closed behind him, Gregson stared at the door for long minutes and wondered whether he'd made the right decision.

Ryan put an urgent call through to his equivalent at Durham CID requesting all the manpower they could spare. He had expected some haggling over protocols, maybe some debate about who should be heading up what would be a joint task force but, for once, he was pleasantly surprised to find they were in complete agreement.

It seemed the Hacker's reputation preceded him, and Durham CID jumped at the chance to help—especially with a police detective as one of his victims.

When Ryan replaced the landline receiver at his desk, it was only to find his mobile phone ringing instead.

"Ryan."

"I've been trying to get hold of you all day," his sister complained. "I thought you were going to try and get back before seven? I cooked something or, at least, I *tried*," she laughed. "Maybe we could spend some time catching up? I feel like we haven't chatted in ages."

Ryan closed his eyes, exhausted both physically and mentally.

Some part of him knew that Natalie wasn't to blame; it wasn't her fault they were facing a threat unlike any they had seen in recent times. She knew very little of the destruction he had witnessed, or of how fractured and impotent he felt as the investigation dragged on. Her world was very different; it was beautiful and innocent and all the things he would wish it to be.

But he couldn't help the anger that rose up and threatened to overflow.

What time did he have to sit around, chatting? There was no time for frivolity, not while there was a predator in their midst.

"... I don't even know if you have a girlfriend," she was saying. "What happened to that girl you were seeing a few months ago? Emma, was it? Or Gemma?"

"Natalie, I can't talk now."

"Okay, so when are you heading back?"

"For God's sake—haven't you seen the news?" he bit out, and immediately wished he could claw the words back.

It wasn't in his nature to strike out in anger. "Sorry. It's just that there's a lot going on. There was another victim today."

Natalie made a sympathetic noise.

"That's awful. You still have to eat and sleep though, don't you?"

He pinched the bridge of his nose to relieve the sudden tension.

"Look, I can't say when I'll be home tonight. I may have to work into the early hours." *He would.* "Once this is all over, we can have that catch up you're talking about, I promise."

"Okay," she said, dejectedly. "Look after yourself."

"You too. Remember what I told you about locking up properly."

"Yeah, yeah, I remember. Love you."

"You too."

Ryan ended the call and set the phone carefully on the desktop within easy reach. Despite himself, Natalie's personality was infectious, and a reluctant smile tugged at the corners of his mouth. He remembered the day she had been born, remembered visiting her in the hospital and stroking her soft dark curls.

"Mummy, what are you going to call her?"

"Why don't you help us choose a name, Max?"

Twenty-five years later and the thought still brought a smile to his face.

CHAPTER 23

He would rather have been sitting in the front row.

It wasn't his habit to settle for second best and he was unaccustomed to anything other than the orchestra stalls or—depending on the theatre—the dress circle.

Unfortunately, needs must.

The music soared, filling the Theatre Royal with sound as she moved across the stage. He'd seen her before, of course, at the Royal Albert Hall in London. That's when he'd first discovered her talent and, he had to admit, felt the urge to crush it. However, the opportunity hadn't presented itself.

Until now.

It had been serendipity that had brought them together and he had a very limited window of opportunity in which to take advantage of it.

He closed his eyes briefly to savour the creamy sound of her voice, felt himself shiver as it touched him somewhere he hadn't thought existed. Somewhere others might have called his soul.

O mio babbino caro,
Mi piace, e bello, bello,
Vo'andare in Porta Rossa...

Of course, Gianni Schicchi was his least favourite of Puccini's operas, and that particular aria had been sung to death.

No pun intended.

He chuckled at his own joke, drawing an irritated glare from the woman seated beside him. He turned to look at her in the semi-darkness and something in his eyes must have frightened her because she looked away quickly and reached for her husband's hand, clutching it for the remainder of the performance.

Mi struggo e mi tormento!
O Dio, vorrei morir!

He turned back to watch his prima donna, noting the line of her arms and the length of her neck. She was so much younger and more vibrant than the usual ageing monstrosities and, to him, she was Christine Daaé, Lolita and Juliet, all rolled into one.

He watched her eyes light up as she sang to the audience; a glorious beacon in a barren landscape.

She looked so much like *her*, the woman he would never, could never kill. The woman he longed to dissect as if she were an insect in a laboratory, an inhuman thing that deserved nothing less.

Hatred flowed like lava through his veins, scalding his skin until the pain was almost unbearable. He cradled himself, rocking slightly at the end of the row, drawing more nervous glances from the woman seated beside him.

When the song ended, he stood up and applauded along with the rest of them.

———

He left just before the end, slipping out of the fire doors and into the side alley that ran perpendicular to the main entrance. It was a wrench to leave so soon without being able to enjoy the remainder of the show, but sacrifices had to be made if he was to create his own finale.

It was risky to stand around, especially as it was still light, but he knew where the cameras were and had already chosen the perfect spot to wait; it was the same one he'd used the previous evening when he'd first begun his preparations.

He was taking far more risks for this woman than with any of the others. He knew he should never return to the same place, he *knew* that. Just standing here, he doubled the chance that somebody would notice him, especially two nights in a row. Some nosy bitch from one of the restaurants or bars would see him and decide he was worth talking to, then she'd veer towards him and start crawling all over him. It happened all the time.

And how could he blame them, really?

He was quite a catch.

Then, it'd be, *Oh, my goodness, Chief Inspector, I remember that man! I was talking to him on the corner of High Bridge Road at eleven o'clock.*

His brow furrowed as he thought of the man who was, at this very moment, out there somewhere searching for him. Ryan was close; much too close for comfort. It was remarkable how similar they were, when you stripped away all the trappings of 'right' and 'wrong'. Beneath the suits they both wore, they were both hunters. Ryan hunted him with the same intensity as he hunted each of his victims and with the same goal: to make the final kill.

Victims.

That was a joke. 'Victim' was a term coined by a society that refused to accept that some people were born to be winners while others were born to be losers. Ryan should be thanking him for his public service, not to mention the restraint he exercised every single day.

How tempting it was, each time they wheeled in a new one. The power was so rich, so potent, he could almost taste it on his tongue. With every drunk vagrant, every drug addict, and every other worthless person who ended up in his hands, he was tempted to put them down. As he felt their wounds, felt the blood run over his hands, he longed to feel it against his skin as he had all those years ago.

But he couldn't afford the luxury.

This one must be the last, he warned himself, at least for now. The memories and photographs would sustain him for a while, although they lacked the effect they once had. Photographs couldn't compare with the real thing.

Across the street, crowds spilled out of the theatre. He heard them chattering and gushing about her performance, some of them attempting to sing a few bars. Apparently, an evening spent in the company of greatness had afforded them delusions of grandeur.

He kept his eyes trained on the door. Unblinking, unwavering, unmoved.

Twenty minutes passed before he spotted her. He could hardly miss her; she stood out like a rare, exotic flower amid a garden of weeds, and she was bundled into a light summer coat in a shade of scarlet designed to attract attention.

She succeeded.

He watched her spend long, tedious minutes signing programmes and chatting with the die-hard fans who stood beside the theatre door cap in hand, then one of the male ushers came forward and they headed out into the evening together.

Yesterday, that had given him some cause for concern.

What was she doing going out after work, late at night, when she should be conserving her voice and letting it rest?

But, to his relief, the usher turned out to be her chaperone. Somebody had decided the star of their show would be safe returning to her aparthotel with one of the puny, acne-scarred ushers acting as bodyguard.

What an insult.

If she had an ounce of self-esteem, she'd have demanded a chauffeur or hired security but that was just another thing to like about her, he supposed. It had never occurred to her that anybody would see her and imagine all the wonderful possibilities.

He pushed away from the wall where he had been standing and began to walk at an even pace behind them, keeping his head ducked low.

He was nothing, if not a man of great imagination.

He watched her enter the foyer of her apartment building, pleased to note there was no doorman to be seen. The usher waved her off at the door, not even waiting until it had closed behind her before he hurried away, presumably to join his friends at the nearest watering hole.

The building itself was nothing to speak of; the fact they had not housed their star performer in anything other than a run-of-the-mill aparthotel told its own story of how difficult things were in the arts industry.

As far as he was concerned, it was another gift.

He watched her disappear out of sight, the ends of her hair swishing behind her and imagined what she would do next. Perhaps she'd pour herself a cup of camomile tea and have a warm bath to ease her aching body after her exertions on stage. Perhaps she'd call her mother, or a lover she'd left behind in London.

He hoped she made the most of it, because this night would be her last.

With a quick glance both ways, he walked across the road and made for the side alley, intending to disarm whatever camera they'd fitted outside the service entrance. He had his little hammer in one pocket and a can of spray paint in the other.

But when he found the service door—left helpfully ajar by the kitchen staff in the hotel's dreary restaurant— somebody had already done the grunt work for him, because the camera hung limply from its holder two metres off the ground. A small mountain of cigarette butts lay on the steps beside the door.

He heard laughter coming from somewhere within and he grinned like the madman he was, eyes almost feral with anticipation of his next kill.

"Thank you," he said. "Thank you very much indeed."

CHAPTER 24

Wednesday 9th July

In the end, Ryan never made it home.

After spending hours at his desk reviewing statements and summaries, he'd allowed himself a brief nap on the foamy loungers in the staff room at CID Headquarters. By the time the new day dawned, he was back at his desk with his head bent over a stack of paperwork. Phillips found him there, noting that his hair was still wet from the staff showers and he was wearing his dress shirt, the only one left inside his locker.

He tutted.

"You need rest, lad."

"Thanks, Dad," came the surly rejoinder.

Phillips decided to let it go, ambling across the room to set a cup of coffee on Ryan's desk.

"Don't mention it," Phillips said cheerfully, noting the sickly pallor of Ryan's face, the shadows beneath his eyes. "You, ah, you find anything useful?"

"If he works at the hospital, he's tied into shifts," Ryan said. "I've got a copy of the shift rotas from the A&E department for the last month, courtesy of Joan Stephenson. It was easier than going through Draycott," he added.

Phillips reached across to pick up a sheet of paper covered in multi-coloured highlighter.

"Who's who? Or, what's what?"

"I've got a key somewhere…here," Ryan handed him another sheet of paper with coloured lines and names alongside. "Green is Draycott, Yellow is Edwards and so forth."

Phillips took a slurp of his milky coffee and studied the dates and lines.

"You're looking at who was off-shift when Isobel Harris went missing? There was a shift change at eight the morning after Harris died, when Draycott, Edwards, Chowdhury and others were due back at the hospital. Harris died the previous evening, which puts them all in the frame."

Ryan nodded.

"Same goes for Cooper's timeline," he said. "The shift started at eight a.m. on Monday. The pathologist puts her death anytime up to seven a.m. but that's a best estimate; there'll be some leeway in that. Say he killed her around six-thirty, after having a couple of hours to work on her, that still gives him enough time to get back across town to start his shift if he hustled."

"Yeah, and the same people are in the frame for that, too."

"I know," Ryan said. "Frank, we need that CCTV. We need to see if any of their vehicles were in the vicinity."

"I've had them looking at it for the past two days," Phillips said. "They won't stop until they've checked every scrap of footage, you can count on it, but they're moving as fast as they can."

Ryan leaned back and scrubbed a weary hand over his face before tapping the spreadsheet again with the end of his pen.

"It gets complicated with Nicola Cassidy," he said. "She left work on Sunday evening for a week's holiday in Fuerteventura. Nobody reported her missing because everybody expected her to have caught her flight and to have been sunning herself abroad. Instead, she was taken and held in her own home."

"What time was her flight?"

"She was due to catch the twenty-past-midnight from Newcastle International," Ryan said. He knew the flight number thanks to a difficult conversation he'd had with Nicola's mother the previous day. His chest tightened as he remembered her devastation, the pleading look in her eyes as she'd begged him to tell her it wasn't true, that her daughter wasn't dead. She'd shown him the text messages her daughter was supposed to have sent, just like the e-mails Sharon Cooper had apparently sent last Sunday.

"—had to have been the window between her leaving the hospital and catching her flight, then?"

Ryan caught the tail end of Phillips' sentence and looked up, then away again.

"Yeah, it had to be. If he missed that window, he missed his chance. He couldn't risk holding her captive for days without somebody reporting it. He had to use her holiday as a cover story."

"He did his research, again."

Ryan nodded.

"He sought out the best match. So, we ask ourselves: who was on shift between, say, eight and ten p.m.? Allowing for the fact she'd have to make her way to the airport a couple of hours early."

Ryan already knew the answer to that, since he'd been through the steps during the early hours of the morning.

"Shifts are twelve hours for the consultants, doctors and surgeons, give or take," Ryan said. "Nurses tend to work a bit longer, so if we focus on the clinicians then we're looking at a mass shift change around eight. Once again, that puts the usual suspects in the frame."

"I've requested the CCTV footage from the hospital," Phillips said. "It's good and bad news. Which do you want first?"

Ryan pulled a face.

"Give me the bad."

"They've already destroyed the footage for the week when Isobel Harris went into A&E after her dizzy spell at work. It's policy to destroy it after three weeks unless there's some kind of incident."

"Damn," Ryan ran a hand across the back of his neck. "Okay, how about the good news?"

"They're sending through the footage for the past week or two, so we can scrutinize it and see who left their shift right on time. We can look for Nicola Cassidy and see who she spoke to, who was on the wrong ward at the wrong time, that kind of thing."

Ryan thought of all the extra hours racking up and resigned himself to it. There was no other way.

"What about the CCTV on Claremont Road? How far have we been able to track her movements?"

Phillips' face told him all the answer he needed.

"You know as well as I do, guv. The Council only keep half the cameras working because it's all they can afford to maintain. The rest of them act as a deterrent."

"Which means we've got nothing?"

"There's the CCTV from the hospital but…yes, we've got bugger all else."

Ryan pushed away from the desk and paced a few steps, trying to shake off the frustration. Nobody knew better than a policeman about the constant balancing of cost versus benefit when providing a public service. But, God, it was hard.

If there was no convenient camera capturing the killer on screen, he had to find another way.

"I need to know what kind of dosage would have kept Nicola Cassidy unconscious and how frequently she would need topping up," he said. "That will give us some idea of how often her killer needed to slip back. Then, we can compare the timings with whoever was on shift."

Phillips smiled.

"Now we're getting somewhere."

Ryan looked out across the city and wondered when they would find another woman dead in her own bed, left like so many bits of rubbish to be thrown on the scrap heap. The man who hunted them was insatiable in his need, and arrogant to boot. It was a deadly combination.

"Let's get there faster, Frank. If it's the same man and we're right about him working at the hospital, that means he killed one woman and took another on the very same day. One in the morning, before his shift, and the other after his shift ended. There are dozens of medics associated with A&E who would've had the opportunity to commit both murders. That doesn't even count the ones who work the red-eye, from six p.m. to four a.m., or the ones who worked a double shift."

"When does the shift pattern change?" Phillips asked.

Ryan turned to face him.

"Friday," he said shortly.

At precisely nine o'clock, Will Cooper kept his pre-arranged appointment to attend CID for questioning. He had a sharky-looking solicitor in tow, one MacKenzie and Lowerson recognised from previous investigations.

"He hasn't spared any expense, has he?" MacKenzie remarked, from their position in the viewing area overlooking Interview Room C.

Lowerson ran through the questions he planned to ask one more time, just to be sure.

"You'll be fine," MacKenzie reassured him. "This one's a doddle. You've got to remember that we're coming at the interview from different directions. Will Cooper probably wants to help us catch his mum's killer, but he's worried about implicating himself in whatever drugs offences he's been committing on the side. We, on the other hand, don't care so much about him dealing, so long as he tells us who and what he's been supplying. We might hit lucky."

She nodded through the glass.

"Underneath the bravado, you can bet he's scared. He's shitting himself that he'll find himself arrested and chucked behind bars, where everyone in this building will look at him like he's something on the sole of their shoe. You can use that," she said. "If he finds himself banged up, he'll be surrounded by people his mother helped put away. They won't give him an easy time. You might want to paint a picture of what it's like to be a guest at Her Majesty's pleasure."

Lowerson nodded, lapping up the advice.

"He isn't here because he wants to be," MacKenzie continued. "But there'll be part of him that knows he's doing the right thing."

"Could be, he's mixed up in something big," Lowerson put in. "Things might have got a bit out of control and he's frightened that, if he blabs, he'll be punished."

"Yeah, there's that too. What're you going to do about it?"

"Convince him otherwise."

MacKenzie smiled and shook her thumb towards the door.

"See? You're all over this. Go get 'em, tiger."

Beneath a layer of fake tan and a liberal coating of aftershave, Will Cooper was just a boy dressed up in his dad's suit. That was MacKenzie's impression as they entered the interview room and seated themselves at the small table, and she thought briefly of how Sharon would have felt to see her son in such a setting.

It didn't bear thinking about.

"Detective Constable Jack Lowerson and Detective Inspector Denise MacKenzie entering Interview Room C at"—Lowerson checked the time for the recording—"seven minutes past nine a.m. on Wednesday, 9th July 2014. Others present are William Cooper and his solicitor, Janet Smeaton. If you could please state your names for the record."

He waited while they did so, recited the standard caution and then shuffled his papers to find the list of questions he wanted to cover.

He couldn't find it.

MacKenzie's face betrayed nothing at all as she continued to watch Cooper, thinking that Lowerson's tactic of drawing things out seemed to be working because the man's forehead was already showing signs of a light sweat.

"Uh, thank you for coming in voluntarily, Mr Cooper," Lowerson began, a bit awkwardly.

"My client would like it noted for the record that he is here of his own volition to assist the police with their enquiries into the death of his mother, a decorated Chief Inspector—"

"We all knew Sharon," MacKenzie interrupted, in a low tone. "We knew what a wonderful person she was. That's why we're all here, isn't it, Will?"

He shifted uncomfortably beneath her penetrating green gaze.

"Yeah, of course."

"Good, I'm glad we're all on the same page," Lowerson said. "Mr Cooper, I'd like to start by asking you about your relationship with your mum."

Cooper shrugged.

"Same as most sons and mothers, I would guess. She nagged me, and I sometimes listened, sometimes didn't."

He smirked, clearly pleased with the answer he'd given.

"Same here," Lowerson said, easily enough. "You must have been devastated when you heard the news of her death?"

"I thought it was a joke, at first. I thought it was somebody prank-calling me from the office. I didn't believe it was true."

His smile slipped, and he looked at his own reflection in the glass behind Lowerson's head.

"Why did you tell DCI Ryan during a conversation on Monday 7th July and with your grandmother, Eileen Spruce, present, that you hadn't seen your mother in a couple of weeks?"

The solicitor opened her mouth to say something about his overwhelming grief, but Cooper overrode it.

"I already told you and the sergeant—Phillips. I was embarrassed because we'd argued the night before she died, and I thought it looked bad. I panicked, okay?"

"Do you also remember telling us that you'd argued over the fact your mother refused to provide a false statement to your supervisor at the Dental Hospital, regarding your current suspension for alleged drugs offences?"

The solicitor leaned in to whisper something in Cooper's ear.

"We argued about my suspension, but I would like it noted for the record that the investigation has not proven any of those alleged misdemeanours and no report has been made to the police."

"Is that because your mum took care of it?" Lowerson shot back.

Cooper's face reddened but he said nothing.

"Should charges be brought, the court may be entitled to draw adverse inferences regarding your refusal to answer these questions," MacKenzie said.

Cooper looked sharply at his solicitor, who could do little to argue with the truth of it.

"Are you intending to bring charges against my client?" she asked. "If so, this interview will terminate."

"That all depends on Will," Lowerson said, reverting to first name terms. "Y' know, Will, most people who peddle drugs don't think about where those drugs end up. They just think about the cash in hand and what it can buy them. That's a nice suit, by the way," he threw in, and watched the solicitor rear up again.

"Are you suggesting that my client has used proceeds of crime to purchase his suit?"

"Did I give that impression? My apologies," Lowerson said. "I thought I was complimenting his tailoring."

"Let me sketch a hypothetical scenario for you, Will," MacKenzie said, leaning forward. "In this scenario, we have a high-achieving young man who's studying...let's say veterinary science."

Cooper rolled his eyes.

"At the university, he meets somebody—maybe more than one person—who tells him he can afford a few of the finer things in life if he nicks some drugs from the pharmacy or carries them from one place to the next. You know, like pass the parcel," she drawled.

Cooper shifted in his seat again and they could smell his body odour wafting across the table.

"The thing is, this bloke didn't know what he was really getting himself into." Lowerson picked up the storyline like a pro. "When he wants to stop, he starts getting threats and maybe somebody roughs him up a bit on his way home or"—and this came to Lowerson in a sudden burst of inspiration—"or maybe, they threaten to hurt his mum."

Cooper raised his eyes and they were dark pools of misery.

"That's it, isn't it, Will?" MacKenzie said gently. "Did they threaten your mum?"

"He said he'd kill her and make it look accidental," he whispered and then, to their collective dismay, burst into tears. "It's my fault she's dead."

The room was filled with the sound of his heart-rending sobs as he rested his head on his arms and let out all the grief and worry, all the lonely hours he'd spent contemplating ending it all.

"I'm so sorry. God, I'm so sorry."

Lowerson began to record the time and put a stop to the interview but MacKenzie stayed him with a subtle hand on his arm.

"Will, your mum's death isn't looking like a revenge kill," she told him. "Whatever might have been threatened, whatever you *think* might have happened, might not be the case. We won't know for sure until you give us some names and some dates."

He swiped the sleeve of his jacket across his face, smearing mucus across his cheek.

"Put an end to this interview immediately, or I'll advise my client to make a formal complaint of police harassment," the solicitor stormed.

"Is that what you want, Will?" MacKenzie asked, very softly.

Two, maybe three seconds passed by before he drew himself up again and shook his head.

"I'm ready to talk."

CHAPTER 25

After Will Cooper had purged himself, Ryan and Phillips went in search of the Head of Emergency Medicine. According to Cooper, he had never stolen any drugs, but he had ferried them from one place to the next. One time, he'd seen a man he recognised making the drop-off and that man was one of the pharmacists at the RVI hospital, located a stone's throw from the Dental Hospital. If pharmaceutical products were going missing regularly, the hospital must be aware of it.

Furthermore, Sebastien Draycott was on the hospital committee, next in command after the Medical Director who was—maddeningly—still out of the country. If anyone was aware of a discrepancy in their logs, it ought to be Draycott. The fact that he hadn't mentioned it when questioned was a black mark against him from the outset.

There was a slight chill in the air by the time they reached Draycott's home on one of the city's smartest roads. It was a towering feat of Art Deco architecture that spoke of wealth and taste, as well as extreme order. The gardens were exquisitely manicured, and a snazzy little Aston Martin was parked behind the tall security gates, polished to a high sheen.

"This is it," Ryan said, executing a nifty parallel park on the kerb outside so that his car was sandwiched between two souped-up Range Rovers.

"It suits him," Phillips remarked, and thought that he much preferred his little three-bed semi. "Looks like the doctor's in residence, too."

"Ah, but he's a surgeon. We mustn't forget that, must we?"

Phillips snorted.

"How d' you want to play it?"

Ryan locked the car and looked up at the house.

"He gets one chance to come clean," he said. "After that, it's open season."

Phillips rubbed his hands together, in anticipation.

"Ma—"

He was cut off by the sound of Ryan's phone ringing.

"No caller ID," Ryan said, then answered. "Hello?"

"H-hello? Is that Detective Chief Inspector Ryan?"

"Yes. Who's calling?"

"This is Eileen. Eileen Spruce, Sharon's mum."

Ryan held back a sigh, thinking that there was no time to spend consoling grieving relatives, much as he might want to.

"Hello, Mrs Spruce," he said. "How can I help?"

"Yes, well, that is—I don't know if it's important or not. Only, I've found something that Sharon left at my house," she said.

"What's that, Mrs Spruce?"

"Well, Sharon had dinner at my house a few days before… It was the Friday night before she died." He heard her take a deep breath as she tried to collect herself and remained silent while she waged her battle. "While she was here, she told me she was a bit worried about Will. To tell you the truth, Chief Inspector, he hasn't been himself lately. He used to be such a kind boy," she said.

"Did Sharon say why she was worried?" he pressed.

"She only said he'd got himself into a bit of trouble at the university. I assumed he'd cheated on one of his exams or something like that," she said. "He hasn't told me and, to be honest, I'm frightened to ask."

Ryan shifted the phone to his other ear and thought that this was nothing they hadn't already learned.

"I'm sure Will can get himself back on track," he said, lamely.

"Yes, I hope so," she said. "But that's not really what I was ringing about. I'm sorry, I seem to have gone off on a tangent."

"Take your time," he said.

"Thank you," she sniffled, and blew her nose loudly down the line. "It's about the file."

Ryan exchanged a look with Phillips and signalled for a notepad and pen.

"What file?"

"Well, it's just that Sharon left a notebook and one of her files at my house. I mentioned it to her at the weekend and she said she'd come by and collect it but, of course…she never did."

"Did you find something in the notebook that worried you, Mrs Spruce?"

"I didn't mean to pry," she said quickly. "I suppose it was just something Sharon had left behind, and it reminded me of her. I haven't been able to go back to her home; the forensic people are still working there."

"I understand, Mrs Spruce, don't worry. As soon as they've finished, I'll be in touch."

"Thank you. Well, I just thought I'd better let you know. It might be important, although I didn't recognise any of the names."

Ryan felt his heart begin to thud.

"What names were they, Mrs Spruce?"

"It was about somebody called Sebastien Draycott," she said. "It looked like letters between a patient's family and the hospital, agreeing to pay £250,000 if they dropped their complaint against him."

Ryan closed his eyes and felt something click into place.

"What was the complaint about, Mrs Spruce?"

"Well, I didn't like to read everything, you know. But I had a little look," she confessed. "They thought it was his fault their dad had died. They said he seemed to be under the influence when they saw him after the surgery."

Ryan made a scribbled note for Phillips' benefit that simply read: 'DRAYCOTT—DRUGS/ALCOHOL?'

She paused.

"Did I do the right thing, telling you?"

Ryan looked up at Draycott's front door and smiled.

"Oh, yes, you did the right thing, Eileen. We'll stop by and collect the file in about an hour, if that's okay?"

"Yes, of course. Thank you," she murmured.

"Take care, Mrs Spruce."

Ryan slipped his phone into the back pocket of his jeans and nodded towards the surgeon's security gates.

"Come on, Frank. Let's go and surprise Mr Draycott."

Draycott took his time answering the intercom but eventually the iron gates scraped open, dragging against the paved driveway as they went.

"Chief Inspector. I don't expect to have my home and private life invaded at all hours of the day," he said, at the front door. "I am happy to assist with your enquiries, but you might at least have made an appointment before turning up on my doorstep."

And put you on notice? Ryan thought. *Hardly.*

"Sincere apologies," he said, with what he hoped was the right amount of humility. "May we come in?"

Draycott threw his hand up to indicate that they should enter but did not invite them into one of the reception rooms.

It made no difference: Ryan took in the minimalist décor, the framed pictures of Michelangelo's anatomical drawings, and the polished marble floor in a single glance.

He came straight to the point.

"Mr Draycott, am I correct in understanding that, aside from the Director, you have general oversight of not only the Emergency Medicine Department but the wider hospital thanks to your position on the management committee?"

"Yes, that's correct."

"I see. Therefore, you are aware of any and all complaints or internal investigations concerning the hospital pharmacy?"

Draycott's eyes turned cool.

"Yes, I am. May I ask where these questions are going?"

"Certainly. I'm trying to understand why you didn't see fit to tell us about the high level of drug theft the hospital is experiencing at the moment, including large quantities of sedatives, adrenaline and various other drugs with a morphine base."

Draycott affected an air of surprise.

"Every hospital suffers a level of theft, as I'm sure you're aware. It's a sad fact of life but hardly worth mentioning and nothing to do with your investigation, in any event."

Ryan was incredulous.

"I'll be the judge of what is relevant to our investigation. Only yesterday, you were asked whether, to the best of your knowledge, there had been any recent theft of drugs from the Emergency Department or from the hospital pharmacy. You said there hadn't. Would you like to amend your statement now, under caution?"

Draycott's hands were beginning to shake and he clasped them behind his back, where they wouldn't be seen.

"To my knowledge, it's not an unusual level of pilferage," he blustered.

"If you fail to cooperate with us, we can do this another way," Ryan said. "We can arrest the hospital pharmacists and compel disclosure of your records."

"Aye, and you know what it can be like down at CID," Phillips put in. "More leaks than a drippy tap. Wouldn't be surprised if the papers got wind of all those drugs being stolen, and when they find out about how the killer's victims were all drugged up before they died…well, that won't go down well, will it? Can't imagine what the hospital trust would have to say about it."

"Or the General Medical Council," Ryan added, ominously.

Draycott looked between them, trying to work out whether it was a bluff.

"Then, there's the small matter of that complaint, Mr Draycott." Ryan piled it on thick and watched his face drain of colour.

"I don't know what you're talking about."

"You should try telling the truth," Ryan said, conversationally. "You might find it refreshing. However, let me jog your memory. I'm talking about the large pay-out made by the hospital recently in exchange for a family dropping their complaint against you, on grounds of negligence."

Draycott relaxed again.

"Grieving families often make complaints," he said, with a bored shrug. "They're always looking for somebody to blame, to divert their anger onto something tangible rather than accepting that it was just their time."

"That's true enough," Ryan agreed. "But the hospital seldom dishes out a quarter of a million just to make them feel better. That'd be a road to bankruptcy. No, Sebastien, I'm talking about the complaint made recently, the one where it's alleged you were operating under the influence of drugs or alcohol."

Draycott let out a nervous laugh and ran a trembling hand through his hair.

"I—I—"

"Is that why you won't turn over your records, Mr Draycott? Is it because you're part of the reason drugs are being skimmed off the top?"

The surgeon turned red and then white again. Unforgiving light filtered through the window and showed up every hollow on his face, every line around his mouth. Here, in his own home, Draycott was just another man and wielded no special power.

"It'll ruin me," he said eventually. "Please. It'll finish my career."

"I want all your files," Ryan said. "Without delay."

"Yes—I…yes. What are you going to do?"

Ryan looked at the man long and hard. Undoubtedly, there had been many patients he had saved, people whose lives continued because he had been there to use his skill. But that was only one side of the story.

"How did it start?"

Draycott looked away, ashamed.

"Tell me where it began," Ryan persisted.

"Eighteen months ago, I was the passenger in a road traffic accident. Nothing serious, except it jarred my back. In my profession, I'm constantly required to lean over patients and the pain was agonising. I went through all the usual treatment and was prescribed codeine. As you may be aware, it contains morphine, which is highly addictive."

He let out a short, self-deprecating laugh.

"I, of all people, know its properties. I knew the dangers of becoming reliant on the pain relief but…it helped. When the prescription ended, I started topping it up with a couple of pills here and there. We keep a box of medicines available in the department to give to patients," he explained. "Nobody noticed a box or two going missing, but I needed more."

"So, you found more."

Draycott nodded, resigning himself to professional ruin.

"But I didn't realise there was already a drugs ring in operation. I swear it," he said, with apparent sincerity. "I didn't know it was already established and it came as quite a shock. But…addiction can change a person."

Ryan looked at him for long seconds.

"I understand that addiction is debilitating but people are placing their lives in your hands every time they pass through the door. I can't let that continue, much as I admire the work you may have done in the past. Your inaction has enabled unscrupulous people to peddle drugs to vulnerable people and God knows who else. It may turn out that it has enabled a murderer to access the tools of his trade." Ryan's face was hard as granite and just as unyielding. "I want every member of the Emergency Medicine Department to submit to a drugs test. I want every locker searched. Do we have your permission?"

Draycott nodded, feeling his life slip away like sand through his fingers.

"Good. Phillips? Get a team together and let's make a start. Draycott? You're with me. I want your staff to see that this is coming from their leader, such as he is."

He stared at the front page of the broadsheet newspaper, reading and then re-reading the headline until the lettering became illegible to his addled mind.

HACKER'S KILLING SPREE CONTINUES

Very slowly, very deliberately, he set the newspaper down.

His anger was so strong it took several minutes to bring himself under control again.

Hacker?

They dared to call him *the Hacker*?

It was such an insult to his sensibilities, he was almost reduced to tears. After all his careful work, all his planning and skill, that was the best they could come up with? It reduced him to little more than a butcher, some bumbling moron with a meat cleaver and not a man of refined taste and judgment, a giver and taker of life.

He spent several more minutes imagining the many and varied ways in which he would punish the person responsible. There would be no pain relief; oh, no. He would take them quickly and silently to a place where nobody would hear their screams and he would kill them slowly, removing their bowels and tearing them limb from limb, like in the old days. If it was good enough for ancient kings, it was good enough for him.

Afterwards, he felt better, the red mist having dissipated enough to allow him to think clearly again.

He decided he should be flattered, really. All the best killers had a title, something designed to strike fear into the masses. Hadn't he always longed to be feared and revered, after so long living in the shadows?

His spirits lifted immeasurably at the prospect.

CHAPTER 26

Ryan had to admit that Draycott put on a good show.

When they returned to the hospital together, there was no outward sign of his earlier remorse or any indication that he was anything other than in complete control of himself and his department. He seemed to take on a cloak of invincibility within the confines of the hospital and they watched the staff defer to him like sheep to their shepherd.

Records were seized, the pharmacist was taken in for questioning and the staff locker room was held under guard as each locker was searched for signs of unauthorised substances or material evidence. Everything was done by the book, with representatives from the Drugs Squad in attendance.

It was, to Phillips' mind, a stroke of policing genius.

"Wouldn't have been able to go rifling through people's things without this drugs hoo-ha," he said. "We'd have needed to get a search and seizure order."

Ryan smiled wolfishly.

"There are very few times in life when you'll hear me say that I'm glad we have a drugs problem, but this is one of them."

"What're we going to do about Draycott?"

Ryan lifted a shoulder.

"He hasn't confessed to any crime except theft of prescription drugs and providing false statements to the police. It'll be a matter for the Drugs Squad and the Crown Prosecution Service as to whether it's in the public interest to prosecute him for it down the line but, whether or not that happens, it's very likely he'll be struck off anyway."

"Still might be more to him than meets the eye," Phillips said, watching as the search moved on to the next locker.

Ryan nodded.

"Draycott spun a sad, sorry tale of human frailty but I haven't forgotten that he, more than anyone else here, had the means, the opportunity and the surgical skill to tear those women apart."

"Aye, but does he have the motive, or the character?"

Ryan considered the question carefully, watching the man himself stride down the hallway as if he hadn't a care in the world.

"We all put on a mask to face the world each day," he murmured. "The question is, what lies beneath it?" He shook his head. "I don't know what drives men to kill like that and I don't much care. We've heard it all before. Mummy didn't love me, so I became a killer. A girl once rejected me, so now I hate all women. I'm sure whoever killed these women has his own pathetic reasons for taking life but, underneath it all? It's not about any of that. They kill because they *like* killing. They like the sense of power, the feeling of omnipotence. So, I couldn't care less if their mum loved them or not, Frank. Plenty of people have a rough start in life and they don't all become serial killers."

"And if he hurt one of your loved ones, if it cut too close to home…would the reasons matter then?"

Ryan gave an irritable shrug.

"I don't believe in an eye for an eye, Frank. I know the law draws a distinction between what counts as sane and insane but, let's face it, whether they were in control of their actions or not, whether they knew their own minds or not…you still need to have a screw loose to be cutting people up like that. I'll be satisfied if we can get them off the streets, by fair means or foul."

"Amen to that."

While the search team continued their task, Ryan and Phillips took another trip down to the hospital mortuary to visit its resident pathologist. There had been a day's grace since their last confrontation, and they judged it was time to mend the breach.

But when they walked into the open-plan room, the welcome they received was even frostier than the air temperature.

"Pinter."

The pathologist looked across and then returned to his task, barely giving them the time of day.

"Jeff," Ryan said. "We came to get an update on Nicola Cassidy's post-mortem."

Pinter sent them a wintry smile.

"I only have one pair of hands and since I'm not allowed to work without *supervision*, that hardly helps to move things along, does it? A fine state of affairs for the Head of Pathology, I might add."

Phillips pursed his lips.

"Howay, man, Jeff. You know it's not just a case of doing things above board, it's about being *seen* to do things above board."

Pinter continued to look down at the inanimate mound of flesh in front of him but found himself softening a bit. If he'd only been straight from the beginning, none of this mess would have come about.

"We had some time to start the post-mortem yesterday evening," he said grudgingly. "Give me a minute and I'll take you through."

Phillips opened his mouth to protest but one quiet look from Ryan had his jaw snapping shut again.

"We had another two come in this morning," Pinter said. "I've put them on the back burner—figuratively speaking, of course."

The other two exchanged a pained look. The jokes never got any better with time.

"She's through here."

They followed him through to one of the private examination rooms—the same one that had housed Sharon Cooper's body only a few days before—and huddled around Nicola Cassidy's remains.

"I think you're going to find a lot of similarities between the injuries on this woman's body and the finished product with Sharon and Isobel. In their case, our killer had time to finish his work."

Pinter peeled back the paper covering to reveal Nicola's face, oddly serene in death.

"With the other two, he only had time to sever their major joints," Pinter said, with as much sensitivity as he could muster. "With this poor girl, he was drawing it out for as long as he could, and she suffered numerous smaller amputations. Here, you can see she lost several fingers. Same goes for her toes, although there doesn't appear to be any particular pattern to it."

Ryan looked at her hands and feet, saying nothing.

"Her body is a road map of what he planned to do next," Pinter said. "He's marked her body with knife wounds in the same way I'd expect to see a surgeon marking up a person's body before theatre."

"He has a ritual, then," Phillips observed. "That confirms what we thought about the bloke's character. He's ordered."

Ryan was looking at the puncture wound on her neck.

"Pressure syringe, again?"

Pinter nodded.

"I'd say so. You see, there was enough time for the skin to bruise," he remarked, using a retractable pointer to indicate the greenish-grey bruise around the point of entry. "And, if you look here, we found a canula still embedded in the skin of her left wrist. He must have done that to enable him to inject the sedative or adrenaline more quickly."

"A&E set up an IV line," Phillips said, but Pinter shook his head.

"That's over here, on her right wrist," he said, pointing to a small red dot on the other side.

There were so many questions to ask, Ryan thought. So many important things he needed to know. But only one answer mattered to him at that moment.

"Jeff, how much of this would she have been aware of?"

Phillips glanced across at him and thought that the man's emotions bubbled so close to the surface, it could be a double-edged sword. Caring for the dead they strived to avenge was admirable, but without detachment, it left the door wide open to heartbreak.

"Impossible to say, for sure," Pinter replied. "We can only hope, for her sake, that she was unconscious for most of it. However, given the killer's track record, that hope may be optimistic."

There was an uncomfortable pause and then Ryan passed a weary hand over his face, blinking several times to refresh his tired eyes.

"What else?"

Pinter shrugged his bony shoulders.

"It's possible—and I only say *possible*—Faulkner can retrieve something from the tissue we found beneath her nails." He directed their attention back to the plastic bags covering her hands. "He's testing it for DNA now. Let's hope for her sake that he comes up trumps."

"For all our sakes," Phillips muttered.

———

Half an hour later, they returned to find chaos breaking out in the Emergency Medicine Department.

"Sir, please stand back. We're under instructions to search your office, too!"

"I told Ryan he could have my files. I didn't say you could go rifling through any *bloody* thing you like!"

"Problem here?" Ryan asked.

The beleaguered constable turned to him with no small measure of relief.

"Sir, I've been explaining to Mr Draycott—"

"Look," Draycott cut across him in a sharp undertone. "I've given my permission for this search to go ahead in the interests of…well, in the interests of safety."

In your own interest, Ryan amended, silently. The man hoped that, by co-operating with the police, those who considered his case at a later stage might be disposed towards a more lenient punishment.

"Yes, you did," Ryan said, flatly. "And I presume safety is your first and only concern. That being the case, kindly stand aside and let us do our jobs."

They were interrupted by the sound of one of Ryan's officers calling out to him, sharply.

"Sir!"

Phillips placed a none-too-gentle hand on Draycott's elbow to prevent him following Ryan as he stepped inside the man's office. Like his home, it was ordered to within an inch of its life.

"Yes, Constable?"

"We found these, hidden up here," the woman said excitedly, indicating the architrave above the folds of a plain blue PVC roller blind decorating the only window in the room. In the palm of her gloved hand, she held a set of house keys hanging from a key chain emblazoned with the words, 'IBIZA ROCKS'.

Ryan pulled on a pair of gloves and took them from her, studying the little keys with mounting anger.

He walked back outside, to where Phillips was holding the man captive by the strength of his personality alone.

"Are these your keys, Mr Draycott?"

The surgeon glanced at the keys in Ryan's hand and shook his head.

"No. Do I look like the kind of person who holidays in Ibiza?"

"I don't know what kind of person holidays in Ibiza," Ryan shot back. "Would you care to enlighten me? Perhaps the young student doctor who died on your table yesterday afternoon?"

Draycott shook his head.

"I have no idea whose keys they are Chief Inspector. All I can tell you is, they're certainly not mine. Now, I think I've had quite enough of this—"

"Do you know how they came to be in your office, hidden above the window frame there?"

Draycott glanced through the open doorway, up at the window.

"I have no idea," he said. "Maybe one of your people planted them there, since you haven't been able to find the real man you're after. You think this is your chance to make a name for yourself, don't you? Well, I won't let it happen. I know people, Chief Inspector, and my name still stands for a lot—"

Ryan looked over Draycott's shoulder at the gathering crowd of consultants and nurses, then made a split-second judgment. He had to.

"Sebastien Draycott, I am arresting you on suspicion of the murder of Isobel Harris, Sharon Cooper and Nicola Cassidy. You do not have to say anything. But it may harm your defence if you do not mention when questioned something which you later rely on in court. Anything you do say may be given in evidence."

Draycott drained of all colour.

"I want my solicitor," he managed.

"That's your right," Ryan said, and led him towards the exit.

CHAPTER 27

"Ryan? In my office."

When he stepped inside Gregson's office, his superintendent surveyed him with a critical eye.

"Jesus. You look even worse than I feel."

"Thank you, sir."

"What's this I hear about you arresting Draycott?"

"What about it, sir?"

"Don't give me the run-around," Gregson warned him. "He's been on telly, for God's sake. He's known, Ryan, a Fellow of the Royal College—"

"He's also a fraud," Ryan ground out. "I don't care how many times he's been on Channel 4 giving his tuppence-worth about cardiothoracic surgery. He's admitted to serious offences including theft of prescription drugs and I've referred it to the General Medical Council for investigation which was, I suspect, what Sharon Cooper intended to do before she died."

"She knew about it?"

"Yes, sir. She had a file on him. There's an established drugs ring in operation between the hospital and the Dental Hospital, and Draycott knew about it. A complaint was made about him operating under the influence and the hospital tried to hush it up." Ryan lifted a shoulder. "It'll be down to other divisions to decide whether to press charges but, at the very least, I expect him to be suspended and ultimately struck off."

Gregson blew out a long gust of air and then his face broke out into a smile as he thought of all the positive press that could come of it. It was hard luck on the hospital but that wasn't his problem.

"Good work," he said. "Are you sure he's our guy?"

Ryan looked at Gregson in surprise.

"Oh, I'm sure he isn't, sir."

There was a two-second delay before Gregson erupted.

"What the bloody hell are you playing at?" he roared. "There's a man's reputation at stake!"

"Draycott ruined that all by himself."

Gregson leaned his hands on the desk and watched his hopes of a victorious press conference go up in smoke.

"What makes you think it isn't him? Why arrest him if you know he's not our man?"

"He would never have agreed to the search so readily if he knew there was something to find. I saw the shock on his face when we found those keys, sir. He had no idea they were there."

"You're saying they're a plant?"

"Yes, sir. They fit Nicola Cassidy's front door and her mother has confirmed she recognises the key ring. Draycott was out of his office all day but people still go in and out. Easy enough for someone to slip inside and stash the keys somewhere incriminating."

"You can't mount a case against someone on the strength of some keys," Gregson nearly shouted.

"I'm well aware of that. But this takes Draycott out of the equation for up to seventy-two hours, if we can manage to hold him."

"The magistrate will never allow it," Gregson argued.

"They might, if you weigh in."

"And why should I do that?"

"Because I expect him to strike again, very soon, and I need to be sure it isn't Sebastien Draycott. He might be many things but, if I'm right, a killer isn't one of them."

Gregson drummed his fingers against the desktop, following Ryan's train of thought.

"And we have no way of knowing who?"

Ryan swallowed, finding his throat painfully dry.

"Not yet, sir, but we're narrowing the field. If somebody wants us to believe Draycott is a killer, then we need to force the issue. They'll have to choose between their better judgment, knowing the man is in police custody, and their overriding need to sate themselves."

"You're talking about somebody's life hanging in the balance, Ryan."

"It gives me no pleasure to say that, sir." *It nearly killed him, knowing he could do nothing to stop it.* "We don't have the manpower to set up surveillance for every person who falls within the frame. There are too many of them. But we'll go over the results of the fingertip search, today. We'll seek voluntary DNA samples and compare them with what we found at the first two crime scenes. We have the hospital pharmacist in custody alongside Draycott and we'll question them both. We'll continue to check every alibi. We won't stop."

Gregson looked up at Ryan with sudden pride.

"I know you won't stop," he said, quietly. "But, sooner or later, you'll have to."

Ryan's body swayed, as if it had heard him.

"I know that, sir. Just not yet."

The interview suite had never been so busy. Aside from the usual rounds of drunken assault and petty crime, the corridors rang with the sound of medical staff giving their version of events. While MacKenzie and Lowerson turned their attention to the hospital pharmacist in the hope of extracting her client list, Ryan and Phillips faced Sebastien Draycott and his solicitor across the metal table of Interview Room A. They might not believe he was the man they were seeking but it was a foolish detective who failed to exhaust every line of enquiry.

"Mr Draycott, you were arrested earlier today on charges of murder. Do you have anything you wish to tell us?"

"No comment."

He had received a thorough briefing from his solicitor, but they were undeterred.

"Sebastien, in a statement dated 8th July 2014, you told us that you were at home on the evening of 20th June and did not leave until it was time to go to work the next morning. Is that correct?"

Draycott looked across at his solicitor, then gave a brief nod.

"Yes, that's correct."

"Is there anybody who can vouch for your whereabouts?"

"No, I live alone."

"You didn't speak to anybody on the telephone, or answer the door?"

"No, Chief Inspector, nobody happened to pass by at an opportune moment."

Ryan turned to the next significant date.

"How about the morning of last Sunday 6th? In your previous statement, you told us that you were, once again, at home throughout the relevant time period. Can anybody vouch for that?"

"No, Chief Inspector, as I've already said, I don't keep a lodger in the house for the express purpose of providing me with an ongoing alibi. The last time I checked, we don't live in a police state. Citizens are usually free to go about their lives without fear of being arrested on trumped-up charges of murder."

Ryan raised an eyebrow at that.

"So, in summary, you do not have an alibi for either of these dates?"

Draycott pressed his lips into a tight line.

"Turning to the most recent events of Tuesday 8th July, we already know you were at your workplace at the Royal Victoria Infirmary at the time Nicola Cassidy died. Can you tell us your whereabouts after your shift ended on Sunday 6th?"

"My client has already given his whereabouts in his statement dated 8th July," his solicitor said.

"I'd like him to remind us," Ryan said, politely.

"I was at work until nearly ten o'clock," Draycott snapped. "I didn't get home until more like eleven, at which time I collapsed into bed." *After taking a hit, to help him sleep.*

Ryan said nothing, but both he and Phillips knew that the time recorded on the hospital's CCTV camera confirmed Draycott's story, at least on that day. He hadn't left work until more like ten-fifteen, which put him outside the timescale for snatching Nicola Cassidy. It would have been too late.

But their faces revealed none of that.

"This afternoon, Sebastien, we found keys belonging to Nicola Cassidy hidden in the architrave above the window in your office. Can you tell us how they came to be there?"

"No comment."

"Oh, and we were doing so well."

"You already denied any knowledge of those keys," Phillips said, reasonably. "You seemed to think somebody planted them there. Any idea who'd want to do that?"

"I have no idea."

"Anybody hold a grudge against you? Anybody who'd want you out of the way?"

Draycott pulled a face.

"Leading a team won't win you any popularity contests," he said, then turned to Ryan. "I'm sure you know all about that."

Ryan said nothing, but had to admit there was a grain of truth in it.

"You're saying nobody stands out above the rest, nobody who springs to mind?"

"No."

"How about this," Ryan tried another tack. "If you were removed from office, who would be a shoo-in to replace you on the hospital committee?"

Draycott's mouth turned down as he thought of that scenario, which would come soon enough once the committee and the GMC got wind of the drugs investigation.

"There are several suitable candidates," he said. "Chowdhury, Edwards, O'Rourke," he rattled off a few names. "They all have the authority, at a push."

Ryan brought up their faces in his mind's eye and agreed that, given the right circumstances, each of them had the gravitas to run a busy department.

The question was whether any of them had the inclination to kill.

CHAPTER 28

Heavy rain clouds were gathering in the sky by the time Ryan's team gathered in the Incident Room at six o' clock, reflecting their general mood. It had taken several hours to take statements from every member of the Emergency Medicine Department. The interview with the hospital's senior pharmacist had elicited no real information; she was lawyered up to the hilt and prepared to give a 'no comment' interview despite their best efforts. It was another blow to their already strung-out nerves.

To counteract the gloom, Ryan flicked on the overhead lighting and looked at the assembly. It was a hotchpotch of stalwarts from his own division, plus a significant number of 'new' faces from Durham CID who had been working remotely until now. It was heartening to know that they had made the effort to be there, in solidarity as much as anything else.

"You've all seen the papers," he began, coming to stand at the front of the room with his hands tucked in the back pockets of his jeans. "You've seen the headlines and you know our killer has a name, just not the one we're looking for."

Ryan looked around at their tired faces and wondered how much longer they could stand to work at the rate he was asking of them.

Not much longer.

"You'll all be aware by now that we have a man in custody," he said, which drew a few claps and cheers from the back row. He waited for the spontaneous outburst to die before crushing their hopes. "I very much doubt he's the man we're looking for."

He watched their shoulders droop and was sorry for it.

"Our killer made a strategic move today," he said. "He planted a set of Nicola Cassidy's house keys in another man's office to incriminate him. We can hypothesise that he did it in reaction to Draycott giving an interview to the press which may or may not have been instrumental in them coining the nickname, *'The Hacker'*. It could also have been done out of professional rivalry, or simply as a means of deflecting attention away from himself. Whatever the reason, Draycott has a partial alibi for the time Nicola Cassidy is supposed to have been taken on the evening of Sunday 6th, so we have to look elsewhere."

He turned to Faulkner, who was leaning against one of the walls in the packed-out room.

"Tom? Can you give us a quick summary of where we are with forensics?"

Faulkner shuffled forward, his face bearing the evidence of many sleepless nights.

"Um, okay. You already know we have trace DNA from the first two crime scenes but, without any record on the database, it's just data. We can't compel a DNA swab from people without some kind of material link to the crime but, since Draycott was arrested, we've been able to take a swab from him to compare with the samples we already have on file. Hopefully, that will eliminate him from the enquiry—or not, as the case may be."

Faulkner scratched his ear, battling tiredness to hold onto his train of thought.

"Before, we couldn't go into the hospital and demand DNA samples without some sort of justification but now that there's enough of a link between the victims and the Emergency Medicine Department—especially after those keys were found—we can start processing voluntary swabs."

"And note down anyone who refuses to provide one," Philips chimed in.

"Exactly," Faulkner said, then turned to Ryan. "We'll get through the samples as quickly as we can, but it would be helpful to narrow the field a bit."

"I'll come on to that," Ryan told him. "How about the fibres at Nicola Cassidy's house? Did you find a match?"

"We couldn't isolate any DNA from the sample, but I can tell you the fibres were a blend of black polyester and cotton. It's the kind of thing you'd find in a core-spun, canvas yarn."

"Used in jackets?" Lowerson queried.

"This particular sample was quite thick," Faulkner said. "It's more likely you'd find it in a rucksack."

Ryan thought back to the scene at Nicola Cassidy's home, stepping through the motions in his mind's eye.

"So, he wore a backpack containing his tools and it brushed against the doorframe as he was moving her into the bedroom," he surmised.

"Who have we seen wearing a backpack like that?" MacKenzie asked, following the trail of breadcrumbs.

"Almost all of them," Phillips replied, turning to face her. To his everlasting shame, he found himself reddening again.

Damn. Damn. Damn.

It was starting to become an occupational hazard.

"Frank's right, unfortunately," Ryan said, providing a timely distraction. "Several of them carry backpacks because they cycle or walk into work. But once we narrow down that field, we can take samples from each of them and compare the fibres."

Faulkner tugged at his lower lip, thinking of the next point he needed to make.

"We tested the semen we found on Cassidy's sofa but, as I thought, it's ancient and we couldn't get a decent DNA profile. The fluid we found in the hallway belonged to Nicola, too."

Ryan chalked that up.

"Okay. Did you have any luck with the tape?"

"Yes, it's definitely surgical tape," Faulkner confirmed. "My team have compared its make-up with three of the best-known brands used by hospitals and I think we can be fairly certain it's Elastikon, by Johnson & Johnson. Comes in a three-metre roll you can fit in your pocket; easy enough to carry about."

"Not big enough to be noticed, if a roll went missing," Ryan said. "And I'm betting you could buy it over the counter at any high street pharmacy, if you wanted to."

Faulkner agreed.

"Yes, the tape's a bit of a dead end, I'm afraid. No handy prints or fluids found on it either, other than Nicola's own."

"Okay, thanks, Tom. I appreciate the work your team's put in to get us this far. We'll start taking DNA samples first thing tomorrow morning and courier them across to your lab."

Faulkner thought about how they would possibly process them all, then simply resigned himself to another few days without sleep. Looking at Ryan, he could see that the man was expecting no more of him than he expected of himself.

"We'll be ready," he said.

"Mac? Lowerson? Any further leads from the hospital pharmacist or Will Cooper?"

"We're fairly confident Cooper's given us everything he has," MacKenzie said. "He blames himself for Sharon's death because he thought it was linked to the drugs ring he managed to get mixed up in. This is just the start of his worries," she said. "But he's got some family left who still care and he's done the right thing, albeit later than anyone would have liked."

"No helpful names?"

MacKenzie shook her head.

"Nope. He says his role was to move the stash from one place to another. His only contact was a bloke named Hopper, who is already known to us. He's small-time but looking to expand."

"How about that pharmacist? What's her role in all this?"

"Drugs Squad are with her now," Lowerson said. "She's totally clammed up, sir. We worked on her for a good couple of hours but she's like a vault."

"We've still got the pharmacy records, although they appear to have been heavily doctored," MacKenzie said. "So, we went all the way back to the pharmaceutical companies, who sent through a record of what they've supplied for the last six months. It'll take some time because there are several different companies and we're still waiting for some of them to come through with their disclosure. But from the ones we've already received, it's obvious there are significant discrepancies."

Ryan nodded.

"Good work," he told them. "What about CCTV?"

The enormous task of reviewing the footage collated from several agencies and businesses had been split into smaller teams, each tasked with managing a different portion of the relevant victim's timeline.

"Let's start with Isobel Harris. We already know there was no CCTV to be had from her previous visit to the hospital and most of the cameras along her journey home were out of action. How about vehicles? Have we found any footage of a vehicle crossing paths with all three victims?"

Lowerson started to raise his hand, then remembered what Ryan had told him about speaking out.

"We haven't found a vehicle belonging to anybody from the Emergency Medicine Department, but we have found something interesting," he said. "We might have found a bicycle."

"A *bicycle*?"

Lowerson nodded.

"Yes, sir. Snapshots of footage along the high street in Tynemouth have captured partial images of a male riding a bicycle in the direction of DCI Cooper's home just after midnight."

"Can't have been long after her son left," Phillips put in.

"Yes," Lowerson nodded.

"Have you picked up a bicycle on any of the other footage?" Ryan asked, but Lowerson shook his head.

"Not yet, sir—and the footage we do have is so blurry it's next to useless. It's mostly guesswork that the rider is male because all we can see is a dark shape on wheels. I've forwarded the footage to the tech team to see if they can sharpen it up."

Ryan gave him an encouraging smile.

"That's good work. Keep looking."

"Who do we know who rides a bike?"

"Nearly all of them," Phillips said, testily. "It's the council to blame, putting in all these bike lanes, pretending to be

Amsterdam. Everybody and their grandma is riding a bike, these days—weaving all over the place, too."

"Don't you just hate it when the council tries to curb your unhealthy lifestyle?" Ryan mused.

"Aye, I do. My car gets me from A to B without any bother. Can't see who'd want to gad about in all weather wearing a bleedin' Lycra jumpsuit—"

"I would, for one," MacKenzie interjected. "Unlike *some people,* I take an interest in my health and keeping fit. Besides, the Lycra helps with the aerodynamics."

Phillips was lost for words, largely thanks to a delectable vision of Denise MacKenzie in skin-tight Lycra.

"On that note, let's take a break and douse ourselves in coffee," Ryan suggested, and was glad they could still find something to smile about.

Natalie Finley-Ryan meandered along the riverbank with a large, multi-coloured umbrella to protect herself from the freak monsoon rainfall that covered the city in a blanket of water. She didn't mind the rain so much; it was the isolation that was the most difficult thing to bear.

She paused to look across the swollen river, wondering how Ryan could stand it.

He was enigmatic at the best of times and always had been, she supposed. He was like their father, bred to be a stoic and toughened by years at one of the country's most famous boarding schools. It was a family tradition, just as it had been traditional for her to attend an equivalent establishment for Young Ladies. Had it not been for their mother, whose natural warmth softened the situation to a degree, either or both of them might have ended up very differently.

She turned her face into the wind, feeling it rush through her hair, and she began to understand what had drawn Ryan to the North. Here, the elements reminded you that you were truly alive; your body hardened to the colder temperatures and, before you knew it, anything more than a few degrees became almost tropical.

Natalie smiled as a pair of rowers skimmed across the water, uncaring of the downpour, and raised their hands to wave.

She waved back, then straightened up again to continue her journey to Ryan's apartment building. As she walked, she worried for him and whether he was coping with the extra demands that went alongside a career as a senior murder detective. There were things he must have seen that haunted him at night and that he may never want to tell her about, she knew that much. She was twenty-five years old but, to him, she would always be his little sister, just a kid.

But there were things she longed to tell him, too.

She wanted to understand what made him tick and to be understood in return. She didn't want to continue their half-relationship; she wanted theirs to be a proper family where regular phone calls and visits wouldn't be unusual, as they were at the moment. She wanted to remind him of all the good things in life, to help him to see that there were still decent people in the world.

She truly believed that.

As she approached the apartment building, she glanced up and noticed that the little CCTV camera above the door was hanging loose from its holder.

Ryan wouldn't like that; she must remember to tell him about it.

Ryan was feeling the full force of long-term sleep deprivation. Caffeine sloshed around his empty stomach and made him jittery. His eyes ached but a quick application of some eye drops had bought a little extra time before he was forced to make up some of the deficit.

Until then, he rounded up his team for the second half of their briefing.

"Let's focus on Nicola Cassidy for a moment," he said. "One of the key features of her death is the commitment it must have required to keep her alive for as long as he needed. She was tied up and gagged—we believe, using her own underwear—but to ensure that the risk of escape remained low, he had to dose her with a sedative. The toxicology report hasn't come back yet but there are needle marks on her body that are consistent with his MO. What I want to know is, how frequently would our perp need to keep topping it up?"

"I had a word with Pinter about that," Phillips said, and popped a stick of nicotine gum into his mouth, wincing at the taste. "Depends on the drug but, assuming he continued to use lorazepam, he needed to tread a very fine line not to give her a fatal overdose. Hence, the adrenaline on stand-by. Pinter thinks, to strike the balance, you'd be looking at upping the dosage little and often."

"How little, how often?" Ryan prodded.

"Every two to four hours," Phillips replied. "According to Pinter, at least."

"We can ask around. If we assume he's correct, they'd need to sneak out regularly. Let's think about this," he said, boosting himself up onto the edge of his desk and picking up the nearest thing to hand, which happened to be a bottle of Tippex. He fiddled with it while he thought.

"If he dips in to see her before his shift, he can dip out again three or four hours later if he has a lunchtime window, or a late morning coffee break. It's a busy department and her flat was only five minutes away; less, if he jogged part-way."

"A lot of them say they go to the staff gym on site, or for a wander around the park," Lowerson said. "Easy enough to make an excuse and say he's going to do the same thing."

"No CCTV in the gym, before you ask," Phillips said, anticipating Ryan's next question.

"Okay, this leads me on to the most obvious question," Ryan said. "Nicola Cassidy was able to escape because the drugs wore off. That's common sense. But why would he keep her alive so diligently and invest so much time in torturing her, only to let her escape before the end?

The answer has to be that it was an oversight, or perhaps an unexpected delay that was out of his control."

Phillips chewed his gum thoughtfully.

"You're looking at the shifts," he said, with approval.

Ryan nodded.

"We've got a problem, though. The rota we have doesn't account for anybody who swapped a shift informally, or worked extra hours, or was off sick. I realised that today when I cross-checked Draycott's story. We know he was at work when Nicola Cassidy came in because we happened to be right there, talking to him. Yet he wasn't listed on the rota."

"Did he swap?" MacKenzie asked.

"No, he was just working overtime, according to him," Ryan said. "All the same, it tells us things aren't quite as straightforward as we thought. Now, we need to go back and double-check everybody who was at work and might have been unable to go back and check Nicola at the usual time."

There were nods around the room.

"That would narrow the field," Faulkner said. "It'd give us a fighting chance to get through the DNA samples."

"That's what I'm hoping, Tom. We're overdue a bit of good luck."

CHAPTER 29

Stephanie Bernard was looking forward to her bed.

It had been a long run these past few months, touring the regional theatres with *Gianni Schicchi*, and she was ready to go home to her own little flat in Paris. She enjoyed visiting new places and spent much of her time in London, but nothing compared to the city where she had been born. Some people preferred the countryside, but she had never known anything other than the urban landscape with its ancient streets and elegant boulevards. She preferred its pace of life, its food, and its fashion.

She spread her arms wide to encompass the audience, who rose from their seats to applaud. She smiled warmly, grateful for their kind reception which made everything easier to bear.

She dipped into a low curtsy and accepted the obligatory bunch of red roses from the stage manager, stepping back as the curtain fell. She smoothed a hand over her hair and straightened her dress until the curtain rose again for an encore and she curtsied again, blowing kisses, playing the part.

Only after the final curtain fell did she hurry off stage and into her dressing room. Usually, she removed her make-up before heading back to the aparthotel the company had rented for her, but tonight she was much too tired.

She'd have a hot bath before bed and take care of it then.

Once the crowds had departed, she made her usual exit from the stage door and mustered a smile for the people who had waited around in the rain to see her, although her back was aching, and her feet wept from hours spent treading the boards.

"Goodnight! Thank you so much for coming!"

She waved them off and hovered in the doorway waiting for Mark, the usher who usually accompanied her back to her aparthotel. She was not normally anxious about these things but, in the present climate, she was grateful for the company. Everyone had seen the news reports and it was the stuff of nightmares for women like her; young women with dark hair. Pride prevented her from cancelling the final days of the tour but, as she stood framed in the doorway of the theatre, she found herself wishing that she had.

"Hi Stephanie, sorry to keep you waiting. I got held up dealing with some old codger wanting to know how he could get Puccini's autograph."

Mark joined her, wielding a large black umbrella.

"With some difficulty, considering he died in 1924," she chuckled. "Shall we go?"

"Are you sure you don't want me to call a taxi?"

"It's only a couple of minutes away," she said. "It'll be quicker to walk, rather than wait around."

"Okay, let's make a run for it."

After a mad dash through the rain, Stephanie said 'goodnight' at the door of her aparthotel, or tried to. It seemed that, since this was the last show, Mark had mustered the courage to ask her out. It was both endearing and awkward, considering he was hovering in the doorway of her hotel.

"So, um, I was wondering if you might want to have a drink before you go? The rest of the cast are heading out for a quick one to celebrate."

Stephanie stifled a yawn and tried to think of a gentle way of saying 'no.'

"Ah, that would have been nice, Mark, but, you know, I don't drink. I have to protect my voice."

Thankfully, he took it well enough.

"Ah well, I had to ask!" He smiled beneath the rim of his umbrella. "Take care of yourself, Stephanie. It's been really nice to know you."

She watched him hop over puddles on his way back to the theatre and she smiled after him. If only every man could be so good-natured.

And she would know.

Two years ago, there'd been a man in London. Over the course of a weekend, he'd waited around after every performance and just the sight of his face had been enough to set her nerves jangling. He'd made no overtures and hadn't insulted her in any way.

It was just something in his eyes.

Remembering sent a shiver across her skin and she found herself peering out into the gloomy night, imagining she would see him standing there waiting for her. Just watching her.

"Don't be ridiculous," she told herself, and pulled the door shut.

A few miles further west, Ryan watched the sun go down over the city and knew that, somewhere out there in the darkness, a killer waged a war with himself. If he went out hunting tonight, there would be no way of pinning anything on Sebastien Draycott, and that would undo all the effort of planting Nicola's keys in the man's office.

And yet, to deny himself would require a level of restraint that was beyond his capabilities. More than twenty-four hours had passed since Nicola Cassidy died, depriving him of his chance to satisfy whatever need compelled him to kill. Ryan suspected there was a paraphilic desire to see inside the human body, or something equally perverse.

But, when all was said and done, he didn't care what motivated him except to the extent it helped to stop him.

He continued to watch as the sun slipped off the edge of the earth and darkness fell. Warm rain beat heavily against the window pane and Ryan watched the drops run down the glass, wondering where the hammer would fall.

Stephanie never saw it coming.

The corridors of her hotel were impersonal and deserted, with yards of worn carpet in a geometric pattern that was hard on the eyes. Faded prints of Van Gogh's famous works hung at intervals in cheap plastic frames and she followed them, counting them off until she reached *The Starry Night* which hung next to the door to her suite.

She already had the key in hand, some odd sense of foreboding having alerted her to move quickly to safety.

Despite it, she still didn't see him until it was too late.

She caught a flash of movement behind her and then a firm hand clamped around her mouth while the other stabbed something sharp into the side of her neck. He used a knee in the small of her back to thrust her forward into the room she'd already opened, and she fought her faceless attacker, twisting so that he lost his grip on the needle.

But the drug was already taking effect and he watched her stagger into the room, trying to pull it out, her arms flailing.

Calmly, he closed the door and locked it from the inside.

"There now," he said. "Together at last."

She collapsed onto the floor and her last thought before she lost consciousness was that it was the same man as before.

He had come for her, at last.

Ryan hadn't been able to settle down to any meaningful work and he acknowledged it was time he allowed his body some rest. His hands shook with fatigue and as Phillips had kindly remarked, he was starting to resemble the arse end of a bus.

"Go on home, lad, and get some shuteye. I'll man the fort here and let you know if anything happens."

Ryan nodded, putting a grateful hand on his sergeant's shoulder.

"Thanks, Frank. You'll let me know—"

"Aye, I'll call you if anything breaks. Go home."

So Ryan drove slowly through the quiet streets, his eyes focused on the road with the kind of intensity known only to drunk drivers and those who hadn't slept properly in several days. He fiddled with the radio until he found a particularly obnoxious station and subjected himself to twenty minutes of house party anthems to keep himself awake until he made it home.

He could have fallen asleep at the wheel by the time he brought his car to a stop in his usual bay in the parking lot beneath his apartment building, but he dragged himself the rest of the way to the lift and punched the button for the top floor.

Natalie muted the sound on the television when she heard the creak of the lift outside and hurried across to the front door, not bothering to check the peep-hole before she threw it open to welcome her brother home.

When she saw him, she was shocked.

"You look awful," she said bluntly, and he laughed.

"You're as bad as Phillips," he said, shrugging out of his coat and tossing it over a chair.

A pot of soup was simmering on the hob and his stomach rumbled loudly as his nose registered the scent.

"Come and sit down," she told him, in the same tone their mother used. "I'll put a bowl out for you."

"You don—" He yawned hugely. "You don't have to."

"I know that," she said to herself. "But I want to."

She watched him spoon a few mouthfuls and, when he would have stopped, she bullied him into finishing the rest.

"That's better. You look like you could sleep for England."

"That's because I could," he said, stumbling towards his bedroom.

When he entered, he found she'd left one of the bedside lights on to greet him and, if he wasn't mistaken, there was fresh linen on the bed.

"Nat?"

She poked her head around the doorway.

"Yeah?"

"Thank you for all this," he said, gesturing to the room and thinking of the soup in his belly. "It's been a long time since anybody looked after me like that. Usually, I don't need it but…it's nice to come home to a friendly face, rather than an empty flat."

She smiled beautifully.

"Goodnight, big brother."

"G'night," he replied, and face-planted on the bed.

It was only after she heard his gentle snores that she remembered there had been something she meant to tell him.

It would keep.

CHAPTER 30

Thursday 10th July

The housekeeping team didn't find Stephanie Bernard until it was almost lunchtime. They had respected the 'DO NOT DISTURB' sign hanging outside her door but, when it remained hanging there for several hours, they decided to risk it. A discreet knock had not elicited a response, so they let themselves into the room she had occupied for nearly a week.

And what they found in there would stay with them for the rest of their lives.

Faulkner stepped carefully over a mound of drying vomit near the doorway, with Ryan and Phillips following closely behind. The team of CSIs were already on site and the aparthotel had been declared a crime scene. Lowerson was overseeing the process of re-housing other residents to provide a clear pathway for the police operation, while MacKenzie took over management of the Incident Room back at Police Headquarters. That was no small task, given the number of police personnel attached to the investigation which had now been given the jovial title of 'OPERATION SUMMER' by The Powers That Be.

The three men stood a few feet from the edge of the bed in full protective clothing, surveying the Hacker's most recent handiwork. It seemed he had taken to his new title because this latest demonstration was less a feat of medical prowess than an act of total destruction.

"God in heaven," Phillips choked out, focusing on his breathing so that he would not embarrass himself.

"He's completely gone now," Ryan said, feeling his own stomach churn. "This is something else."

The woman was in pieces, laid out like chopped vegetables on the bed and decorated by rose petals taken from the bouquet she had been given at the end of her last performance.

"Do you realise who this is?" Faulkner asked.

Phillips could barely recognise the gender of the body parts, let alone determine an identity.

"Who?"

"I think this is Stephanie Bernard. She's a French opera singer, a soprano."

Ryan thought of what was playing across the theatres and musical venues and came to the correct conclusion.

"*Gianni Schicchi*?"

"Yes, she was playing Lauretta. I wanted to go and see it but couldn't get a ticket," Faulkner explained.

"You said she was French?" Ryan thought of the cross-jurisdictional complication and immediately hated himself for it.

"Yes," Faulkner replied. "There was a write-up in *The Guardian* about the opera coming up to Newcastle as part of a tour of the UK. She was a real emerging talent."

"He's created a bit of his own theatre," Phillips remarked. "Look at how he's arranged the petals coming out of her mouth, to look like a song."

Ryan nodded.

"I want a total press ban," he said. "He's peacocking, showing us what he can do to live up to his new name. I told them," he raged, softly. "I tried to warn them, you can't glorify a person like that."

"He's more animal than person, now," Phillips said.

Ryan nodded, and stepped outside to put a call through to Gregson.

———

His superintendent answered after a single ring.

"This is Ryan. There's been another one."

Pause.

"Who?"

"He's escalated again, sir, as we suspected he would. His victim appears to be an opera singer called Stephanie Bernard, but we haven't confirmed her identity formally yet."

"I know her," Gregson said. "Or, at least, I saw her in *The Marriage of Figaro* at the Royal Albert Hall a couple of years ago. She was luminous."

Ryan didn't comment but thought it was funny that a celebrity was afforded a greater degree of sympathy from his superior than a shop girl or a student.

For his own part, he tried to treat every victim alike. Death was a great leveller, after all.

"She's French or Italian or something," Gregson continued. "We'll need to manage that situation carefully because the last thing I want is the continental press picking up on our inability to bring this man to heel. This thing's already going viral."

Again, Ryan said nothing. He could have spoken of all the hours they had been searching, of all the spent resources and personal cost to every member of his team, but it would have been like water off a duck's back.

"She's French, sir."

He knew, because he'd already looked up her *Wikipedia* page. Stephanie Bernard had been twenty-seven years old, born in Paris, and with a permanent home there on the Left Bank.

"Ryan, this breaks new ground," Gregson said. "If you can't put an end to this, this *orgy*, I'll hand it over to someone who can. I've already had the Murder Squad on the blower, offering to take over."

Ryan knew the team in London very well, since he'd completed his training with the Met years earlier. He knew them to be capable but no more so than the team he had the privilege of working with right now.

"Look, the nation is watching us, and people expect action," Gregson said. "When this latest news hits the press, it'll send shockwaves around Europe."

"I want it suppressed for a few hours," Ryan said. "At the moment, he doesn't know that we've found his latest victim. We might be able to use that."

"How?"

"It'll give us time to get hold of the footage from the theatre, the ticket lists and anything else we can. If there's a name or a face we recognise, we can move in without him rabbiting away."

"You've got until three o'clock," Gregson said.

The line went dead.

———

A series of discussions with Stephanie Bernard's production company confirmed that the last person to see her alive was Mark Pepper, a thirty-year-old usher at the Theatre Royal. It was pushing one o'clock, but he answered his front door in a pair of rumpled tartan pyjamas and a t-shirt with a picture of a dancing frog embroidered on the front.

"Yeah?"

"Mr Pepper? DCI Ryan and DS Phillips from Northumbria CID. May we speak to you, please?"

The acronyms had an instantly sobering effect.

"Uh, yeah, sure. Am I in trouble?"

He thought of the bag of weed sitting on the window ledge in his bedroom and broke into a cold sweat.

"No, Mr Pepper. We're here because we hope you might be able to help us."

"Oh," he said, relieved. "What with? Is it about the bloke at the pub the other night? Look, honestly, he was all over the place. The bouncer should have thrown him out before he got into that state."

They followed him down a narrow hallway to a small living room that was decorated in what Phillips would call 'man style'. An ancient sofa had been plonked against the wall and boasted a variety of food stains, while a gigantic television dominated the other wall and was flanked by freestanding speakers that must have cost a small fortune. A games console with four handsets was lying on the floor beside it, and every surface was littered with dirty plates and mugs.

"Sorry, I haven't had a chance to clean up," Pepper said. "D' you want to sit down?"

His face was such a picture of hospitality, they were almost sorry to decline the sofa.

Almost.

"No, thanks," Ryan said. "But perhaps you'd better take a seat. We have some bad news."

Pepper sank onto the edge of the sofa.

"What is it?" he said. "Is it my mum? My dad?"

"No, lad. Far as we know, your family's safe and sound," Phillips said. "We're here because Stephanie Bernard was found dead in her hotel suite, not long ago, and we understand you might have been one of the last people to see her before she died."

They watched the changing emotions on Pepper's face, from shock right the way through to grief and, finally, denial.

"I-I can't believe it. Are you sure?"

Phillips held back any smart comments and simply nodded.

"Aye, we are."

Pepper held his head in his hands.

"I can't—*Stephanie*? Was there some kind of accident?"

Ryan side-stepped the question.

"If you could just tell us, in your own words, what happened after the show finished last night. We're going to take a note you can check over at the end."

Pepper nodded.

"Okay. Do you mind—can I get some water?"

"Sure."

They waited while he gulped down a pint of water, then filled another glass and brought it back with him.

"The performance finished around ten-forty-five," he said. "Stephanie usually takes…*took* fifteen or twenty minutes to get changed and ready to go back to her aparthotel but she was a bit quicker last night. I usually try to meet her at the stage door on the dot of eleven, but she was there at five-to."

"That's very helpful," Ryan said. "Go on."

"Okay. Um, she'd finished signing programmes and chatting to the people at the stage door and she was waiting for me. I'd been held up a bit by some old bloke," he remembered.

"Did you see anybody at the stage door when you joined her there?"

Pepper tapped his fingers against the glass.

"Yeah, there was a woman in her fifties with someone—I guess he was her husband. They were telling her how much they'd enjoyed the show, but they headed off straight away."

"Nobody else that you could see?"

"No. Well, I mean, obviously, there were people passing by, but I can't remember exactly. It was raining, and people were rushing to get indoors."

"Okay. Then what happened?"

"Well, the company liked me to make sure she got back to her hotel safely. They didn't spring for the Rolls Royce service, so she had to make do with me," he said, with a shrug.

Tears filled his eyes.

"She was lovely," he said, suddenly. "A real class act, you know?"

Ryan nodded.

"She never complained about anything and never had a bad word to say when things went wrong. She just got on with it, like a true professional. I thought she was amazing."

He looked down at his glass and took another sip.

"I feel—um, I feel awful. Last night, I asked her out for a drink. Don't know what I was thinking," he said. "Must have had a rush of blood to the head or something. Anyway, I gave it a go and asked her."

"What did she say?" Phillips murmured.

"Oh, she knocked me back. But she did it in the nicest way," he said. "Like I said, she had class."

He looked up at their sombre faces.

"Somebody hurt her, didn't they? You wouldn't be here, if they hadn't."

They said nothing, but their silence was confirmation enough.

"Carry on telling us what happened," Ryan advised. "It's the most helpful thing you can do."

Pepper nodded.

"We chatted on the way to her aparthotel. It's only a few minutes away from the theatre, down on Dean Street... although, I guess you know that," he said. "I don't really know what else to tell you. I dropped her off as usual and made a fool of myself, asking her out, then said 'goodnight' around twenty-past-eleven."

"Did she give you any indication that she was worried, or that anybody had frightened her?"

"No. Yes," he remembered suddenly. "She told me that the reason she never likes to go home alone when it's dark is because she had this fan a couple of years ago who had freaked her out, or something like that. She wasn't exactly the nervy type, especially not on stage, but she was quiet in real life, y' know? Sort of...gentle."

"I don't suppose she ever mentioned a name or a physical description of this fan? Male or female?"

"Definitely male," he said. "But I don't know anything else about him. Sorry."

They stayed a few minutes longer covering the same ground to make sure they had his best recollection, then left Mark Pepper to his hangover and his grief.

Outside, Ryan turned to Phillips with blazing eyes.

"It was him. The fan, two years ago. I know it was him, the man who killed her."

Phillips had the same feeling, deep in his gut.

"Aye. I think you might be right."

"He couldn't have known two years ago that she'd be in Newcastle right now, so it has to be a case of opportunism. He must have been delighted."

"He needed to do his research quickly," Phillips said. "The company were only here for a week and he needed to find out where she was staying, whether she was alone, whether there was a camera on the door and all that."

"And he'll have wanted to see the production," Ryan said. "It was a juggling act, considering he had Nicola Cassidy to manage alongside his regular work, but there's no way he would have missed the show. Question is, which one did he go to?"

"He probably paid for his ticket in cash, if he did go, but I'll check with the box office."

Ryan thought back to the events of the past week.

"We need to go back to the hospital," he said. "It's imperative we fill in the gaps on that rota, now we know Draycott is out of the running."

CHAPTER 31

The time was edging closer to three o'clock when Ryan and Phillips stepped inside the A&E department once more. Ryan didn't concern himself with the arbitrary deadline handed down by DCS Gregson and concentrated on doing what he did best.

There was a different atmosphere in the Emergency Medicine Department now that Draycott had been arrested; a sense of unrest and disorder, and they reminded themselves that his staff knew nothing about Stephanie Bernard's murder, nor of Draycott's likely innocence.

"Hello, Chief Inspector."

Keir Edwards spotted them entering the main waiting area and headed them off.

"Doctor Edwards. How is everyone faring?"

The other man pulled an expressive face.

"Oh, you know, there were a few grumbles here and there about the search and about having to give a DNA sample but, for the most part, everyone was happy to help. Understandably, it's been a shock to find out the truth about Sebastien."

Ryan gave him a bland smile.

"What truth is that, Doctor Edwards?"

The other man gave a funny little laugh.

"Well, he's been arrested—we assume for the murders of those poor women. Is that not the case?"

"We can't discuss an active investigation," Phillips said, then jerked his head towards the treatment area. "We were hoping to speak to Joan about a staffing matter, if she's around?"

"I'm afraid Joan doesn't start until four today," Edwards replied. "Is there anything I can help you with?"

Ryan smiled, noting that Edwards was seamlessly transitioning into the role of Acting Head of Department.

"Perhaps you can," he said. "Shall we use Mr Draycott's office?"

"Certainly."

Edwards seated himself at Draycott's desk and spread his hands.

"How can I be of help?"

Ryan took out his dog-eared copy of the staff rota for the last week and laid it out on the table so that Edwards could see.

"This is the original rota that was drawn up two weeks ago by Mr Draycott, and Mrs Stephenson on the nursing side," Ryan explained. "It's since come to our attention that changes were made in the interim owing to sickness, overtime and staff swapping shifts. We were hoping you could help us to fill in the gaps."

Edwards made an expressive face.

"Well, I'll do my best. Let me see, now."

He made thoughtful noises.

"Ah, yes. I can see my own shift pattern hasn't been updated on here," he said, and began making notes with a pencil in the margin. "Likewise, I know that Doctor Chowdhury had to swap on Tuesday…mm hmm…"

He spent some time making notes and then sat back and pushed the piece of paper back across the desk.

"That's all I know of," he said. "Joan should be able to fill in the blanks on the nursing side and she's due back here in half an hour."

"Thank you, this is very helpful," Ryan said, skimming his eyes over the notes.

"I suppose you'll need to take some more statements," Edwards added. "Would you like me to arrange a meeting room, so you can talk to the staff in private?"

Ryan inclined his head.

"It's good of you, but no. That won't be necessary just yet."

"It's a terrible tragedy, what happened to that woman. Such an enormous loss to the world."

Ryan thought of Nicola Cassidy's wish to be a paediatric consultant and nodded his agreement.

"Every victim of crime is a loss, Doctor."

"We feel the same, here, with every patient we lose," Edwards said. "But it isn't every day that you get somebody like that, is it? It must be quite a task for you."

Ryan's forehead crinkled as he studied the rota, only half listening to the small-talk.

"Yes, I suppose so."

They stood up, preparing to leave.

"Thanks again for this," Ryan said, tucking the paper into his breast pocket. "We'll be in touch."

"Ah, Chief Inspector? Sergeant?" Edwards' voice lowered to a stage whisper. "About Mr Draycott. Some of the patients and staff have been asking where he is. What should I tell them?"

"You should tell them the truth, Doctor. It's always preferable."

Ryan had barely gone fifty yards when the truth hit him and, when it did, it fell like a thunderbolt.

He stopped dead, just outside the automatic doors of A&E, oblivious to the people coming in and out, oblivious to the rain that had begun to fall.

"Frank."

Phillips had continued walking and was startled to find Ryan had not kept up. He trundled back to where his SIO stood, looking as if he'd seen Caesar's ghost.

"What's the matter?"

"He wasn't talking about Nicola Cassidy. When Edwards said it was an *enormous loss to the world* losing somebody *like that*, he wasn't talking about her. He was talking about Stephanie Bernard. The bastard was talking about his latest victim."

It took Phillips a couple of seconds until the penny dropped.

"Nobody knows about Bernard yet. Nobody but us."

"Exactly. Nobody but us and the man who killed her." Ryan lowered his voice, thinking quickly. "Get a team down here, fast as you can, sirens off. If he thinks we know, he'll make a run for it, or he'll attack."

Phillips nodded, already reaching for his phone to put an urgent call through to the Control Room.

"What are you going to do?"

"I'm going to keep him occupied until they get here," Ryan growled. "He's a danger to the public and he's volatile. If I can keep him talking, we might be able to do this without any more bloodshed."

Phillips kept a sharp eye on the door.

"Be careful, lad."

CHAPTER 32

Ryan made sure his face was completely neutral when he stepped back inside the Accident and Emergency Department. A man who had killed three women with obscene brutality was not above threatening the public to save himself, and he couldn't have any more lives on his conscience. The waiting room was awash with mothers and babies, children with sporting injuries as well as the elderly, and all age groups that lay in between.

Ryan's heart thudded against the wall of his chest as he made his way towards the reception desk, where he forced himself to smile.

"Hello, me again. I was just speaking to Doctor Edwards. Do you know where I can find him? I forgot a couple of questions I meant to ask."

The receptionist returned the smile and thought she would miss seeing him around the place when his investigation was all over.

"Yep, I think he was called through to the resus department."

Ryan considered the best approach.

"If it's okay, I'll wait for him through there. I need to have a word with some of the staff, anyway," he lied. "I promise I won't get in the way."

"Oh, go on then," she said, jerking her thumb in the right direction.

Ryan thanked her and made for the resuscitation department, running through all the possible outcomes in his mind. Some of the staff spotted him and waved or smiled, but he didn't see them; his mind was focused entirely on one thing and one thing alone.

Safety.

He peered inside open curtains, listening for the sound of Edwards' voice.

When he heard it, white-hot anger gushed through his body and he took a couple of deep breaths until he could be sure none of it would be visible. Just a few more minutes until reinforcements arrived, he thought. It couldn't be longer than that.

"How's she doing?"

Through the crack in the curtain, Ryan could see Edwards speaking to one of the nurses monitoring the heart machine.

"She's back down to 72 bpm, Doctor."

"Great work, everybody," he said, leaning down to place a gentle hand on a child's head. She couldn't have been more than twelve or thirteen. "You're going to be okay, sweetheart. You've been very brave."

He delivered the words with such sincerity, it might have caused a lesser person to doubt themselves.

But Ryan *knew*.

It wasn't just the slip Edwards had made in their conversation earlier; the notes he'd made on the rota failed to include the double shift he'd worked on Tuesday, a double shift that would have made it very difficult for him to slip away and top up the medication in Nicola Cassidy's system. He was the only one to fit the profile for every murder; the only one who couldn't provide an alibi for any of them.

His stomach rolled as he listened to the child's mother.

"I'm so grateful, Doctor. Thank you, so much."

He heard the good doctor give a trite, humble reply, then the curtain whipped back, and they came face to face.

How had he failed to see the truth before? Ryan wondered. It was written there, in the man's eyes. They stood facing each other, icy grey clashing with darkest brown.

"Chief Inspector." Edwards studied Ryan's face closely. "Did you forget something?"

Ryan managed to produce an easy, social smile.

"Yes, as a matter of fact, I wondered if you had time to give me your expert opinion," he lied.

Something flickered in Edwards' eyes; something like suspicion.

"I understood Mr Draycott had already provided you with his *expert* view," he replied, and Ryan could see it now.

The anger, the jealousy, the festering realm of hate that simmered so close to the surface. It was there for all to see, if they only knew how to look.

"Yes but…" Ryan made a show of checking they would not be overheard, then put a light hand on Edwards' arm to lead him to one side.

And away from the child.

"I don't like to admit when we make mistakes," Ryan said, conspiratorially. "But—and this is highly confidential—we're very close to charging Mr Draycott with the murders of four women."

"Four?"

Oh, he was clever, Ryan thought. He would not reveal himself a second time.

"Ah, yes. Unfortunately, we found another body earlier today, but it hasn't been made public yet." Ryan affected a sigh. "To tell you the truth, I'm as shocked as you are. Draycott put on a good show, didn't he? He had us all fooled."

Edwards smirked.

"I would have thought his, ah, *superior* surgical skill would have ruled him out of those murders. If the press is to be believed, the killer was little more than a *hacker*, was he not?"

Careful, Ryan thought. *Softly, softly.*

"You know how the press like to sensationalise these things," Ryan said. "But we understand that the person who killed those women was unmatched in his field. Draycott naturally fits the bill."

Edwards said nothing but stepped slightly further away, closer to the girl who still lay recovering on a hospital bed. They could hear her mother murmuring to her, telling her she would be better soon.

"I must be getting back to my patient," Edwards said. "If you'd like to discuss anything, I'm sure I can make myself available later in my shift."

Ryan's eyes caught a small movement over Edwards' shoulder and the other man caught it too, turning to see Phillips hurrying down the corridor. When his sergeant spotted them, he came to an awkward stop and, in doing so, gave himself away.

When Edwards looked back at Ryan, the monster had been unleashed.

"Like I said, I must check my patient," he snarled. "It's amazing how quickly they can deteriorate, if left for too long. Children are so fragile."

To Ryan's horror, he stepped back into the recovery area.

"How are we doing, here?" he purred.

"Oh, fine, Doctor. Daisy's doing just fine," her mother said. It was nauseating, just to hear the gratitude in her voice, to see it etched into the worried lines of her face.

"Let's just have another check, shall we? I hope you don't mind if these two gentlemen observe? They're visiting consultants, from one of our sister hospitals," he lied.

"Oh, no, no. Not at all. Doctor Edwards has been marvellous," she told them. "Really marvellous."

"Long may it continue," Ryan said, holding the man's eyes across the table. He watched as Edwards reached into a locked cupboard and retrieved a fresh syringe, which he held in his hand like a weapon. "You're due a little holiday, aren't you, Edwards? You've been a busy man, lately."

"Exceptionally busy," Edwards agreed, flicking the little girl's nose as they watched in disgust. "But then, I've always kept myself busy."

Ryan's jaw hardened as he interpreted the message and knew that his suspicions had just been confirmed. The man had been operating quietly for years.

"You've really outdone yourself recently, it has to be said."

"Oh, you must be exhausted," the woman said. "Honestly, I don't know how you do it."

"If I had a penny for all the times I've heard that," Edwards said, and grinned at his own joke. "I consider my work to be…a kind of vocation."

"We need more doctors like you," she said.

Edwards looked across at Ryan and Phillips, and they could see the mania in his eyes as they heard the gentle tear of the syringe packet.

"Well, I think we've seen all we need to," Ryan said, feeling his blood race as he watched Edwards lift the girl's hand and check the IV link, every movement a greater threat than the last. "What do you say we move on, Edwards?"

"Oh, but I haven't finished checking little Daisy," he said. "I'm concerned about her breathing and I wonder if she might need a little more help."

Her mother's face instantly fell as she looked at her daughter, then at the man she thought had saved her.

"Your shift is ending soon," Ryan said, firmly. "We can take over here."

"That's very good of you," Edwards said, tapping the syringe as if giving the matter thought. "Unfortunately, I left my car at home this morning. I wonder if any of our mutual friends will be along to give me a lift?"

Phillips bunched his fists, thinking of the response teams that were on their way.

"Aye, they'll be along soon."

"Well, in that case, I might just take your advice."

A second later, Edwards disappeared behind the screen and they heard his running footsteps retreating down the corridor, leaving the woman and her daughter looking on in shock.

"Main entrance!" Ryan shouted to Phillips, and raced after him.

CHAPTER 33

The red telephone began to shrill again as Ryan sprinted down the corridor after Keir Edwards. He saw the upturned trolleys and shocked faces of the doctors and nurses Edwards left in his wake and almost barrelled into them as they milled in the corridors to witness the uproar.

"Move!" Ryan shouted, only narrowly avoiding a collision with Joan Stephenson as she threw herself back against the wall.

He heard shouts behind him as the ward fell into pandemonium, heard his shoes scraping against the linoleum floor as his legs pumped faster to keep up with his quarry.

He almost fell over a wheelchair user as he rounded the corner into the waiting area and stumbled past, ignoring the calls from the receptionist who demanded to know what was happening.

"What's happening? What's going on?"

They'd find out, soon enough.

He caught a flash of Edwards' scrubs as he shoved people aside and hurtled through the main entrance. Ryan burst out of the doors soon after and almost fell into the path of the blue-light ambulance pulling up nearby, stopping himself just in time.

He used his hands to push against the side of the van and then he was off again, sprinting full pelt across the tarmac in pursuit of the man who was less than thirty paces ahead of him. He saw Edwards pause at the pillared gates leading into the hospital car park, unsure which way to turn, then he ran straight ahead into the busy road.

As Ryan approached the gates, he understood what had spooked him. Patrol officers were approaching from both directions at a run, and the traffic was parting for squad cars whose screaming sirens and flashing lights told him their earlier orders to approach quietly had been overridden.

Everything had changed.

Edwards had made it across the street and was heading into the centre of town via a cut through some of the old, red-brick university buildings. The patrol officers acted swiftly and held back the cars so they parted like the Red Sea, allowing Ryan to pass across the street and continue the chase on foot.

Back at CID Headquarters, MacKenzie was kneading a low-grade tension headache and wondering whether she should have another coffee when the alert came through from the Control Room, via Phillips.

"Sweet Baby Jesus," she muttered, and contacted the Air Support Team, whose helicopter had a heat-tracking device and a sophisticated, long-range camera that might allow them to stay on Edwards' tail.

"Jack!"

Lowerson's head popped around the side of his computer.

"We've found him! It's Keir Edwards. He's making off on foot. Ryan's going after him."

Lowerson nearly fell off the chair he'd been swinging on.

"Right. Right," he repeated. "What now?"

MacKenzie told herself to be patient; he was still very new to all this and it wasn't as if they uncovered a serial killer every day of the week, let alone chased him through the streets.

"I need you to contact the railways and the airport and put them on notice. We're setting up a command centre here—"

Gregson burst into the Incident Room.

"Denise, tell me what the hell is going on."

"Jack, get on with it," she said, before turning back to the Superintendent.

"Sir, Control have just informed me that Ryan is pursuing a suspect on foot heading east from the Royal Victoria Infirmary. I've requested immediate Air Support—"

"It'll take too long," he cut across her. "I'll ring the local news channel and ask them to send out their press helicopter.

It'll cost us, but it'll save some time. I'll tell them to patch us into the live feed."

MacKenzie nodded.

"Phillips already has squad cars and foot support coming in from all directions. It seems they were already on the way by the time Edwards left the hospital grounds."

Gregson smiled slightly. Ryan had delivered a suspect just in time for his three o'clock deadline, after all.

"Keep me posted," he ordered, and headed back out to brief the Chief Constable.

Ryan's feet slid against wet flagstones as he ran through the university quad connecting the hospital compound and the city centre. Ordinarily, it was a peaceful corner of the city with a mixture of old and new architecture, housing budding architects and fine artists of the future.

Today, it provided the pathway for a killer as he fled beneath its hallowed arches and emerged into a wide, open pedestrian zone outside the Student Union building and the Northern Stage theatre. Further ahead, Edwards could see the city's spires and rooftops and a chance to lose himself among the crowds.

He also saw the police cars coming to a screaming halt before he could get there, blocking his pathway to the east. Behind him, Ryan was still coming on foot and off in the distance he could see more police following.

Edwards took it all in at a glance and then jerked to the left, hurrying down a single flight of stairs until he re-connected with Claremont Road and started to double back towards the hospital, having run in a wide circle.

Ryan's hand barely touched the metal rail as he flew down the stairs after him, along the pathway that would lead them back to Claremont Road. Nicola Cassidy had lived at the opposite end, but he had no idea where Edwards planned to go. He was surrounded by approaching police, either on foot or in cars. Over the sound of the traffic, he thought he heard the distant chug of a helicopter.

There was nowhere for Edwards to run.

But when Ryan's feet touched the pavement and he burst back onto the road, the man was nowhere to be found.

Panting from the exertion, Ryan spun in either direction, searching the street. To his right, the road into the city centre was quiet, with just a couple of pensioners walking along slowly, oblivious to the drama playing out nearby. To his left, he saw the flashing blue lights of approaching squad cars, but no sign of their suspect.

"Where the—"

One of the cars pulled up beside him and Phillips jumped out of the passenger side, having done the decent thing and hitched a ride to save himself a heart attack.

"Where is he? Which way did he go?"

Ryan made an angry sound and continued to search the street, jogging further along to crane his neck this way and that.

A bus moved ahead as the traffic lights turned green, revealing the entrance to the Hancock Museum of Natural

History. It was a classical building built upon raised ground overlooking the city centre and accessed via a footpath ramp from the road.

At the bottom of the ramp, a man dressed in work gear was swaying against the railing, clutching a wound to his head.

"There!" Ryan shouted. "Get a medic out here!"

With a quick glance both ways, he took his chance and sprinted across the road to where the man had now collapsed to the ground.

Phillips wasn't far behind and produced one of his all-purpose handkerchiefs, which he pressed to the side of the man's head.

"Which way did he go?" Ryan asked. "Which way? The museum?"

With every passing second, they were losing ground.

"Down there," the man gasped, feeling sick. "The tunnel. Down there."

Ryan looked around and saw something he had never noticed before. Cut into the side of the small hill where the museum rested was a circular wooden doorway standing open to reveal a pitch-black tunnel beyond. Yellow cones and red triangular signs had been arranged around it, warning, 'DANGER—MAINTENANCE WORK IN PROGRESS'.

"Let's get after him!" Phillips shouted, jogging towards the entrance to the tunnel.

"No," Ryan replied. "I need you to stay above ground. Find out where this tunnel leads and make sure we've got every exit covered. I'm not losing him again. I'll try to catch up with him and flush him out."

"Here! Take this with you!" Phillips said, chucking his radio across to Ryan, who caught it one-handed.

Ryan shoved the radio into his back pocket, took a deep breath and stepped inside.

CHAPTER 34

Ryan stepped carefully over the threshold and into the Victoria Tunnel, a subterranean wagonway running beneath the city of Newcastle for nearly four kilometres from the old Spital Tongues Colliery in the west of the city all the way to the River Tyne in the east. It lay sixty-five feet beneath the ground with a series of partially hidden entranceways, such as the one Ryan had just found. Large sections of the tunnel had already been renovated and were open to guided tours for the public; the remaining sections had either been left to dilapidate or were still being reconstructed.

But Ryan knew none of that.

He entered slowly and was grateful to find the first section of tunnel had been illuminated by makeshift lighting left by the unsuspecting workman who was injured outside. Scaffolding had been erected to support the crumbling inner walls and Ryan walked carefully beneath it, wary of the long shadows further ahead and of who might lurk within.

He was right to be wary.

Edwards stood at the far end of the scaffolding, his eyes trained on the entrance until he judged the time was right. When Ryan passed beneath the main scaffolding, he began to kick it away, grunting with the effort until the metal leg collapsed, bringing the rest of the structure down with it.

Ryan turned to run back but it was too late. He heard the creak of metal as it buckled overhead, and a fine sheen of dust rained down from the ceiling.

At the tunnel entrance, Phillips heard the thud of Edwards' boot against the scaffolding and hurried inside, only to be forced back again as the scaffolding tumbled down in a heap of solid metal.

"Ryan!" He gave an involuntary shout.

Inside, Ryan heard the ceiling splinter and threw himself to safety, looking back to watch the last light of the tunnel entrance disappear, taking his means of escape with it.

Trapped.

He was covered in a billowing cloud of dust which coated his skin and clogged his airway. He crawled away from the fresh pile of rubble, coughing the grit from his lungs until he could breathe freely again.

When the dust settled, only darkness remained.

Ryan heard muffled sounds coming from the tunnel entrance and knew it must be Phillips, but couldn't make out any words. He still had the radio in his pocket but, if he turned it on, it would alert Edwards to his location.

He kept it off and felt his way through the darkness, trailing his fingertips against the damp wall until he came to a fork in the main part of the tunnel. Each direction was pitch-black and completely silent except for the echo of his own breathing and the quiet drip of leaking moisture against the thick stone walls. As he descended deeper into the tunnel, the comforting thrum of civilisation disappeared and, in that moment, Ryan felt completely alone.

But he was not alone.

To his right, he heard something scrape against the edge of the tunnel, sending a faint echo down the length of it.

Ryan searched the darkness, fiddling with his mobile phone to bring up the torch setting and shine a light into the shadows. Its meagre light was swallowed by the all-encompassing darkness so that it barely illuminated more than a couple of feet ahead of him.

His fingers slipped and the torch switched off, plunging the tunnel into total darkness again. Ryan did not immediately switch it back on but held his breath, waiting for another sound. He stood completely still, shivering slightly as his body reacted to a sudden drop in temperature, listening for the sound he knew would come.

There.

It was almost impossible to judge distances, especially as it was unfamiliar territory and Ryan felt a momentary doubt.

He should turn back, wait for them to dig him out.

But as Phillips had known from the off, he would never be able to live with himself if his inaction led to more death, more waste and destruction.

He took a step forward, his feet sounding impossibly loud as they crunched against the floor, and he stopped dead again.

There was a taut silence, and then he heard soft laughter echoing down the tunnel, circling around his head.

"We were too late getting the helicopter in," MacKenzie told the superintendent, as they stood around a map of the city Ryan had pinned to the wall.

"Where is he now?"

"He's gone into the Victoria Tunnel, sir," she replied. "It runs beneath the city from east to west, built to transport coal from the colliery to the river in the Victorian era."

"How the hell did he get down there?"

"Phillips seems to think the route was unplanned, but we can't be sure. If he'd planned several murders in detail, it isn't outside the realms of possibility that he would have considered an escape route, if the time came."

"Get Ryan on the phone," he ordered.

"That's not possible, sir. Ryan went down into the tunnel in pursuit and the scaffolding collapsed behind him, probably orchestrated by Edwards. He hasn't made contact via radio yet and there's no telephone signal down there," she explained. "Phillips has a team working to dig out the rubble and go in after him."

Gregson swore.

"Show me the access points," he said.

"We haven't been able to find a map of the tunnel," she said, not bothering to hide her concern. "I've got Lowerson looking into it now. He's speaking to Northumbrian Water and Newcastle City Council to see what they have because there's nothing online."

Gregson thought of one of his best detectives trapped underground with a killer and felt something he hadn't experienced in a long time.

He felt frightened.

———

The rain continued to fall as Phillips stood with a team of police personnel outside the Hancock Museum entrance on Claremont Road, watching and helping as a crew from the renovation works team dug furiously to clear a safe pathway through the rubble.

Phillips tried the radio again.

"Ryan? Ryan, come in. Over."

Nothing.

Phillips gnawed at his lip, wondering what to do for the best, then rang MacKenzie's number.

She answered immediately.

"Frank, tell me some good news."

"I wish I could, love," he said unthinkingly, and immediately suffered a coughing fit.

"You alright?" she asked.

"Aye, sorry. I had some dust caught in my throat. Listen, it's been nearly twenty minutes and we still haven't got through the worst of it—and I haven't heard from Ryan. I'm worried."

"We've heard nothing here, either," she said. "We've got a team watching Edwards' house, in case he finds another exit and tries to go home."

"He can't hope to get out of the tunnel without being caught," Phillips said, then felt his stomach dip. "Unless he doesn't plan to escape."

"What do you mean?"

"Ryan's down there with him, alone."

Back at CID Headquarters, MacKenzie looked across at the photograph of their friend, Sharon Cooper, and felt her heart tighten.

"Get in there after him, Frank, as quick as you can."

"Yes, ma'am."

CHAPTER 35

Ryan continued onward, heading along the tunnel as it passed beneath St Thomas's church, a quarter of a mile further east of where Phillips worked hard to clear the entrance beside the museum.

"There's no way out of this! Turn yourself in!"

His voice ricocheted around the walls, spiralling until it was lost somewhere in the darkness.

There was no reply.

His feet continued their careful progress and he was grateful to find that the floor had been laid with rough concrete at some stage or another, which made the going easier underfoot.

He raised his phone torch again to shine a miserable white light a few paces ahead, then heard the ominous 'beep' that signalled his battery was running low.

"Uh-oh," a voice called out, sounding closer this time.

Ryan held the torch aloft and peered into the darkness, but he could see no further than the end of his own arm.

"You want to know *why*, don't you, Ryan?"

Edwards' voice whispered along the scaly edges of the wall, reaching into Ryan's mind and toying with what he found there.

"You're desperate to know, aren't you?"

"You're desperate to tell me," Ryan called out. "Why don't you?"

Why don't you...why don't you...

More soft laughter.

"I've watched you, Ryan. I watched your face when the woman died and wondered what it would be like to *feel* the way you do for all the miserable nobodies in the world."

Ryan followed the voice, edging closer while Edwards spoke.

"Come now, this is very one-sided," Edwards said, and his voice sounded further off again. "Tell me, how did a man of your breeding and education come to be a murder detective? Surely, your future was mapped in a very different way."

Ryan stopped again, unnerved to know that Edwards had looked into his background.

"You like playing the hero, don't you, Maxwell? The name suits you, by the way. Can't imagine why you'd want to change it."

Ryan walked into something solid and stumbled backwards, bracing himself for impact, ready to face another attack, but it was only a concrete wall blocking the pathway ahead.

It seemed Edwards had vanished into thin air.

Ryan ran his fingertips around the edge of the concrete and found a narrow gap running down the edge, just narrow enough for a man to squeeze through. He realised he had stumbled into a blast wall and common sense told him it must have been installed sometime during the Second World War. It presented another challenge because the tunnel had gone quiet again and it was impossible to know if Edwards would be waiting just around the other side, if he risked moving around it.

Once again, Ryan thought of turning back and taking his chances that Phillips would have cleared the entrance at the Hancock Museum, but he had gone too far to turn back now. Instead, he flattened himself against the wall and edged slowly, moving inch by inch as he felt his way around it.

The blast wall curved around into a zig-zag, a tunnel within a tunnel that he followed with extreme caution until he emerged on the other side and back into the main tunnel.

Suddenly, he sensed a presence nearby.

"Hello, Ryan."

Instinct alone had him sidestepping Edwards' arm as it swung out to attack and Ryan felt a slight gust of air against the side of his face. He could see nothing; there wasn't a single shard of light inside the tunnel and his movements were guided by his other senses.

He hunkered to the floor, listening.

There.

Ryan wasn't sure if he heard or felt the tiny motion, but he took his chance, rising up to catch Edwards in a tackle that brought them both crashing to the floor. He heard the air gushing out of the man's chest and then they were writhing, spitting, clawing at one another, little more than two animals battling for survival.

He tried to pin Edwards' arms, but they were a physical match and Edwards would always have the upper hand for he had nothing to lose and everything to gain.

He was also entirely without scruples.

Ryan felt something sharp sink into the skin of his upper arm and realised it was Edwards' teeth. He kicked out, bucking away from the animal that sought his blood, and a moment later there came the sound of light footsteps retreating into the darkness.

His skin burned, and Ryan stemmed the blood flow as best he could. His hands were shaking as he reached for the police radio in his jeans pocket, but he found it missing.

Ryan felt around the ground in case it had been dislodged during the tussle and was relieved to find it had been thrown clear. He grasped it again, clutching it tightly as his only means of communication with the outside world.

CHAPTER 36

Phillips told himself not to despair when the workmen retreated from the entrance to the tunnel, shaking their heads despondently.

"Sorry," they said. "The ceiling's completely caved in. Every time we clear a path, more starts falling down. We'd need to get a proper scaffolding team in here and a bigger team just to make a dent."

Phillips put a call through to MacKenzie.

"Mac? I need to know where the other entrances are to the tunnel. There has to be more than one."

"We're looking for them now, Frank," she said, and he took comfort from the warmth of her voice resonating across the wires. "Lowerson had no luck with the council or the water board, so he's trying to chase down one of the volunteers who give tours of the tunnel. If anybody knows, it'll be them."

"Tell him to hurry up," he said. "We can't get through here; the entrance is completely sealed, and it'd take too long just trying to make it passable. God knows what might be happening in there while we waste time trying."

Suddenly, his radio crackled into life and he ended the call abruptly, hurrying to snatch up his receiver.

"Phillips? This is Ryan. Over."

Phillips breathed a sigh of relief.

"Ryan? You gave us a run for our money there, lad. Are you okay? Over."

"I'm okay, just a couple of scratches. He's still in the tunnel, approximately a quarter of a mile ahead if he's moving at a steady speed. Have you been able to clear the rubble from the entrance? We need an armed response team and some lights down here. Over."

Phillips wished it could be that easy.

"There's no way in. The entrance is still blocked and can't be cleared. We're looking to find the next available exit. Over."

Ryan felt a shiver of fear as he leaned back against the blast wall. The cold was sinking into his bones and the darkness was beginning to play games with his head.

For one thing, he thought he smelled gas.

He did smell gas.

"I think there's a gas leak somewhere nearby," he told Phillips. "I need to move forward because it'll spread. Contact me when you have a map of the exits. I've just passed the first blast wall after the museum, heading east. Over."

"Will do. Chin up, lad. We'll get you out of there as quickly as we can."

Ryan clipped the radio onto his belt and left it crackling. The noise alerted Edwards to his location, but he didn't care anymore; he needed the familiar sound of it fizzing away as he was forced to continue into the darkness that seemed never to end.

Lowerson re-entered the Incident Room at a run, armed with a faxed copy of an archive map belonging to the trust who operated guided tours.

MacKenzie hurried across to meet him.

"What've you got for me, Jack?"

He caught his breath after taking the stairs two at a time.

"There are technically seven entranceways into the tunnel," he said, rolling out a civil plan dating back to wartime. "This plan was made when the council was converting the tunnel into an air raid shelter, so you can see where the blast walls are located."

"Phillips heard from Ryan. He's okay. He says he passed the first blast wall after the museum entrance on Claremont Road."

"What about Edwards?"

"Somewhere down there, not far ahead of him. Let's focus on getting Ryan out and getting some teams in place beside the other entranceways."

They found Ryan's last known position on the hand-drawn map and estimated he had walked half a mile east of the museum.

"The tunnel follows Claremont Road," she said. "It runs past the hospital into the city centre, skirting past the Hancock Museum and St. Thomas's church, then through the city centre towards Byker and Shieldfield in the east, eventually ending up in Ouseburn beside the water."

"Only two entrances are in general use," Lowerson said. "The entrance beside the Hancock Museum wasn't supposed to be operational and the same can be said of an entrance on Crawhall Road. According to the tour guide I spoke to, an emergency exit was installed at Crawhall Road around 2008 or 2009, which could be opened from the inside and gives access to street level. They say the entrance beside St Thomas's church is impassable as the ramp leading to ground level hasn't been cleared of years' worth of debris, but you never know."

MacKenzie nodded.

"We need teams on the ground outside all working exits," she said. "We'll flush the bastard out."

"What about Ryan?"

"He has to follow the same direction as Edwards," she said. "We'll tell him to head for Crawhall Road."

"It's a way off," Lowerson said. "Another mile further along the tunnel. That's a long way in the dark."

"I know that, Jack. But there's no other choice."

CHAPTER 37

Police response teams were stationed outside every known entrance to the tunnel and roadblocks were set up in a quarter-mile radius of each one. While Ryan made his slow, painstaking journey through the long tunnel below, Phillips traced its pathway above ground, estimating Ryan's position.

"Sir, it would be easier if we just headed to the first exit," one of the constables suggested, and Phillips rounded on him.

"Don't tell me what would be easier. Easier for who? For me?" He shook his head. "My lad's trapped down there with that bloody nutter gunnin' for him and a gas leak spreading. I'll walk alongside him, even if one of us is below ground."

He spoke into his handset again.

"Ryan? You still down there? Over."

The radio crackled into life.

"Where else would I be, Frank?"

Phillips smiled.

"I dunno. Might have dug your way out, by now. That's the trouble with your generation; always expecting to have things handed to them on a plate."

Somewhere beneath the ground twenty metres further east of where Phillips walked, Ryan managed a laugh.

"Yeah. Nothing but lazy. If it'd been you down here, I'll bet you'd have dug a new tunnel, by now, eh, Frank?"

"Darn right, I would," Phillips told him, keeping an even pace as he consulted the directions MacKenzie had given him. "You passed that second blast wall, yet?"

"No, not yet."

"It'll be coming up soon. There'll also be another disused entrance coming up on your left, in around fifty metres," he said, looking up at St. Thomas's church. "Sorry to tell you, there's no way out of there."

There was a prolonged silence as Ryan dealt with that blow.

"How much further, Frank?" He asked quietly, as his feet stumbled onward through the darkness.

Phillips heard the anxiety in Ryan's voice and did his best to keep things light.

"Ah, just a bit further. I'm walking with you, lad."

Ryan thought of his sergeant tracing his footsteps above ground and was deeply moved.

"Frank?"

There came a crackle.

"Aye, lad?"

"Don't think you're going to get a pay rise out of this, mind. You just had one, back in January."

Phillips grinned.

"It was worth a try."

Ryan continued his slow journey east, stopping every so often to touch a hand to the wall. It was stupid, he supposed, but after walking so far in complete darkness a sense of unreality had crept in, as if it were all a bad dream conjured up by his imagination.

But the dream was real. He felt the damp wall on either side of him and could sense there was not much clearance above his head. He had no way of knowing whether Edwards was fifty paces ahead of him, or five; he might have passed him along the way.

His body was attuned to every change in atmosphere, every scent on the air. If the man was near, he would know it.

"You still there, lad?"

Ryan lifted the receiver again, feeling the wound in his upper arm ache.

"Yeah, I'm here."

"Not much further now," Phillips said.

"You said that half an hour ago," Ryan muttered.

"Yeah, but this time I mean it. The Crawhall Street exit is coming up in another thirty yards or so."

Phillips spotted the police vehicles up ahead and it was like reaching the Promised Land.

"Any sign of Edwards?" Ryan asked.

"No word yet," Phillips replied, and found that odd. Edwards must have heard the police presence above ground and decided to push on towards the next exit. "There's only a finite number of ways he can get out of that tunnel. He has to show himself, eventually."

As they were talking, Ryan paused to sniff the air. It was heavy with the thick aroma of sewage and a thought struck him, suddenly.

"Is there a sewage track nearby?"

"I can ask MacKenzie to check," Phillips told him. "Why'd you ask?"

"I can smell it," Ryan said. "And rats are drawn to sewage, aren't they?"

"Aye, they are. I'll get onto it."

Ryan felt a light gust of rancid air hit his face at the side and knew he must be passing an adjacent tunnel. He couldn't be sure, but he thought there was a sliver of light shining from somewhere inside it, from the streetlamps above.

"I think he found a manhole," Ryan muttered. "He's back on the streets."

CHAPTER 38

When Ryan reached the emergency exit at Crawhall Street, he understood for the first time what it meant to see light at the end of the tunnel. Up ahead, Phillips was waiting for him just inside the entrance and was surrounded by several film lights on loan from the CSIs, creating a blinding halo around his stocky figure.

"Took your time, didn't you?"

Phillips clasped Ryan's hand and tugged him the rest of the way out into the open air, then watched him turn his face up to the sky and inhale a series of deep breaths. After a moment, he slipped his anorak over Ryan's shoulders and steered him gently towards one of the squad cars, where he slumped against the car seat.

"Thanks for keeping me sane," Ryan muttered.

"Some things are beyond the power of my magic," Phillips quipped. "But, as far as it goes, you're welcome."

The car moved away, back towards CID Headquarters.

"I'm going to drop you off at home," Phillips said. "You need some rest."

Ryan's eyes flew open.

"No, Frank. I can't rest while Edwards is somewhere out there. We've got a manhunt on our hands. People are depending on us to bring him in."

"You're dead on your feet," Phillips argued.

"That won't stop him."

Phillips couldn't argue with that.

"Have we got a team stationed at Edwards house, in case he tries to go back?'

"Aye, MacKenzie took care of that. Faulkner's going through the place and they've seized boxes of stuff, already. They found photographs," Phillips added.

Ryan fell silent, thinking of the gruesome images a man like Edwards might choose to capture and keep for posterity.

"He needs the photographs to keep him going, between kills," he said, in a voice devoid of emotion. "There may be other trophies. Other women."

"He has a type," Phillips said. "With the exception of Sharon Cooper, they've all been young brunettes. That'll be for a reason."

"We may never know the reason why," Ryan said. "He as good as told me that, himself."

Phillips gave him a considering look and wondered what passed between Ryan and Edwards in the tunnel. Perhaps that was another thing he would never know.

———

There was a rapturous welcome awaiting Ryan as he stepped back inside the Incident Room. The staff of

Operation Summer broke into spontaneous applause and there was plenty of the kind of back-slapping that Ryan normally detested.

"Thanks," he said, after the noise died down. "As you can see, I'm still in one piece. We have a name, we have a face. Let's find him."

The room was re-energised now that its leader had returned, and police staff scattered back to their desks dealing with a constant stream of information that was trickling through. Every media source was reporting the manhunt and the country was gripped in a state of fear and limbo, afraid once again to leave their homes or answer their door to strangers.

"Mac, tell me what we've got," Ryan said, pouring himself a generous cup of what he assumed was coffee from an urn sitting on the side.

"We've issued an All Ports Warning," she said, running a sharp eye over his face. "The stations, ferry ports and airports are on red alert. Gregson's managing the press and they've plastered his face all over the news."

"Good," Ryan said. "People need to know what to look for."

"That's what we thought. Durham CID have drafted in extra patrol officers, so we've got a bigger presence on the streets."

Ryan nodded.

"What about his credit card company? His bank? Has there been any activity?"

"Already spoken to them," Lowerson said. "There's been no activity on any of his bank cards since early this morning, when he bought a coffee on his way to work."

"He's smart," Ryan said. "He won't make it easy for us. He didn't keep his bag of tools on site at the hospital and he didn't leave them at home—or did he?"

MacKenzie shook her head.

"We found photographs hidden in his study but nothing that looks like a murder weapon. Best guess is, he keeps a storage box or locker somewhere and stores everything there."

Ryan thought for a moment.

"Does his house have a garage?"

"No, it's a terrace in Jesmond," MacKenzie replied, referring to one of the city's most expensive areas. "Most people park on the road."

"Or buy garage space, somewhere," Ryan suggested. "Jack?"

"On it, boss." He bustled away to start searching.

"Let's assume he keeps a ready-bag in a separate, secure location," Ryan said. "It'd be the first place he goes after leaving the tunnel."

"He might still be in there," Phillips said. "Every exit is covered and there's been no sign of him."

"Even the one at St. Thomas's? He could have found a way through," Ryan said. "And we didn't account for the sewage pipe that runs as an offshoot. One of the drain covers was ajar."

"How could you tell?"

"It was the only light source in the entire place," Ryan said shortly. There would come a time when he'd have to think about the time he'd spent inside that tunnel, but it would not be now. He could not allow the remembered fear to hinder the work they needed to do.

Phillips understood.

"We've already got a team doing a search of the area around that drain cover. I'll get in touch with the team on the ground and tell them to check the other manhole covers for any sign of tampering. It'll give us a starting point and we can look at the surrounding CCTV once we know his exit point."

Ryan took a long drink of the lukewarm coffee in his hand.

"What we really need to understand is what he hopes to achieve. Does he believe he'll get away, or does he have some other goal in mind?"

"We'll find out, soon enough."

CHAPTER 39

The city entered a state of lockdown.

The Lord Mayor conducted a televised conference alongside DCS Gregson and a number of local officials with the notable absence of DCI Ryan, who was of the view that his time was better spent searching for Edwards than merely talking about it. The people of Newcastle and the surrounding areas were warned to remain indoors and not to venture outside unless it was an emergency, and to report anyone acting suspiciously or matching Edwards' description.

But, in their experience, there was nothing worse than well-meaning 'do-goodery', as Phillips called it. Armed with a very small amount of information, suddenly every man and woman in the city fancied themselves as Columbo and weren't shy about it, either.

The telephones in the Incident Room rang off their hooks as people reported near-constant sightings of the Hacker, with conflicting reports of people claiming to see

341

him at a pub in Gateshead whilst simultaneously claiming to see him stealing a car on the opposite side of town. It was a gruelling task to sift through all the reports and try to make sense of them, but that was only the tip of the iceberg.

Moments of panic and disorder were the perfect breeding ground for career criminals and there had been a spate of thefts reported in the last couple of hours as they took advantage of the city's weakness. Police resources were already at breaking point and they could spare very few personnel to go through the motions of taking down statements and providing crime reference numbers.

Armed police guarded the railway station and the airport, and army reservists had come down from their barracks in the Otterburn Ranges in Northumberland to assist.

Throughout it all, Ryan couldn't help but think of Stephanie Bernard, whose death had not yet been reported and had, in any event, been superseded by the manhunt.

How Edwards must be enjoying himself.

―――――――――

Natalie Finley-Ryan watched the news from the comfort of Ryan's large, corner sofa. Every now and then, she dipped her hand into a bag of crisps and munched while she listened to reports of a foot chase that had taken her brother down beneath the city. Photographers had captured images of him arriving back at CID, and he'd looked exhausted.

As if she had conjured him up, her phone began to ring.

"Nat?"

"Hey," she said. "I'm so glad you're okay. I've just been hearing about it on the news. Are you hurt?"

Ryan thought of the bandage on his arm covering the small chunk Edwards had ripped from his skin, but it was minor in comparison to what could have been.

"I'm fine. Just a few scrapes."

Natalie would believe that when she saw it.

"It's going to be another long night here," he said, and she heard him stifle a yawn. "I just wanted to check everything was alright with you. Did you remember to lock the doors and windows?"

She looked across at the enormous floor-to-ceiling windows and wondered how anybody would manage to scale a wall that high.

"The front door's locked, the windows are secure," she said. "Mum was on the phone, earlier. She's worried about you."

"She's always worried about me. It's part of the job."

"This seems different," she said, refusing to be fobbed off. "Look after yourself out there. I don't know what any of us would do without you."

Ryan was taken aback by the strength of her emotion.

"I love you, kid."

"I love you, too."

They searched every nook and every cranny while Ryan contacted everybody at the hospital who had worked with

Edwards and sent officers around to their houses to double-check they were not harbouring him. Keir Edwards had been universally liked and respected, to such a degree that some of his colleagues refused to believe it could be true that he had murdered four women, maybe more.

It was startling, the extent to which he had cultivated his 'nice guy' persona. Nobody could believe that *lovely* Doctor Edwards could be a cold-blooded killer. They would not accept that they had been duped, conned into believing that he'd been anything other than what he was.

A raider. A killer. A man without any compassion for his fellow human beings.

Ryan had already observed that people were predisposed to apply positive attributes to people they found attractive, and Edwards fell squarely into that category. It was all too easy to see how he could have charmed the women he later murdered, using his eyes and his smile against their better nature. He chose carefully, too. Aside from Sharon Cooper, his victims had all been young brunettes in their twenties; not children, but not yet sufficiently seasoned by life experience to see the danger until it was too late.

The search continued.

CHAPTER 40

It was nearly two o'clock in the morning by the time Faulkner's team called it a night at Edwards' home and MacKenzie told the surplus patrol staff to stand down for the night. They maintained an army presence, but the city was like a ghost town, its streets empty and glistening from the rain that had fallen on-and-off throughout the day.

"It's time you got some rest, lad. I'm surprised you're still upright," Phillips said.

Ryan admitted he was only barely standing, and his eyes were so blurred he could barely see his computer screen.

"Come on, I'm driving you home."

Ryan had already sent half of the team home for the evening to catch up on some rest, but a skeleton staff remained.

"I'll watch over things here and let you know if there's any word," Phillips promised. "You know it makes sense.'

"I can drive myself," Ryan protested, nearly falling over as he stood up.

"I bet you haven't eaten, either," Phillips said sternly. "Howay, the Pie Van's still open."

"At this hour?"

"Why, aye," Phillips said. "He's canny, the bloke who runs it. He knows we've all been stuck in here and none of us can face the pasta bake in the staff canteen. He's been doing a roaring trade all day."

After they'd made an obligatory stop for a steak and ale pie and washed it down with something equally nutritious, they made their way across town.

Within minutes, Ryan's eyelids drooped, and he fell asleep against the passenger window. Phillips glanced across at him and allowed his face to soften as he looked at the man who was his closest friend. Neither of them had said as much because they didn't need to, but he would never forget how Ryan had been there for him when Laura had passed away. Ryan had put up with his anger and grief all those months with quiet sympathy. He'd bought him a pint when he'd needed it and given him work when he'd needed the distraction. They could not have come from two more different worlds and, yet, they had forged a friendship.

Hell, it was more than that.

They were like family.

Ryan could feel the shirt clinging to his back as he slammed out of Phillips' car. The day had dragged on, hour after painful hour, and there was still no end in sight. Edwards was still out there, somewhere in the night.

The river shimmered to his right like a black snake, rippling its way towards the sea. His eyes were like pinpricks after endless hours without rest and the burden of stress he'd carried for days. His heart was weary with failure, knowing there could be another one tonight.

"Try to get some sleep, son," Phillips said, from the driver's seat.

Ryan mumbled something unintelligible and headed towards the entrance of his apartment building. The streets were empty and only a handful of lights flickered in the other apartments. He looked up at the top floor and realised that one of them was his.

Natalie must have waited up for him.

He thought of his sister: bright and beautiful with a mane of long dark hair and eyes the same shade of grey as his own, inherited from their mother. He didn't expect her to come and look after him and, in some ways, he would rather she wasn't there to witness the aftermath of the day he'd put in.

All he wanted was bed and oblivion.

He waved Phillips off, making sure the door was shut behind him, then dragged himself over to the lift. Normally, he took the stairs, but he couldn't find the energy to manage them tonight.

As the doors swished open and he stepped onto the top floor landing, the first thing he noticed was that his front door was ajar.

———

Had Natalie left the door unlocked?

Ryan frowned, black brows drawing together in an angry line. At a time when women were living in fear of attack, and knowing there was a man out there killing women just like her, she had no right to be so reckless.

He pushed the door open, preparing to deliver a few choice words about home safety, and froze in the doorway. Fear hit him like a wall.

Blood rushed in his ears as he moved slowly forward to see what rested on a small white tray on a table in the hallway. Three greying human fingers had been arranged into a teepee, propping up a card bearing the message, 'CATCH ME IF YOU CAN'.

His stomach performed a series of somersaults and his teeth began to chatter, but he reverted to training. His eyes scanned every corner of the room, searching every crevice for signs of Edwards but there was nothing. Nobody.

His hands fumbled to find his phone and he pressed speed-dial for Phillips' number.

"Pick up. For God's sake, pick up."

But the man was driving.

Ryan put a call through to the Control Room, requesting immediate assistance, and slid the phone back into his pocket. He moved carefully from room to room towards his bedroom and the authorised firearm he kept in a locked box on the top shelf of his wardrobe.

He never made it that far.

He pushed open the door to his spare bedroom and saw that his sister was seated on a chair in the centre of the room, so he would see her as soon as he came in. The central lights blazed overhead, illuminating the sickly colour of her skin. Her head slumped forward, and her body was unmoving, tied into place by long strands of surgical tape.

He didn't know if she was still alive.

Exhaustion and training forgotten, Ryan surged forward to check her pulse and release her from the ties. Panic and love swamped him in equal measure, overtaking self-preservation.

The man who watched him judged it the perfect moment to strike.

Edwards lunged from behind and Ryan turned too late, seeing a flash of movement as a pressure syringe plunged into the side of his neck. He tried to fight, to pull it from his skin, but his body was already shutting down as he fell to his knees and into the oblivion he had wished for.

CHAPTER 41

Ryan opened his eyes to a blistering headache.

He was in the living area of his apartment and, remarkably, his arms and legs had not been tied. They didn't need to be, he realised.

They would not move.

Across the room, he saw the monster hovering beside his sister and he tried to leap up from his chair, but the drugs prevented his body from responding to the frantic order.

Edwards glanced behind him to where Ryan now lay in a heap on the floor, struggling to drag himself up.

"Sedative," he offered. "It's obviously working well."

The bastard was right, Ryan thought. He couldn't feel a thing in his legs as he lay beached on the floor, but there was movement in his arms. With silent, subtle movements he reached behind to the pocket of his jeans, feeling around for his mobile phone.

It wasn't there.

He looked across to the dining table and spotted the contents of his pockets sitting on the top.

"What do you want?" he managed, not recognising the sound of his own voice.

"For one thing, I'd like this ridiculous game of cat and mouse to end," Edwards replied. "It's been fun. Don't think I haven't enjoyed knowing you were always a few steps behind me, plodding along in your interminable way, but I'd like to regain my freedom."

"Get out!"

"Tut, tut. After all the time you've spent trying to find me, I'd have thought you'd be a bit more welcoming. If I hadn't invited myself over, who knows when you might have found me, if at all?"

Ryan used his hands to grip the carpet and drag himself along, inch by painstaking inch. Unperturbed, Edwards strolled across to one of the dining chairs and dragged it across to where he had placed Natalie, in the centre of the room like a showpiece. He seated himself beside her, crossing one elegant, suit-clad leg over the other. Ryan thought he recognised the suit as one of his own.

"Get away from her!"

He tried to heave himself upwards, crying out in frustration when his body would not cooperate.

Edwards trailed a finger over Natalie's unconscious cheek.

"She should be coming around any time now. We'll have a nice little chat, the three of us."

"Not her," Ryan begged. "Please, not her."

Edwards raised an eyebrow.

"I bet that hurt your pride, just a little. The mighty DCI Ryan reduced to begging. On his *knees*, no less."

"If you want me to beg, that's what I'll do. I'm begging you now. Please don't kill her. Don't kill my sister."

Edwards smiled.

"You don't understand, do you? Didn't you ever think that I might be following your movements, just as closely as you were following mine? Having her here in your home, you placed her in front of me like an offering. A challenge to the brave. You must have known I wouldn't be able to resist her."

He trailed another finger across Natalie's bare thigh, dressed in the short pyjamas she'd worn for bed.

"She's a real beauty, this one."

Ryan felt bile rise in his throat.

"Take me, instead."

"Oh, I will."

Edwards gave Natalie a couple of sharp slaps. Her head rolled back as she struggled to the surface, and he drew out a long, surgical knife.

"No!"

Ryan clawed his way across the carpet, willing his body to move. Edwards watched him as if he were a strange oddity.

"Save your energy," he said. "You may need it."

"My team are on their way!" Ryan shouted, wondering where the hell they could be. It had been a long time since he'd called through to the Control Room.

Edwards smiled again.

"I took the liberty of calling again to explain there'd been a false alarm. We sound very alike, you and I, and you'd given your passcode in such a helpful way, earlier."

Ryan felt the last of his hopes dwindle to nothing.

Natalie's eyelids swept upwards. Confusion and terror played across her face and she looked away, meeting Ryan's desperate eyes across the room.

He read the acceptance, the dreadful knowledge of what was to come.

"*No!*" He dragged himself forward again, like a dead weight.

"Say 'goodbye'," Edwards said.

A scream broke free as Ryan watched him take a handful of Natalie's hair and tug it back, exposing the slim column of her throat. Adrenaline surged through his body, finally propelling him upwards. He stumbled across the floor, arms outstretched to prevent the fall of Edwards' knife.

But he was too late.

The blade swept a long graceful line across her neck and a river of blood gushed forth, fanning a warm arc over Ryan's upturned face.

He watched her body fall to the ground, as if in slow motion. He felt her fingertips brush his own and he tried to grasp them, to hold her close. But in his heart, he knew he was too late. Wild anger surged through his veins and he rounded on her killer, acting on instinct alone. He caught the look of surprise on Edwards' face before his hands clamped around the man's throat. He never knew where he found the strength, but he saw Edwards' eyes bulging in his head, felt the rush of his blood straining through his arteries as he gasped for air. Ryan realised he was crying, tears coursing down his face as he did what he had sworn never to do.

To take another life.

His arms were shaking by now, but he felt nothing; only a hollow emptiness where his heart had once been. He felt Edwards' hands scratching his face, trying to claw his way free, and he knew that the end was close.

Dimly, he heard somebody burst through the door behind him. He thought he heard Philips shout to him.

"No! No, lad!"

The mist faded and his hands loosened on the man's throat. He fell back, shivering and sobbing while the police rushed forward to where Edwards lay in the foetal position, dragging air into his burning lungs. Ryan was shaking so hard, his teeth chattered. His body was reacting badly to the cocktail of drugs and adrenaline, but he forced himself to crawl across to where his sister lay in a heap on the floor.

"*Natalie*," he whispered, brokenly.

He kneeled beside her, cradling her head gently in his lap, smoothing back the hair from her forehead. He began to rock back and forth.

Philips watched him with a heavy heart, and shooed away the medics who would have interrupted Ryan's final moments with his sister.

"Give him a minute," he murmured.

Eventually, he laid a gentle hand on Ryan's shoulder.

"It's time to go," he said gently.

"I'm not leaving her," Ryan said, and continued to rock.

"You can go with her. We'll make sure she's well looked after."

"It's my fault, Frank. She was here because of me and she died because of me."

"No—" Phillips began, but Ryan wasn't listening.

He watched them drag Edwards to his feet, restraining his hands as he continued to fight. For a moment, their eyes locked and a single message of mutual hatred was exchanged before he was led away.

EPILOGUE

There were candid photos of Ryan that morning as they'd transported him by stretcher to the hospital, but even the worst rags refused to buy them. Instead, they printed Edwards' face next to those of his five known victims and paired it with the headline:

HACKER TAKES FINAL VICTIM

Phillips had ordered a complete media ban in the hospital room where Ryan lay, having been transported from the emergency ward onto the psychiatric ward for observation. He had not uttered more than a handful of words since he'd arrived, not since his parents had visited him and been turned away.

"Your mum and dad are here again," Phillips told him, from the single armchair in Ryan's private room. "They want to see you."

Ryan shook his head.

"Your mum—she's in a bad way, lad. She needs to see you."

Ryan turned on him with such a look of despair, it brought a lump to Phillips' throat.

"I can't stand to see her, to see the look in her eyes. It was my fault," Ryan said again. "She'll never be able to think of me in the same way again."

"You're wrong," his mother said, from the doorway. "You're very wrong."

Eve Finley-Ryan stepped inside the room, her cheeks hollowed and her eyes shadowed by grief. Ryan's father was beside her, an older version of himself with a shock of white-grey hair and eyes that were pools of incredible sadness.

Phillips stood and moved aside, to give them the privacy they needed.

Eve sank onto the chair beside her son, her strong, handsome son who carried the weight of the world on his shoulders. It was too much for anybody to bear.

She took his hand and held onto it when he would have pulled away.

"I want to tell you two things," she said, and her voice shook with emotion. "The first is that we love you, so very much."

A tear tracked down his face, but he would not meet her eyes. Eve moved to perch on the bed beside him, so she could reach up and smooth the dark hair away from his face.

"The other thing you need to know is that it *wasn't your fault.*" Her daughter was lost to her and there was a hole in her heart, one that would never heal. But her boy was not to blame for that.

Ryan's face crumpled and she rubbed her palm against his cheek, as she used to do when he was a child.

"My boy," she murmured, though he was a grown man.

"I almost killed him," Ryan whispered. "With these hands, I almost killed a man."

Eve's lip trembled, then she took both his hands in her own, warming them.

"You witnessed something nobody should ever have to see. But you're better than that—that monster, Ryan. You stopped yourself, before it was too late. You have nothing to reproach yourself for."

Ryan heard the words, but could not bring himself to believe them.

"Please, son. Come back with us," his father said. "Let us look after you."

Ryan turned away, and his eye caught on a decorative coaster sitting on the bedside table. It was an image of the castle on Lindisfarne, a tiny island separated from the mainland twice a day, sixty miles north along the Northumbrian coastline. They said it was a place of sanctuary where it was possible to think, to reflect. Perhaps it would be a good idea to turn his back on the world, at least for a few weeks.

"I need to get away for a while," he said, in an odd, emotionless voice. "I'll keep in touch, I promise. I just—I can't be around people, for a while."

His mother looked down at their hands but nodded, trying to understand.

"Where do you plan to go?"

"Holy Island."

The sixty-mile drive from Newcastle city centre to the remote island of Lindisfarne was faster than Phillips would have liked. There hadn't been nearly enough time to try to talk him out of it, nor to remind his friend of all the people who cared about his wellbeing and would rather have kept him close. He stole a glance at Ryan's profile in the passenger seat and then back at the scenic lane which wound its way through the countryside towards the sea, then heaved a sigh.

It had been a week since Ryan had been discharged from the hospital and four days since they had buried his sister at the family home in Devonshire. Phillips had been in attendance, at Ryan's invitation, alongside MacKenzie and Gregson. He'd stood a few rows behind his friend inside a pretty little church packed to the rafters with family and friends who had come to pay their last respects to Natalie Finley-Ryan, and had watched Ryan standing tall, his spine ramrod straight as a priest spoke of healing and forgiveness. He'd watched Ryan's mother reach out to him, needing to hold her remaining child close, and had seen that spine stiffen through the material of his fine black suit. With quiet admiration, he'd watched his friend shake hands and thank well-wishers, his face shuttered as they subjected him to endless reminisces about his sister, which only served to remind him of the enormity of what had been lost.

Pain, Phillips thought. So much pain.

The sun broke through the clouds overhead and cast long, hazy rays of dappled light through the trees lining the roadside but Ryan saw none of it, his thoughts were far away and remote; snatched memories of his sister he tried to capture and hold close to his heart. He saw her as a child playing hide-and-seek, then as a teenager arguing over something trivial. A thousand flashing images of a life only half lived.

"Penny for them," Phillips murmured, breaking into his reverie.

Ryan merely shook his head and turned to stare out of the window at the passing landscape. As they rounded a bend, the island appeared before them, rising up from the sea like an apparition, shrouded in mist. The tide was out, revealing an ancient causeway that allowed safe passage across from the mainland twice a day. It had been the pathway for saints and pilgrims since time immemorial and, though he would not consider himself a religious man, there was a sense of peace in the air; a serenity awaiting him on the little scrap of earth where a community had endured wind and sea for a thousand years after its priory was first built.

Perhaps he, too, could learn to endure.

"I can walk from here, Frank," he said quietly.

"I can give you a lift across—"

"I appreciate it," Ryan cut in. "But I could use the walk."

"It'll do you no good, hiding away from the world, away from your friends—"

"It'll just be until the worst is over," Ryan said. "I need time, Frank. I'll ask Gregson for a sabbatical; it's what the psychologist recommended, anyway."

Phillips nodded, wishing there was more he could say, more he could do.

"You'll call me, if you need me?"

Ryan paused in the act of reaching for the door and gave his sergeant a hard hug, which was returned.

"Mind how you go," Phillips said, with a catch in his voice. "They say, God and the Devil both walk on that island."

"There's only one way to find out."

With that, Ryan stepped out of the car and into the crisp morning breeze, lifting his face to the salty wind. He slung a small weekend bag over his shoulder and, with a final wave for Phillips, set off towards the causeway. He paused to toe off his boots and let his feet sink into the sand, enjoying its texture against his skin. A number of wooden stakes had been erected at intervals across the causeway to guide the way for pilgrims and, across the expanse of sand, the island awaited.

He took the first step, following in the wake of countless others who had sought solace and solitude.

Phillips watched the tall, lone figure walking across the sand until he was little more than a shadow, a mirage in the rippling light as it glimmered and bounced off the distant waves, and wondered what he might find on the other side.

Time would tell.

DCI RYAN WILL RETURN…

The Infirmary is the prequel to the DCI Ryan Mysteries series. Readers who are new to the series can follow Ryan's story chronologically by reading *Holy Island*, which covers the events immediately after *The Infirmary*.

If you have already read the ten existing DCI Ryan books, look out for the next release *The Moor*, which will be available in all good bookshops in October 2020!

AUTHOR'S NOTE

Since my debut novel, *Holy Island*, was first published in 2015, many people have asked to know a little more about what led DCI Ryan to seek sanctuary on the remote little Northumbrian island. I wrote another nine chronological books and explored the struggle between Ryan and his nemesis, 'The Hacker', over the course of those books, but the story of their first psychological duel was never fully told. This is, in part, because the prospect of writing a prequel story is quite daunting: having developed all the characters throughout the series, it is a challenge to step back in time to their fictional world as it would have been in 2014. Was the story important enough to tell? Ideas and storylines have been percolating over the past three years until the timing seemed to be right to reveal the world of DCI Ryan before experience had taught him caution.

Writing *The Infirmary* led me to rediscover parts of the city of Newcastle upon Tyne I was already familiar with but also revealed new and exciting discoveries such as the

Victoria Tunnel which runs beneath the city from Leazes Park to the west all the way to the river at Ouseburn, to the east. Taking a tour of part of the tunnel (which has served several purposes over the years, including coal transportation and air raid shelter during the World Wars) was an eerie experience and allowed me to imagine all manner of scenes where Ryan might find himself trapped inside. By necessity, the storyline is a darker thriller than some of the books in the DCI Ryan series but is not, I hope, without humanity. As the friendship between Ryan and his co-workers develops, there are flashes of humour and sentiment to offset their daily grind. Likewise, their interactions with the ordinary people they are tasked to serve and protect reveal a fundamental compassion that underpins all they do.

There are 'good' and 'bad' people in the world and their employment takes many forms. In this fictional story, the antagonist has created an alternate personality in which people believe him to be kind and caring towards those who appear vulnerable. However, *The Infirmary* is a story about Good versus Evil and, without a truly 'evil' baddie, the climax of the story would carry far less weight.

In some quarters, there is an intellectualised debate raging over whether writers of crime fiction ought to create male characters whose aggression tends to focus on women. To some, this succeeds in painting women as perpetual victims. For my part, the choices I have made in this novel reflect reality: to acknowledge that women are (sadly) often victims of serious crimes such as rape or murder does not overlook the opposite scenario, nor is it intended to be reductive. A victim of crime is not the sum total of their experience; their character is much richer and broader, which is why DCI Ryan fights so hard on these pages to avenge their memory. It is equally true to say that deviant personalities and perpetrators of serious crime can belong to women and, indeed, I have written their characters in other books.

No doubt, I will explore another female character whose infamy rivals the Hacker in the coming years… Until then, it will suffice to say that *The Infirmary* is the story of Ryan's personal journey to becoming the much-loved character he is now.

LJ Ross
January 2019

ABOUT THE AUTHOR

LJ Ross is an international bestselling author, best known for creating atmospheric mystery and thriller novels, including the DCI Ryan series of Northumbrian murder mysteries which have sold over five million copies worldwide.

Her debut, *Holy Island*, was released in January 2015 and reached number one in the UK and Australian charts. Since then, she has released a further eighteen novels, all of which have been top three global bestsellers and fifteen of which have been UK #1 bestsellers. Louise has garnered an army of loyal readers through her storytelling and, thanks to them, several of her books reached the coveted #1 spot whilst only available to pre-order ahead of release.

Louise was born in Northumberland, England. She studied undergraduate and postgraduate Law at King's College, University of London and then abroad in Paris and Florence. She spent much of her working life in London, where she was a lawyer for a number of years until taking the decision to change career and pursue her dream to write. Now, she writes full time and lives with her husband and son in Northumberland. She enjoys reading all manner of books, travelling and spending time with family and friends.

If you enjoyed reading *The Infirmary*, please consider leaving a review online.

ACKNOWLEDGMENTS

The Infirmary is the eleventh DCI Ryan novel I have written but its storyline is a prequel to the series. As such, it was an interesting and enjoyable experience to cast my mind back in time to 2014 and to the fictional events preceding the events in *Holy Island*. It was a creative challenge to write and I hope you have enjoyed reading it, discovering Ryan and Co. as they were before many of the events that subsequently shaped and moulded their characters.

I am grateful to all my family and friends who have offered unstinting support throughout my journey as a writer and whose love has sustained me during intense periods of writing during which time I am less sociable and more like a grizzly bear than usual (the difference may be marginal). In particular, I am thankful to my husband, James, who is always on hand to lend a patient ear and read my manuscript, to be encouraging and unfailingly positive which is one of the many reasons I love him.

I would also like to thank Doctor Alexandra Baker, Doctor Waleed and Mary El-Kinini, not only for their friendship but for offering very useful terminology and advice which I put to good use during the scenes in the Emergency Medicine Department of the fictional hospital. They, and many others like them, are shining examples of why I'm grateful to have such highly-skilled and compassionate people working for our shared National Health Service.

If you like DCI Ryan, why not try the bestselling
Alexander Gregory Thrillers by LJ Ross?

IMPOSTOR

AN ALEXANDER GREGORY THRILLER (Book #1)

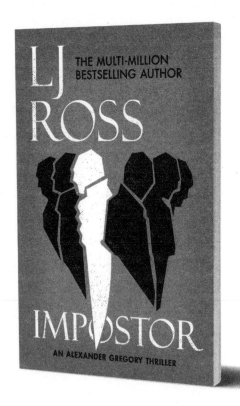

There's a killer inside all of us...

After an elite criminal profiling unit is shut down amidst a storm of scandal and mismanagement, only one person emerges unscathed. Forensic psychologist Doctor Alexander Gregory has a reputation for being able to step inside the darkest minds to uncover whatever secrets lie hidden there and, soon enough, he finds himself drawn into the murky world of murder investigation.

In the beautiful hills of County Mayo, Ireland, a killer is on the loose. Panic has a stranglehold on its rural community and the Garda are running out of time. Gregory has sworn to follow a quiet life but, when the call comes, can he refuse to help their desperate search for justice?

Murder and mystery are peppered with dark humour in this fast-paced thriller set amidst the spectacular Irish landscape.

IMPOSTOR is available now in all good bookshops!

LOVE READING?

JOIN THE CLUB...

Join the LJ Ross Book Club to connect with a thriving community of fellow book lovers! To receive a free monthly newsletter with exclusive author interviews and giveaways, sign up at www.ljrossauthor.com or follow the LJ Ross Book Club on social media:

#LJBookClubTweet

@LJRossAuthor

@ljrossauthor